The Tamar Black Saga – Book Eight

P ANTHEON

BY NICOLA RHODES

ISBN: 978-0-9561495-8-9

In the same series

Djinnx'd
Reality Bites
Tempus Fugitive
The Day Before Tomorrow
Faerie Tale
Anything But Ordinary
Rise of the Nephilim
Pantheon

~ Chapter One ~

THEY WERE RUNNING away; that was the thing. Not forever or anything, just for a little break. It was really a second … a honeymoon. (What with one thing and another – stolen Rheingold, crashing the mainframe, stopping Ragnoroc, half angels taking over the world, reigns of terror, that sort of thing – they had never got around to it after the actual wedding.)

It had been Denny's idea to go to Greece, it being a place he had never visited but had heard a lot about. It was a decision he would live to regret.

Of course, modern Greece is nothing like the Greece that Tamar had known before becoming a Djinn. That was the only reason she agreed to go.

The last thing she expected to see, as she lazed on the beach while Denny went off to see the Parthenon and other old ruins that Tamar was not interested in revisiting, was Poseidon.

But there he was large as life – prehistoric life that is. He was the approximate size (and probably weight) of a Tyrannosaurus Rex and with a similarly ferocious expression.

That made her sit up.

Pantheon

***

There was an enormous crowd at the Parthenon. Of course, it was a big tourist attraction, but this, Denny thought, was ridiculous.

Not only was there a large crowd, but they were, he noticed as he watched them, mostly locals, not tourists. This made about as much sense as the growing and palpable excitement that was spreading throughout the crowd.

'Okay', he thought, 'there's definitely something funny about this.'

He drifted onto the astral plane and wandered unheeded through the crowd. The throng of people was really so thick that there was no other practical way of getting to the action.

As he reached the front of the crowd, as if a starting signal had been fired, every single person, as one, fell on their faces in prostration. Then there was an almighty flash and a loud bang and a huge and fearsome figure appeared as if from nowhere. Now Denny had seen far worse in his time but still his mouth fell open in shock. The reason being, that this particular enormous individual was unmistakably the ancient warrior of the Greek gods, Athena herself; and Athena was supposed to have been dead for a long, long time.

'Oh shit!' said Denny.

Denn-eee!' He heard the shriek in his head, it was Tamar.

'*Not now*!' he thought. Then he thought better of it and teleported to her, just in time to see what he had half expected to see.

'Athena!' he told her shortly.

'Oh God!' said Tamar, catching his meaning immediately. 'Poseidon,' she told him, pointing at the gigantic figure swirling the sea around him like a giant bowl of soup.

'Yeah, I got that,' he replied dryly. 'What's the matter with him? Seems like he's in a bad mood.'

'He's ... he *was*, always in a bad mood,' said Tamar.

'That's the point, isn't it?' said Denny. 'The "was" part. What the hell is he doing here *now*? And how could we not *known* about this?'

'Why should we have?' said Tamar, puzzled.

'Because ... well look around you. Does anyone look surprised to you? It's as if ... as if they never went away. And when Athena appeared, people were *waiting* for her. They fell on their faces before she even arrived.'

'Yes, obviously, if they're here now, then it's because they never died off at all, but ... Oh I see what you mean,' she said. 'If they never went away for everyone else, how is it that *we* know that they did?'

'What?'

'As far as *we* are concerned, the gods vanished thousands of years ago into a deleted file ... Oh!' she stopped in horror as a light dawned.

'They never did, did they?' said Denny, as he also saw the light, 'because I crashed the damn mainframe.'

'*We* crashed it,' said Tamar automatically. 'At least, you wouldn't have done it if I hadn't given you the idea.'

'So ... *what* happened?' said Denny. 'The files never got deleted after mainframe restarted. Fair enough, I get that. But ...'

'Why now?' said Tamar. 'And why is it that we can remember it the other way, not the way it's actually happening now?'

'More or less, yeah?' said Denny.

'I have no idea,' she said.

'Could we be in a parallel universe?' he said.

'Ha!' said Tamar. 'That'd be handy, wouldn't it? But somehow I don't think it's that simple.'

'Can't we do something about him?' said Denny. 'He's making a right mess of the beach.' He pointed at Poseidon. 'And I can't hear myself think with all that racket he's making.'

'What would you like me to do?' said Tamar dryly.

'Just ... shut him up. I know you can do it. He's only a *god*.'

'*You* do it then.'

'All right then,' said Denny. 'I will.' And he directed a lightning bolt at Poseidon's head, which knocked him cold and sent him crashing into the water with an accompanying tidal wave of diminutive proportions. But, small or not (and it was still higher than most buildings) Denny had an unreasoning fear of tidal waves, and he yelped and leapt backwards as this one washed over the beach.

'I guess I didn't think that one through,' he said ruefully, as water dripped off him and left him standing in a puddle.

'Yes, well, if you've *quite* finished,' said Tamar. 'Maybe we should ...'

'Tamar Black!' A sharp voice cut across her words. 'You've really done it this time. You're in big, big trouble.'

It was, of course, Clive.

'You know, technically, it was *my* fault,' said Denny. 'I mean, I was the one who actually...'

'We know all about it,' snapped Clive. '*This* is where you are staying?' he added, *apropos* of nothing, looking around the room in distaste.'

'If you don't like it, you can always bugger off,' said Tamar. 'We know what we have to do you know. No one invited you to stick your big nose in anyway.'

'Ha! It never stopped *you* now did it?' said Clive with perfect truth. 'That's how we ended up with this mess on our hands in the first place.'

'No,' said Tamar with dangerous calm. 'We ended *up* with this mess, because your little friends in mainframe tried to trap us all in a deleted file.'

'Because you are always interfering in things that don't concern you,' parried Clive.

Tamar bristled dangerously, and Clive looked nervously at Denny for support.

Denny, however, just shrugged. 'Don't look at me,' he said. 'I agree with her.'

Clive held his hands up helplessly. 'Look, I'm just the messenger this time,' he said, 'and I had to do a lot of begging to get them to send me along. I *told* them, I told them and *told* them that you would do something bad if they tried it, but they wouldn't listen to me. I'm *persona non grata* up there at the moment. The price of being right when everyone else was wrong. No one likes a know-it-all, you know. You point out the flaws in the master scheme, and then you have to hope like hell that you're wrong because you just *know* the stupid bastards are going to do it anyway, and then they blame *you* for telling them it wasn't going to work in the first place, as if you put a hex on the whole thing just to prove you were right all along. Anyway ...' He pulled a face. 'That is now irrelevant as it goes. You did it, and now you *are* going to fix it. The bosses upstairs are howling for your blood you know. And you *are* going to need my help. You don't know what you're dealing with, believe *me*.' He paused for breath. 'Questions?' he asked.

Tamar and Denny looked at each other with bemused expressions.

Eventually Denny said. 'What?'

'I'm glad you asked,' said Clive apparently not noticing the form of the question. 'The fact is ... it's like this you see... oh *hell*. It's so hard to explain this stuff to – humans. Basically, what's happened is this. You crashed the mainframe, and all the files went back to startup yes?'

'We know this part,' said Denny. 'I was there. Remember?'

'How could I forget,' said Clive sourly. 'Then you know that deleted files are, well it's a bit of a misnomer really, the *data* in the files is deleted, but the files – no, that's not it. Wait a minute. There are two kinds of deleted files in mainframe. The files where all the data has been deleted from them and the files themselves stand empty and the other kind, where the data that has been deleted from the history files is stored. Actually, that's not exactly accurate either but it'll have to do. Anyway, as you have probably reasoned out already, the mythology files for the Greek gods were ... reactivated is the only appropriate term although it's completely wrong – however, from the point of view of the earth, the twilight of the gods never happened. I mean, it did, but then, after you crashed the system, it didn't. See?'

'But why are we only seeing it now?' asked Tamar. 'Denny ... *We* crashed it over sixteen years ago.'

'One thing at a time,' admonished Clive. 'You need to understand this. Now.' He paused. 'Where was I? Oh yes ... you changed history – all over the place as it happens, but this was a big one, because ... well it's made a mess that's all. Originally, the old gods became obsolete because of new gods moving in and such like. Socrates had a big impact on belief when he introduced the Greeks to natural philosophy and openly declared that the gods didn't exist – that sort of thing. And, as you know, when a god becomes obsolete, he dies. QED. But now, we have the old gods *and* the new gods all together, because the old history never got overwritten and turned into legend as it should have been. And, do you know, there isn't a damn thing we can do about it. We've tried, believe me, but it's too late. The only way now is to find a way to kill them off at the appropriate time some other way.'

'What do you mean it's too late?' said Denny. 'How can it be too late? Can't you just ...'

'What's done is done,' said Clive. 'The old legends said that the gods were destroyed in some unspecified manner. And then *they* became a legend anyway, so no one believed it really happened, which it didn't anyhow, because they died off through a lack of belief really. The tale of their so called destruction was just a convenient explanation for the end of the story. But now the story has changed see? And it's up to you to see that it changes back – but for real this time. You have to go back and destroy the gods in the past. After that, they should revert to legends again, and it will all be as if none of this ever happened.'

'Okay,' conceded Tamar. 'I didn't know *that*!'

'Destroy them how?' asked Denny not unreasonably. 'I mean they are technically immortal, aren't they?'

'Yes,' said Clive, 'and that's where it gets tricky see. That's why the story of the destruction of the gods is so damned vague I reckon. Not to mention that in the *stories*, the gods were supposedly destroyed around 600 BC. But they *weren't* you see, that was just back story written in afterwards. In reality, they lasted until the death of the last Tyrant of Athens which happened in 527BC, and even then it took a few years for them all to go. Well more than a few years really, some people were still believing in them up to 200 years later. Well, maybe it wasn't *actual* belief as such, more like – you know when you follow a religion but really you aren't sure, because there are other alternatives, like science and philosophy and even other religions and so on? Of course you don't, what am I saying? But people do do that you know? Anyway, it was like that. And that's more or less what happened after the last Tyrant died, what was that chap's name? Pisistratus, that was it – not that it matters – because he was the last champion of the old gods and after his death, his sons encouraged a lot of new ideas that *he* would never have stood for. And, it is a fact, that the old gods were never actually *seen* again after around 590BC or thereabouts, which might account for the date given in the story of 600BC. Belief is fluid you see. There wasn't just one day when everyone all at once decided not to believe any more.' He shook his head. 'Why couldn't you have just left well enough alone?' he said wearily.

'We had no choice,' said Tamar.

'Not *you*,' said Clive, surprisingly. '*Them*!' He shook an angry fist at the heavens. 'If *they* had left *you* alone in the first place, then none of this would be necessary.'

'Oh,' said Tamar. 'I see what you mean.'

'Anyway,' resumed Clive, 'to answer your earlier question. You are only seeing this now, because there is technically no time within the mainframe and mainframe is where the problem originated. I can't put a better explanation on it than that. At least not one that you could understand, I'm afraid. But in any case, they've been here all along *now*, and it doesn't make any difference to what you have to do.'

'We shouldn't be *seeing* it at all,' said Denny.

'I can't argue with you there,' said Clive.

'No, I mean, why is it that we know … what *you* know? We aren't inside the mainframe now. How come, when history changed, our memories didn't change with it like everyone else's?'

'Because you know better,' said Clive obscurely.

'Clive!' said Tamar warningly. 'No bollocks now or we may decide not to do anything at all about this. It was *you*, wasn't it? *You* gave us the memory.'

'Did you?' Denny turned to Clive, startled.

'Not exactly,' said Clive, which was as good as an admission that he had had *something* to do with it. 'Let's just say, I made sure that you didn't forget what you already knew. Mainframe is inside your head,' he added mysteriously. 'Everybody's head actually. But especially *yours*,' he told Denny. 'Once you've been inside, you're never quite the same again you know. Harder to fool for one thing.'

'Everybody's *head*?' said Denny incredulously. 'That's … actually I think I understand. In memories and stories and everything that people know or think or believe, it's all a part of the mainframe too, isn't it? I remember now.'

'Yes, but you are unique,' said Clive. 'Once you have seen the many layers of reality within the mainframe, a few alternate realities inside your own head are no problem at all to sort out.'

'Most people just see what's in front of them,' said Tamar. 'And then they don't believe whatever they can't handle anyway.'

'But you,' Clive resumed, addressing Denny, 'have literally been hit full in the face, so to speak, with the entire universe, as it really is – and even you,' he turned to Tamar, 'have spoken with the central control system. It gives you a different perspective. Sort of opens your eyes.'

'Anyway,' said Tamar briskly, 'so what's the plan?'

'The plan, as you call it, is up to you really,' said Clive. 'You understand the situation now. So fix it. My job here is done.'

'And that's *it*?' said Denny. 'No well-meaning but ultimately misleading advice? No long winded pontificating about danger and free will and other specious crap? Just "go and kill all the gods and do it fast"?'

'He did that bit actually,' said Tamar. 'The pontificating I mean.'

'Oh, yeah, so he did,' said Denny. 'Well, okay then, I guess we can do without the advice. So get lost then. We'll handle it from here.'

'There is one more thing actually,' said Clive.

'Yes, I thought there might be,' said Denny, sounding resigned.

'A little help with the time-travelling,' said Clive. 'I really wouldn't show your faces in mainframe at the moment if I were you, so ... Well, there is another way to go back without using mainframe as a conduit, and frankly it's a lot more efficient too, *and* more precise than just entering random files and hoping for the best as you did before. Now, before you ask,' he hurried on, 'we couldn't tell you the last time, because we weren't supposed to interfere because of free will ...'

'Aha!' interrupted Denny. 'There it is. I *knew* it.'

'I'm not really supposed to be telling you now actually,' said Clive, ignoring this. 'But frankly I don't give a gulong anymore. If you ask me, the stupid sods asked for this, and expecting you to just "fix" it without any help at all is pretty unfair. Of course, you can always decide not to do anything at all – free will...' he looked sidelong at Denny as if daring him to say anything about it. '... being what it is,' he continued. 'But I'm trusting that you won't do that, so if you want to hear it, my advice is all yours.' He waited expectantly.

'You know we're going to do it,' said Tamar. 'You wouldn't have bothered coming here if you didn't think so. So let's hear it. How do we travel through time without the mainframe?'

'You don't,' said Clive irritatingly. 'But you have to remember, you're *in* the mainframe *now*, one file of it anyway.'

'By God,' said Denny suddenly. 'That's clever. I should have thought of that myself.'

'What?' said Tamar.

'He's talking about file jumping,' said Denny. 'We do it all the time in a manner of speaking, when we teleport. We use the astral plane to go from place to place. Time is just ... a different direction – yes?' He looked at Clive interrogatively.

'Clive nodded. 'You *are* a quick study,' he said, sounding genuinely impressed. 'I always said you couldn't be as daft as you look.'

'Charming!' put in Tamar. She always got irritated when people commented derogatively on Denny's looks.

'All the files – places, times, everything, are accessible from wherever we are,' said Denny glossing over this with the ease of long practice – it happened all the time – well, he *wasn't* handsome and never would be, so why get bent out of shape about it? But Tamar could never accept this.

'Of course, you have to be able to access the astral plane,' said Clive. 'It's not as if just *anyone* can do it. But you two, at least, should have no problems.'

'Well, I wish you *had* thought of it,' said Tamar to Denny. 'Years ago. It might have saved us all that pissing about in mainframe looking for Askphrit.'

'What would have been the fun in that?' said Denny.

* * *

'So where are we going then?' asked Denny. 'I mean what year?'

'Are you certain that you know how to do this?' said Tamar.

'Easy as winking,' he said confidently. 'You know it too, just think about it.'

Tamar thought. 'I'm not sure,' she said. 'I mean I can understand it in principle, but ...'

'Okay, trial run,' said Denny. 'Let's go back to say, last week.'

'We'll run into ourselves,' objected Tamar.

'No we won't,' said Denny. 'The reason being, we weren't *here* last week. We were at home.'

'Oh, okay then.'

'So, ready?' he said.

They drifted onto the astral plane. That was the easy bit; they had done this so many times before without even thinking about it. Now for the hard part. But Denny had been right; when you knew what you were looking for it was easy. To teleport to another time rather than another location *was* just a matter of going in a different direction. Now that she could see it, she wondered that she had never seen it before.

'Oh, it's easy,' she said in delighted surprise.'

The previous/current occupants of their room weren't quite so delighted.

'Well, they shouldn't have still been in bed at that time of the day,' said Tamar afterwards.

'At least they were too busy to register exactly *how* we arrived,' said Denny.

'So, now that we know we can do it,' she said. 'We have a few decisions to make. Like, do we go alone, just the two of us, or do we contact the others? And most important, like you said, what year do we go to?'

'We can't ask Hecaté anyway,' said Denny. 'She's *from* that time …'

'Yeah, well, so am I,' pointed out Tamar. 'I'd already been a Djinn for two and a half thousand years by the time the gods faded out.'

Denny stared at her. He had forgotten this.

'Will it make a difference?' he asked.

Tamar shrugged. 'I shouldn't think so,' she said. 'So, do we call in the troops on this one or not?'

Denny narrowed his eyes. She was being entirely too dismissive on the subject in his opinion. On the other hand, they *had* done this before. They had even met Tamar in her other incarnation once, and nothing much had happened. So maybe she really thought it would be okay.

'It's a long way back,' he said. 'Hecaté was a god at the time – well, she still is of course, but back then …'

'I know,' said Tamar. 'She was one of *those* gods, and we all know what can happen when two of the same person end up in the same time and place.'

'They merge into each other.' Denny knew this because it had happened to him. 'She'd become the Hecaté from *that* time. We wouldn't know her anymore.'

'Oh, God,' he said as he suddenly realised. 'She's *still* the Hecaté from that time. She's *still* one of those gods. I mean, history changed, didn't it? Our Hecaté, she doesn't exist anymore. She's one of *them* now – again – whatever! Which means …'

'She's probably not married to Jack either,' said Tamar. 'I mean why would she be? They probably never met at all.'

'And Jack himself?'

Tamar shook her head. 'We have no way of knowing how much has changed,' she said. 'I can't remember the way things are now. You try it.'

Denny tried. He also shook his head. 'It's not there,' he said. 'I don't know…'

'Damn!' said Tamar. 'Why didn't Clive say anything about this? He could have filled us in, the little weasel.'

'Well, he didn't have to, did he?' pointed out Denny. 'We worked it out by ourselves. Besides, he always does it this way, little dribs and drabs of information and then we have to figure the rest out on our own. At least we didn't find out too late this time.'

'Yeah, okay, but what *else* hasn't he told us?'

'I guess we'll find out.'

'We're on our own this time, aren't we?' she said. 'We're the only ones who know the truth. I mean even if we could find Jack, even supposing he's still our friend – and he might not be you know – and even supposing he understood the situation, and he agreed to help us, he's not a part of this. Neither is Cindy or … anyone else. They all belong in *this* world. Only *we* don't.'

'But Jack and Cindy … we met them *before* we met Hecaté …'

'Ha!' snorted Tamar. 'We met Cindy *because* of Hecate. She is now the goddess of witches, or should be, but she probably isn't now, because she wasn't then – if you understand me. I bet we never met Cindy at all. And as for Jack and that whole vampire plot, I doubt it ever happened. Askphrit wouldn't have got away with, it regardless of us, not with all these other gods running around large as life.'

'And … and… our Iffie?'

'She won't be a witch even, let alone have the power of the dragons. Without Hecaté to train her as a witch or Ashtoreth, who never would have existed at all if it wasn't for Cindy meeting Eugene and then falling for you … sorry I know you don't like to talk about that … But anyway, no Cindy and Eugene – no Ashtoreth, no dragon power.' Tamar shrugged. 'We definitely can't drag her into this.'

'I wasn't suggesting that we did,' said Denny. 'You know, you're talking as if you *know* all this is true,' he added.

'It just makes sense,' she said.

'No, it's more than that,' insisted Denny. 'Intuition?'

'I just think we're on our own this time,' said Tamar stubbornly. 'I know how this stuff works. Call it intuition if you like. All I know is that the whole world changed two and half *thousand* years ago, that's a hell of a knock on effect. We need to put it back how it should be. Clive was right. We have to fix it. We have no choice.'

'I suppose we should consider ourselves lucky that we even met each other,' said Denny gloomily.

'How do you know we did?' said Tamar. 'Only kidding, we obviously did. But poor Iffie never met young Jack, that's a certainty. Even if he was Cindy's adopted son, in the same way as before, I mean, if Cindy *did* have a kid, (just not with Eugene) and Finvarra *did* swap them over like before and all the rest of it, he wouldn't have been a part of *our* lives. Oh, we just have to fix this, for everyone's sake.'

'And if Cindy *didn't* have a kid?' said Denny.

'Then young Jack will have died along with the rest of the Faeries – or … but it was Jack who destroyed the Faeries with

Leir's gauntlet … Oh god, this is too confusing. Are there still *Faeries* out there too?'

'Like you said,' said Denny. 'A hell of a knock on effect. Let's just get on with sorting it out, shall we? We could speculate on this forever. It won't do any good. Let's just make sure that whatever *has* happened, we'll never have to worry about it.

'We *are* on our own,' he continued. 'And it's because, since the world changed, we've *always* been on our own.'

'I can think of worse things,' said Tamar with a gentle smile.

'Yeah, and they're probably all happening right now,' said Denny pragmatically.

'Right!' said Tamar. 'So … we have to decide. 527BC, the *real* beginning of the end, or 600BC, when the story *says* it was the end?'

Denny shrugged helplessly. 'Clive said we have to change the *story* back to how it's supposed to be,' he said. 'But supposing we kill them all seventy years before they *really* started to die off, what will that do to the timeline? Can we even kill them before the belief is all gone anyway? Will people continue to believe in them even after we kill them, and if they do, will that mean they won't be dead after all?'

'When we killed Ran-Kur,' said Tamar thoughtfully; dextrously untangling this metaphysical maze that Denny had woven around himself. 'The actual *belief* remained behind. It was used by Askphrit, but that's not the point here. It *is* possible to believe in something that's not real – or not real *anymore*. Clive said as much. He even said that religions can carry on even after all the belief is gone.' She scratched her head in puzzlement. 'I don't really understand that very well,' she admitted. 'However, Ran-Kur was dead, but the vampires didn't know that, so they still believed in him, but it didn't bring him back to life.'

'So, we go back to 600BC?' said Denny.

'Yes!' said Tamar sounding a lot more positive than she felt.

'And when we get there?' said Denny. 'Just how exactly are we going to kill a lot of immortals anyway?'

'Beats the hell out of me,' said Tamar. 'I'm making this up as I go along.'

'Oh good,' said Denny. 'That always works.' He said this without a trace of irony. The most meticulous plans, as they had discovered again and again, usually just ended up getting in the way.

* * *

600BC was not that different, at first glance, to the present day; at least, not in Greece. Of course, the Temple of Athena– where they had decided to set off from as a constant landmark that they knew existed in both time periods – was a lot less ruined looking, but the basic landscape looked much the same – and oddly enough, not at all like rural New Zealand. Up close, it would no doubt be possible to see many differences in the local buildings, market places and people and so on, but just from here, they might as well not have gone anywhere.

Except for one thing.

'I feel different,' said Tamar. 'Sort of strange … weaker.'

Denny was frowning. 'Me too,' he said. 'Sort of … powerless.'

They looked at each other in horror.

'We don't have our powers!' they said in unison.

'Which also means we're stuck here,' said Denny.

~ Chapter Two ~

TAMAR COVERED her face in a panic. 'What do I look like?' she demanded unreasonably, since he could not see her face anyway.

'What?' he asked nonplussed. 'What are you talking about?'

'My face,' she whimpered. 'Is it … am I … ugly?'

'What? No, you look like you always do. Is this really important right now?' Denny was annoyed. He knew she was vain, but at a time like this …

'Yes,' she said. 'If I've lost my powers, then my beauty is really the only weapon I have left. Besides …' She left the thought unspoken. But he knew what she meant. She was worried that *he* would not like it.

'Well,' he said, 'I always seemed to manage with my ordinary old face.'

'Yes,' said Tamar, too distracted to issue her usual denial that he was not unattractive. 'But that's not what people like about *you*.'

Denny took her hands. 'It's not the only thing people like about *you* either,' he said.

'Oh, yes it is,' she said positively. 'Except you maybe.'

Denny shook his head wearily. He would never convince her. She was brave to the point of recklessness, loyal to the point (sometimes) of stupidity, generous to a fault, selfless, kind, forgiving and wise, and she never, ever gave up on anything or anybody. But she could not be made to see … She even thought that *he* – of all people – would not love her any more if she lost her beautiful face. It was ludicrous. It was also her armour against the world; and that he *did* understand. All of her phenomenal self-confidence came from the way she knew she affected people simply by the way she looked. And she was right, in a way. Without her powers, she was going to need all that self-confidence, amounting to arrogance, to get through this.

She uncovered her face apprehensively. 'Are you sure,' she said. 'I look the same?'

'Exactly the same,' he said. 'I told you ages ago that *is* your face now, so stop worrying about it.'

'Oh, God, I'm an awful person, aren't I?' she said, sitting down suddenly. 'Here we are in this terrible mess and all I can think about is …' She made a helpless gesture toward her face.

Denny hunkered down beside her. 'You know you aren't an awful person,' he said reassuringly. 'You just had a little panic. People often panic about irrelevant stuff when they feel overwhelmed and, let's face it, this is quite a problem.'

'I don't understand it,' she said. 'We didn't lose our powers the last time we went into the past, why now?'

Denny shook his head. 'I don't know. I thought it might happen to *me*,' he admitted. 'I mean we don't know when the Athame was forged, maybe my powers don't even exist yet. But we know that yours definitely do. So why…?'

'But you still *have* the Athame,' said Tamar.

Denny was startled by this revelation. He looked down at his belt and sure enough, there it was, the sheath tucked into his belt as always. 'What the …?' he said.

'Hang on to it,' advised Tamar, 'At best, it's still a power-stealing Athame, and at worst, it's a very, very sharp dagger.'

'Yes, okay, but …'

'I know, I know, none of this makes any sense,' she interrupted. 'You should still have your powers if you still have the Athame. And I shouldn't be able to maintain this face without my powers, and yet … and yet…'

'Well, one thing's for certain,' said Denny. 'We won't be killing any gods without our powers. And we can't get home without them either, so what are we going to do?'

Tamar examined her fingernails.

'I have no idea either,' said Denny.

'Maybe if we could just figure out what happened …'

'Do you think Clive knew this would happen?' said Denny suddenly.

'I wouldn't put it past the little rat, why?'

'Well, you said you wondered what he hadn't told us. Guess this was it. But … it doesn't make sense. How could he expect us to kill the gods in this condition?'

'Maybe that wasn't the point at all,' she said. 'It wouldn't be the first time the clerks had tried to get rid of us.'

'Not Clive,' said Denny. 'He knows us too well to believe for a moment that it would work. It *never* works. There *is* a way out of this. We just need to find it.'

'We need powers,' said Tamar. '*Any* powers, just …' She frowned.

'Eureka?' asked Denny.

'I might know where there are some powers going,' she said.

'Oh?'

'We need to find me,' she said. 'Who else is going to help us, after all?'

Denny thought this was a good idea until he asked. 'Where are you now?'

'600BC.' She thought for a moment and then her face darkened. 'Rome,' she said. 'I'm in Rome.'

'Rome?' exploded Denny. 'Without our powers, it might as well be darkest Africa.'

'I've been there too,' she said. 'It was hot.'

'Well, we can't stay here forever,' said Denny. 'Suppose we go and …' He had been slapping the Athame against his palm all the time they had been talking and now a sudden thought struck him. 'Er,' he said. 'Not that it matters – just out of curiosity – what do *I* look like?'

Denny was technically nearly fifty years old; only the power of the Athame had allowed him to remain at the same physical age (twenty five) that he had been when he found it. So it was yet another mystery that he also looked exactly the same as he always had, but no more of a mystery, as Tamar pointed out, than the fact that not only had she retained her good looks but, the more she thought about it, if the loss of their powers was going to result in instant ageing, then she ought to have crumbled into a pile of bone dust the instant they arrived, like Dracula or something.

'Not necessarily, said Denny. 'You've only been human for twenty odd years, before that you were a Djinn and immortal anyway.'

'They didn't wear stuff like this on Xena,' complained Denny of his toga, which he was wearing over his jeans, completing the overall picture of a complete and utter twerp. 'I never saw a single toga on that show.'

'That was set later on,' said Tamar, 'and it was completely inaccurate anyway. You know this is right. We nicked them off those people who came into in the temple. And it isn't a toga, it's a chiton. And you look f-f-fine – ahem.'

'Oh, yeah, so why are you having such a hard time keeping your face straight?' he demanded.

Tamar herself was looking stunning as usual. Her own chiton resembled a long and flowing dress, with delicate long sleeves and a dainty rope belt around the waist – *she* looked like a princess. Denny looked like the frog (albeit a frog wrapped up in a pillowcase). But since he was well used to this being the case, he did not really mind all that much. But, unusually for him, he did mind a bit.

'I look like a character from Carry On Cleo,' he said. 'Infamy, infamy, they've all got it in for me,' he quoted. 'I really need bigger shoulders to carry off this style,' he added. 'I look like a matchstick man.'

'Is there anything you *don't* think you look like?' said Tamar acerbically. She was not used to this Denny. What had happened to his usual take-me-or-leave-me attitude?

'A normal human being?' he said. 'Look, it's one thing to look like a scruffy git, because you *want* to. It's something else to feel like a complete fool in a bad fancy dress costume, because you *have* to. Sorry,' he added, 'I know we have more important things to worry about. I guess I just can't get rid of the feeling that people are going to stare. Or that I'll be arrested by the fashion police.'

'Oh, all *right*,' said Tamar, exasperated. 'Wait there.' And she disappeared out into the street alone.

Denny had a feeling that he should not have let her do this. They had decided to remain inside the temple until it was dark – this was principally so that their appearance would not be noticed, of course, which was no longer a problem, at least in Tamar's case, since a couple of worshippers had provided a gold plated opportunity for robbery, which Denny was against in principle but in practice ... Well, in practice, he had hit the man on the head with a heavy stone with barely a qualm. It is all very well to stick to your principles when it does not cost you anything, but under the, rather desperate, circumstances ... Denny shrugged. What was done was done, but what was she up to now?

He was feeling far less distressed than Tamar about the vanishing of his powers; he had always had a feeling that this day would come, that his powers were on temporary loan from the universe and that someday they would be repossessed. But it did not prevent the old feelings of hopeless inadequacy from resurfacing. The daft looking toga was not helping. Tamar was right though – under normal circumstances it would not have bothered him as much.

Clearly Tamar understood how he was feeling better than he could have explained it because she returned after about half an hour carrying a long cloak, which she told him to put on. He felt better immediately; he did not ask where she had got it from.

'Okay.' She surveyed him critically. 'The hair's all wrong, it needs to be shorter. Men in this time kept their hair neat and tidy. Your haystack-in-a-windstorm look will draw too much attention. You'll need to shave too. And the trainers will have to go too. But no one will think too much of bare feet around here.'

The man's sandals had been far too small for Denny, but they fitted Tamar beautifully, which was lucky for her since the larger footed woman had been barefoot anyway.

'Cut my hair?' said Denny, horrified. 'Shave? I'll look like a twelve year old.'

This was not far from the truth; Denny had a decidedly juvenile looking face, and without his stubble and long scruffy hair, he would indeed look like a schoolboy.

'People will think you're my mother.' He tried appealing to her vanity.

But Tamar was not having any of it. 'Fifteen,' she pronounced. 'Maybe sixteen or even seventeen. You're too tall to be twelve.'

So they hacked off Denny's hair with the Athame – a pair of handy scissors not being in their current arsenal – and Tamar made a surprisingly good job of it. But when it came to her shaving him with the lethal blade, Denny drew the line. 'I'm not having that thing near my neck,' he told her obstinately.

'What if I could get a proper razor?' she said.

'More stealing?' he said. 'Well okay, but I'm doing it myself.'

'Ever used a cutthroat?' she asked. 'I have. I'm an expert. I bet I could even do it with the Athame if you'd just let me.'

'How are *you* an expert?' said Denny doubtfully.

'Five thousand years as a slave,' she said. 'It was a regular duty. I've shaved masters with knives, daggers … you name it, even a sharpened axe head once.'

Denny sagged. 'Okay, I surrender. Just don't cut my head off by accident.'

'What do I look like *now*?' he asked eventually.

Tamar had been staring at him in wonder for five long minutes without saying a word, and it was making him twitchy.

'Really… pretty,' she said. 'I like it,' she added as he frowned – no *glowered* at her.

'*Pretty*?' he snorted. 'Oh God, my father was right.'

'No, no, I don't mean like a girl or anything, it's just … well I can see your face properly now. You look like Iffie – sort of, but boyish. Man-pretty, that's what they call it, isn't it?'

Denny did not believe a word of it. 'Bollocks!' he said dismissively and signalled that, as far as he was concerned, this conversation was over. 'How are we going to get to Rome?' he asked, effectively bringing them back down to practicalities with a bump.

'We walk,' she said, 'unless we can hitch a ride from someone.'

'*Walk*?' said Denny aghast. 'To *Rome*? You've got to be kidding.'

'Sorry,' she said curtly. 'I forgot my broomstick. Look these are the times. Travellers go on foot or horseback or by boat – which we can't afford. Cheer up. It's only six hundred and fifty miles.'

'Straight across,' said Denny. 'By boat, in other words. How far is it overland?'

'That is how far it is overland,' she said. 'We could go to the coast and try to steal a boat I suppose. Do *you* know how to sail?'

'No, but you know *everything*, don't you?'

'I never had to,' she admitted. 'I never needed to do things the mortal way before.'

'Maybe we could stow away somehow,' he suggested. 'How far is it to the coast?'

'About ten minutes,' she said. 'Same as in our time. But I'm telling you, we won't get a boat to Italy from here. We'd be better off going to the port at Igoumenitsa and catching a boat to Brindisi. Or whatever they call it here – I mean now.'

'And then at least we'd be in Italy,' said Denny. 'Okay, why don't we do that then?'

'You know, you were right,' she said. 'It's 350 miles to the west coast. We should get a cart and horse or something.'

'Oh God, and we're going to have to eat too. What the hell are we going to do?'

'There's food on the altar, it looks pretty fresh. There might be some valuables up there too. Maybe we could trade some stuff. They don't go much on cash around here anyway.'

'You think we should rob the *temple*?' said Denny shocked despite himself.

'Denny,' she said as kindly as possible. 'We came here to kill the gods. It's a bit late to be worrying about blasphemy don't you think?'

'Oh, yeah I suppose when you put it like that. And I *am* starving.'

'It's only going to get worse,' said Tamar gloomily.

* * *

They managed to hitch a ride to the port. Tamar had never had to do this before and had, therefore, been unaware of the usefulness of a pretty face in the successful prosecution of this activity. Although whether it was *her* pretty face or Denny's that clinched the deal remained unclear.

Three boring, slow going days on the back of a smelly cart, listening to the driver's boring tales about pigs (Denny was lucky here – he did not understand a word of it) and she was beginning to wish they had walked it after all.

But the carter was kind and friendly. He shared his food with them, their temple pickings having amounted to very little, and he left them at the dock with some helpful advice on how to stowaway on a boat, it apparently being a favourite pastime of his in his youth. Yes, he had been as far as Crete, he said, and Tamar tried to look suitably impressed.

By asking around, and it really was amazing how a language that she had not used for over a thousand years came back to her so fluently, Tamar discovered that there was a ferry leaving for an Italian port in the early morning. It was a few hours before dusk at the moment, and they were hungry and weary.

Fortunately some traditions have lasted for many thousands of years. There was a temple dedicated to Hestia, a pretty small affair compared to the temple of Athena that they had sheltered in previously, but at least it was a roof and the offerings to Hestia, if Tamar remembered rightly, tended towards the edible. Denny, who was starving and who did not have any better ideas anyway, was in no position to argue. But there was something inexpressibly disrespectful, he felt, about their sheltering in the various temples dedicated to the gods they had come here to destroy.

It was a period of peace in Greece at the moment. That is to say, there were no actual wars going on – well, not major wars anyway, but banditry and other nefarious occupations were rife. The temple was occupied when they reached it. Several rough looking characters, who did not feel inclined to share, were lounging at the altar having apparently had the same idea as Tamar and Denny.

Had they still got their powers, of course, these vagabonds would not have represented a particularly formidable proposition, in the present case, however, it was as simple as five against two. Or rather five against one, as Denny had no intention of letting Tamar fight under the circumstances. Of course, he might as well have tried to hold back the tides.

The leader, a louche looking character rose languidly from his position at the foot of the altar and gave a signal to the others to attack. Denny tensed.

Time to see how much he remembered. Before receiving the Athame, he had trained himself to fight in the old fashioned way and had actually become fairly proficient in several forms of both armed and unarmed combat. He was wishing now that he had not let it slide for so long – he had kept up his training program for several years after he no longer really needed it, but after a while, he had become complacent about his powers and this foolishness was now being brought home to him sharply.

Like riding a bike, apparently. As the first one came at him, Denny reacted instinctively and with a smooth, well-practised move, which the man evidently never saw coming, Denny dodged and caught his sword arm, and completely ignoring the blade as irrelevant, twisted and then brought the full weight of his body into the back of the man's outstretched and thus weakened arm and broke it. It made a horrible snapping noise. The sword clanged on the floor, and Denny picked it up and, without hesitating, brought it down on the man's head. Then he lowered the sword, as Tamar, who had never trained herself to do anything, was caught by two men and held fast with a dagger to her throat.

Denny weighed his options. Tamar *knew* how to fight. He had good reason to know this, in the beginning, she had taught him. But she was now frozen rigid with fear.

'Πτώση αυτό,' said the leader.

'He said "drop it",' translated Tamar. 'But don't,' she added. 'He'll just kill me anyway.'

'I know,' said Denny. It was a stalemate for the time being; he had to find a way to break it to his own advantage.

'Πτώση αυτό,' repeated the leader. 'ή θα την σκοτώσω.'

Denny gathered that this was some kind of threat. Oh well, he appeared to be out of options. He dropped the sword and the two men holding Tamar relaxed slightly. This was a mistake. Denny had dropped the sword onto his foot, and he now kicked it upwards, caught it and threw it with remarkable accuracy at the leader, who was forced to dodge out of the way and fell on his face, Denny was on him in a second, the Athame out. Meanwhile, Tamar had taken full advantage of her captors' momentary inattention as Denny had hoped. Powers or not, they had fought together so often that they no longer needed to read each other's minds. It was all instinctive. She escaped easily simply by dropping to the floor and rolling away, but she no longer had the strength to follow up her advantage as she once could. Once upon a time, they would have been mere smears on the wall. However, with their leader down and Denny rising from his body brandishing a bloody dagger with such a look on his face as would put the fear of God into a Berserker, they both decided that this fight was not for them, and they ran.

The fight had done Denny good. In fact, he felt on top of the world. The feelings of inadequacy that had assailed him since the loss of his powers had receded into nothing.

Tamar was a little shaky however.

Denny knelt down to her. 'Are you all right?' he asked.

'Fine,' she said with a brightness that was a little forced. 'You did well,' she added. 'Not bad for a man with no magical assist.'

'You know, I was a bit worried about that,' he admitted. 'I've been feeling pretty useless since we lost our powers,' he grinned suddenly. 'But you know what?' he said. 'I *am* good.'

'Your nose is bleeding,' she told him.

Denny wiped it with the back of his hand in a rather uncouth fashion and looked at the blood on his hand curiously. He had not seen his own blood for many years. 'Would you look at that,' he said. 'I *am* bleeding. It feels weird after all this time.'

'Weird good or weird bad?' asked Tamar.

'Kind of good actually,' he said. 'I won that fight on my own – no Athame I mean, no special help. I feel … hungry actually. Did those scags leave any food?'

'If they didn't we could always eat him,' said Tamar indicting the fallen leader. Denny chose to take this as a joke.

He helped her up and went to investigate the offering plates. There was a surprising amount of food there. He helped himself and took a plate to Tamar who merely picked at it. The sight of Denny's bleeding nose had shaken her more than she wanted to admit. They were mortal now; they could be hurt – perhaps badly, perhaps even killed. She decided that this was not the time to point this out, though. Apart from the fact that he knew it as well as she did (he was not a fool, after all) he seemed to be on a high at the moment, and she did not want to bring him down. The elevation of his mood was confirmed to her when he began to sing in a loud and hearty voice. Even she had to smile, though, at his choice of song. He was singing, with ironic appositeness, David Bowie's "Golden Years".

~ Chapter Three ~

THEY WERE NOW on the second leg of their journey, and Denny's mood had taken a sharp dip due to the return of his seasickness. A mortal failing that he had forgotten he ever suffered from. Getting on board the ferry had been easy – they had simply paid passage using the money that they had found on the dead leader of the bandits or whatever they were. He had had quite a large bag of coins on him, and Tamar estimated that they would have enough to see them to Rome assuming the currency was good in Italy.

Tamar herself was feeling pretty good. She liked the sea, and the wind on her face was refreshing and calming to her strung out nerves and best of all, they were on their way now. Denny was throwing up over the side, but even in this condition he did not fail to notice the anxious demeanour of the crew.

'They're worried about something,' he said to Tamar during a lull in his ongoing nausea.

'Yes,' she said. 'It's Poseidon they're worried about.

'All sailors are superstitious, said Denny dismissively.

'Poseidon isn't a superstition around here,' Tamar pointed out. 'He's a very real threat.'

'Well,' yes,' agreed Denny. '*You* don't seem too worried,' he added.

'What will be will be,' said Tamar. 'Besides, didn't Clive say that the gods hadn't been seen much around this time period?'

'You aren't taking *his* word for it, are you?'

'Good point,' she said. 'But I still ... Of course, I could be wrong,' she said, her face suddenly white as a sheet.

Denny turned sharply; he had been leaning against the rail with his back to the sea facing Tamar, who had been looking out to sea.

'Do you think it's us he's after?' he asked in a deceptively calm voice.

'I don't see how it can be,' she said. 'They can't *know*, can they?'

'So it's just a horrible coincidence then?' said Denny sceptically.

And Tamar looked at the expression on Poseidon's face. 'Maybe not,' she conceded, and then she smiled to herself.

The crew were panicking as the sea began to boil and churn and the boat was tossed on twenty foot waves.

'We're going to capsize,' said Tamar serenely.

'Oh *great*!' snapped Denny. 'Do you have to sound so bloody happy about it?'

'The fool,' was all she said, and she even smiled. 'We'd better get below,' she added.

'I think you're forgetting something,' said Denny sharply, trying to bring her back to reality from whatever happy cloud she was currently resting on. 'We can *drown* now. Do you even know *how* to swim?'

'No,' she said. 'And I don't have to.'

'What the hell are you talking about, have you completely ... lost ... mind ...?' His voice was lost in the great tumult of crashing waves as the boat was lifted high in the air and then dropped sharply, with a thunderous noise, back on to the surface of the ocean.

Tamar climbed up onto the side of the boat and balanced precariously there, her hair streaming behind her, a look of pure defiance on her face as she caught Poseidon's gaze and held it for a second. Even in the midst of his terror, Denny stopped panicking for a moment to appreciate her. Even with no powers at all, she really was magnificent. She looked like some wild goddess of the sea herself.

'You'll have to do better than that,' she told the wrathful sea god. 'You can't stop us so easily.' And she leapt down lightly on to the deck as Poseidon sent a huge wave crashing over the boat which sent it rocking and rolling headlong. They had finally taken on too much water and were about to capsize any second.

'You had to say it, didn't you?' shrieked Denny as they slipped and skidded across the deck towards the hold.

'Stop bitching,' said Tamar. 'I know what I'm doing.'

And the boat capsized just as she pulled the door of the hold shut behind them.

They were sinking slowly to the bottom of the sea in an upside down boat. But, on the bright side, at least Denny was not seasick any more.

The hold was surprisingly watertight, very little water was coming in, but, on the other hand, they were running out of air.

'Okay,' said Denny, forcing himself to remain calm. 'How are we going to get out of this one?'

'You mean you haven't worked it out yet?' said Tamar.

'Worked *what* out?' said Denny, thus inadvertently answering her question.

'Wait,' she said mysteriously. 'And while you are waiting, ponder on this. This is the age of mythology.'

'I noticed that,' he replied sourly.

'Oh, and we don't belong here,' she added.

'No kidding.'

'Not in this age and not even in this world,' she said calmly. 'We don't exist.'

Denny frowned as he tried to figure out what she was getting at.

'We're still going to drown,' he said eventually.

'Maybe,' she said. 'But I doubt it.'

It was at least half a heart-stopping hour, before something happened. Denny had passed from the depths of sheer panic to the shallows of relative calm and was even feeling slightly sleepy when he was brought to by the boat rocking sharply. He sat up as panic returned. 'What's happing now?' he demanded.

'Automatic file reset,' she said. 'I just had to hope …'

'File reset?' said Denny. 'I don't …' He was cut off as the boat began to rise slowly up to the surface of the ocean. The water that had been gradually leaking in was now leaking back out again. It was a very weird thing to watch. 'Time's running backwards?' he said in complete mystification.

'Only for us,' she said. And that's not really…'

'And you *knew* this would happen?' said Denny angrily. 'And you didn't *tell* me?'

'I-I wasn't certain,' she admitted.

Denny forced himself to calm down as they reached the surface and the boat bobbed up like a cork in a barrel and slowly turned over in the wake of a receding wave.

'What the hell was all that about?' said Denny as the boat righted itself and the crew were manoeuvred back into position by some unseen force as the sea calmed itself and Poseidon sank harmlessly beneath the waves.

'You were right,' she said. Poseidon *was* after us, and that's the only reason the boat sank – but we don't belong here. If we weren't here, it never would have happened at all. It wasn't supposed to happen, it only happened because of us, so the file reset itself as if it never *had* happened. I called him a fool because if he had just killed us outright, without sinking the boat and killing those men before their time, that would have worked fine. But he never could resist a dramatic spectacle.

Even the gods can't fight the organising power of the mainframe,' she said. 'Lucky for us.'

The rest of the voyage continued without incident.

* * *

They would be safe from the wrath of any more gods for the time being. For as long as they were in Italy, in fact. It would be another few hundred years before the Greek Pantheon began to get mixed up with the Roman one and the Roman gods were nothing much at the moment, according to Tamar, just small gods – local deities of tree and stream etc. Besides, Tamar and Denny were not after *them*. And although gods do not respect very much they do respect boundaries.

But it did not alter the fact that they had a long journey before them. 230 miles to Rome. But at least the roads were good.

'They'll be waiting for us,' said Denny, meaning the gods. He looked back at the sea as he spoke.

'Yeah, well, we'll be ready for them when we get back,' said Tamar. 'They'll never even see us coming.'

'Assuming this works,' said Denny.

'It will,' she said confidently.

~ Chapter Four ~

IT WAS CALLED a council of the gods, but it was more like a collective argument/birthday party/orgy all rolled into one.

Zeus sighed despondently. They were like children, he thought. Always fighting and sulking and competing with each other when they ought to be working together. *What a family!*

And then of course Poseidon had to come to him recently with another of his ridiculous conspiracy theories. Not that he was ever taken seriously. He said that he had his ear to the sea bed, and he heard things. He never specified *what* things exactly, just things. Of course, living at the bottom of the sea could make a person a bit strange, sometimes. Poseidon claimed to have seen visitors from another world – he even said that there were the ruins of an ancient civilisation down there. But Zeus had never fancied going down there for a look.

This time he had claimed a couple of would be assassins were after them all, but it had turned out to be nothing more than a couple of mortals who were, as Zeus understood it, on their way *out* of Greece anyway. Well, they were no doubt at the bottom of the ocean now, poor things. He really would have to have a serious word with the old sea god. That sort of thing made them all look bad.

After all, they had *people* for that sort of thing – priests and whatnot. And Nemesis of course for the really bad cases. Although she had been getting uppity lately – kept wanting to know what the wretched person's crime was – as if it was any business of hers. She should do as she was told and never mind the reasons, which he was compelled to admit, if only to his own private ear, were sometimes not particularly clear.

No, the days of *personal* vengeance were over, Zeus had never particularly liked mortals, and he strongly deprecated the idea of making contact with them any more than he had to (except for some of the prettier girls of course – but even that had lost its charm of late) and damn it, was he the king of the gods or was he not? If *he* did not like going down to the Earth then *none* of them should like it. But some of them still did.

Apollo, for example, seemed set on taking over his own role as lady-killer among the immortals, even though Zeus had given him strict orders to stick to his own kind. They wanted no more mistakes like Heracles. Not that he was not proud of the boy, there he was, twinkling away in the heavens to prove it, but the trouble he had caused was nobody's business. But there, there was no respect these days. Zeus was aware that these were the thoughts of an old man. But what was wrong with that anyway? He *was* an old man. Old and experienced – not like these whippersnappers of only a few hundred years who thought they knew it all. Ha!' how would they have stood up to the Titans or the Giants or …

A shrill voice broke across his musings. '*Daddy*! You aren't listening to me.'

This was true of course. And as for the "Daddy"… Zeus focussed his gaze on Aphrodite, her parentage was uncertain at best, he thought. He was not at all sure that he *was* her "Daddy", as she put it.

He allowed his gaze to sweep the halls of Olympia ignoring the importuning of his "daughter". What a bunch of immoral, squabbling, bickering, backbiting, squawking, selfish, arrogant, blundering, megalomaniacal misfits. Perhaps their time *was* coming to an end. And perhaps, if it was, that was not such a bad thing.

Of course, he did not mean that.

* * *

They had been forced to walk after all; the currency of Greece being useless in Italy. Since Tamar had never been out of her native land as a human being, she could hardly be blamed for not realising this, but it made Denny grumpy anyway.

'What's that smell?' said Tamar suddenly.

'Me probably,' said Denny. 'I haven't had a bath for over a week.'

Tamar thought about this and then raised her arm and gave a cautious sniff. 'Ugh,' she said. 'It's *me*. That's disgusting. I *smell*.'

'One of the joys of being mortal,' said Denny unconcernedly.

'I need to *wash*,' she said. 'I can't believe it. Even my *hair* smells.'

'Yeah, well ...' Denny did not have an answer to this particular dilemma. 'Remember when you *wanted* to be ordinary?' he said. 'Be careful what you wish for.'

'I used to be a Djinn,' she said. 'You don't have to tell me that one. I *invented* that one – practically anyway.'

They had been walking for four days and were footsore and weary to a degree that they had never thought possible. And it was around this time that Denny began to have the uncanny feeling that they were being watched. He did not mention this to Tamar, knowing full well her utter disdain for all such chimera. But still the feeling persisted, until his attention was distracted by an even stranger phenomenon.

'Tamar.' He stopped her suddenly. 'Your nose is bleeding.'

Her hand flew to her face. 'It is?' she said. 'What do I do?' she added in a panic.

'Here,' he led her gently to a low wall and sat her down. 'Just put your head back, it'll stop in a minute.' He gripped the bridge of her nose and tilted her head back, and then he noticed a dark bruise on her cheek. He frowned. Where the hell had *that* come from? And then, as she raised her hand to grip her nose herself, her sleeve fell back to reveal another large bruise on her arm.

'What's going on?' asked Denny in considerable confusion. 'You look like you've been beaten up.'

'Well, I have,' she said, 'in a manner of speaking. At least, it isn't *me*, it's the *other* me. I did spend quite a lot of my time during this period being smacked in the face.'

'*What?*' Denny was horrified.

Tamar smiled at him. 'I don't think you ever really appreciated just what you had rescued me *from* when you set me free,' she said.

'But ...but ... *this*?' he indicated her bruised face.

'It's not exactly what you think,' she said. 'My master at this time had me fighting as a Gladiatrix, in his private arena. He made a fortune off me actually because I couldn't be beaten.'

'But that's actually *worse* than what I thought,' said Denny.

'It's the way a lot of slaves are treated at this time in Rome,' she said. 'At least I couldn't actually be killed.' She shrugged. 'He used to put me up against these really massively built men, and I'd knock them down like nine pins. It was quite funny really.' She looked, however, less than amused as she said this.

'And that makes it all right, does it?' said Denny getting worked up.

'Different times,' she said indifferently. 'And it certainly sharpened up my fighting skills; I mean I had to make it *look* real at least. Hence the bruises and nosebleeds and all that. Mind you, it's a bit inconvenient to be having them now,' she added. 'Bit of an unforeseen side effect of close proximity to myself. Especially as it bloody well hurts this time.'

Denny was shaking his head in disbelief. 'Why didn't you *tell* me?'

'Because I knew you'd react like this,' she told him. 'Hey,' she said cheerily. 'At least we know we're definitely going in the right direction.' As she spoke, a split appeared in her lip causing Denny to wince.

'You ... you were never *stabbed* or anything like that were you?' he asked as a nasty thought struck him.

'Oh, no,' she said blithely. 'I was far too quick for that.'

Denny breathed out. His face became serious. 'I am never, *ever* going to let anyone hurt you like that again,' he vowed.

'This is really upsetting you, isn't it?' she said. 'Why?'

'Because I love you, of course,' he said, as if it was a really stupid question. 'In fact, I'm not sure that you really understand just how much I do,' he said. 'You seem to think that it's your beautiful face that I love. It's not. I mean, I'm not saying that I don't appreciate it, or your fabulous body, because I do. You still have the power to turn me to jelly just by walking past me, or with that look that you do, and you probably always will ...'

Tamar grinned happily at this assessment of her charms.

'But,' he continued. 'What you need to understand is that even without that, I would still love you just as much.'

'Like a sister or something though,' she took it upon herself to qualify his statement for him.

'No' he said, much more than that. *You* don't care that I don't look like ... like ...' He could not think of an example. 'But, I know that you love me anyway,' he finished.

'That's because *you* are a much better person than me,' she said.

'That doesn't make any sense,' he said. 'You're accusing me of being shallow, and saying that the only reason that you aren't as shallow as you think I am, is because *I'm* the better person?'

'No, that's not what I meant. I just meant there are other things about you that are worth loving. Qualities that I don't have.'

'But you *do*,' he insisted. 'I wish you could just see yourself as I see you, just for a day. Then maybe you'd understand.'

Tamar had not got a good answer for this so she changed the subject.

'Do you get the feeling that we're being watched?' she said.

Denny rolled his eyes.

'What?' she said. '*What*?'

'You know,' said Denny on the sixth day, 'we really can't go on like this. We need food and better transport. A pair of sandals would be an improvement,' he added exhibiting his bloodied feet for her inspection. 'Anyway, the sooner we get to Rome, the sooner you'll stop looking like you just went ten rounds with the Minotaur.'

'Met him' said Tamar absently. 'He was actually a big softie. At least, he wasn't nasty to *me*.'

'Wonderful,' said Denny nastily. 'What are we going to *do*?'

'Well, I think that *I'm* going to … pass out,' she said, and then suited the action to the word.

'Oh Christ,' wailed Denny bending down to pat her face. 'If this is what living on nature's bounty does for you, you can keep it.' *

And then – a miracle. They had been walking this dusty coast road for almost a week without seeing anybody at all, but, just as they really needed it, a cart came rumbling along. Denny ran out and planted himself resolutely in front of it and began waving his arms frantically, thinking as he did so, that Tamar would have been so much better at this than him.

However, the carter stopped – well it was either that or run right over Denny, although that had been a distinct possibility – it had happened to him before.

Since he could not speak a word of the language, Denny had to try to make his case by signing and pointing. He took the bemused carter over to the prostrate body of Tamar and tried to indicate that they were starving and weary.

---

* They had been living on scrumped apples mostly for the past few days, not enough to keep body and soul together really.

The carter gave a brusque nod to show that he understood and picked up Tamar and carried her over to his cart. He then indicated that Denny take his place beside him and offered him some food. Then he made a gesture unmistakeable in any language. He rubbed his forefinger and thumb together, clearly he was asking if Denny had any money. Denny nodded uncertainly, and the carter laughed heartily at his little joke and slapped Denny hard on the back. Denny answered with a grin of relief.

As they drove off Denny looked back at Tamar anxiously, and the carter grunted and retrieved a bottle of what smelled like some sort of strong liquor from within his voluminous garments. 'Hé,' he said gruffly pointing at the bottle and then at Tamar. Denny nodded uncertainly. Tamar drunk – now that would be a sight to see. 'Hé,' the man repeated insistently and Denny shrugged his shoulders, and took the bottle and climbed over the back of the cart with it to Tamar.

Although Denny managed to force some of the vile smelling liquid between her lips she did not wake up. However, some colour came back to her cheeks, and she seemed to be breathing easier so Denny relaxed. She was probably exhausted. God knew, *he* was.

The carter patted the seat beside him to indicate that Denny come and sit up front with him again. And they... talked. Well communicated after a fashion anyway. First they exchanged names by the simple expedient of pointing at themselves and repeating their own name. The carter was called Ateius. Which Denny thought sounded appropriate, but when he told Ateius his own name it caused gusts of laughter from the cheerful carter. 'Deneee,' he repeated gleefully, 'ha ha ha ha!'

They worked out, after a lot of pointing and shouting and finally drawing a crude map, that the carter was heading for Naples. Denny told him that he wanted to get to Rome. This seemed to be understood. 'Roma,' the carter nodded to show he understood. 'Roma.' Then he pulled a sorrowful face to indicate that he could not oblige his new friend by taking him so far. 'Pfft,' said Denny dismissively to indicate that he did not mind. They were getting along quite well until Ateius showed his hand, as it were. The real reason he had picked Denny up on the road. It was getting dark, and Ateius pulled the cart over to the side of the track and climbed out. This was fine as it went; time to park up for the night, Denny understood.

He climbed out after him and began to help him to collect wood for a campfire when suddenly he found himself grabbed from behind. It was not exactly an aggressive move, more like a very friendly hug. Startled Denny jumped only to find himself turned around, and now he was in what can only be described as an embrace. Ateius grinned at him showing a lot of stained teeth. Then he reached out a hand and began to stroke Denny's hair.

So Denny hit him on the head with a rock and stole his cart.

It was nearing midnight when Tamar awoke to find herself bowling along on the back of an inexpertly driven cart.

'What happened?' she said when her eyes got used to the darkness, and she could just about make out the fact that the cart was being driven by Denny. 'Where did this cart come from?'

'Highway robbery,' said Denny. 'Mine.'

'You *stole* it?' Tamar did not know whether to be shocked or impressed.

'There's plenty of food,' he said without turning his head. 'Help yourself. Can't stop yet, got to get away from the scene of the crime.'

Tamar laughed for the sheer joy of relief. They had transport *and* food. Things were finally going their way. She did not want to know how he had done it, nor why he had suddenly decided to turn to a life of crime. She must be having an adverse effect on his morals (up until now, she had been the main instigator of their various thefts).

Tamar took her turn at driving after she had had some food.

'*Cooked food!*' she had rhapsodised. '*Meat*! Oh I never thought I could be so *hungry*!'

She turned out to be a far better driver than Denny. She did not hit nearly so many potholes for one thing, and she had also mastered the complicated art of stopping.

Denny, however, was far too exhausted by this time to fully appreciate her talent in this area. He would have been fast asleep had she tied him to the back of the cart and dragged him along the road.

They were jogging along at a fair pace now, and taking it in turns to drive so that the other could sleep might have been a little lonely, but it certainly made up the time. In a few more days (if the horse held up) they would be there. Of course, they had to stop occasionally to let the horse rest. This, Denny said, was the main advantage of a motorbike over your average domesticated quadruped. The other being that you could get a motorbike up to seventy on a decent road. The horse's fastest speed seemed to be around ten miles per hour, and it was interminably slow to Denny who liked to go fast – the faster the better.

'Grass is cheaper than petrol,' was what Tamar had to say about it. 'And it's not as of you don't get there in the end.'

But getting there in the end was not the point of travelling as far as Denny was concerned. Watching the scenery whiz past in a blur was the only point in going anywhere his opinion. This meant that he had never actually seen proper scenery before. He was finding it boring.

'At least it's faster than walking,' she said.

'Only just,' he countered grumpily.

'More comfortable too,' she added, as if she had not heard him. Since Denny's unshod feet were now beginning to heal up, he had to concede that this was true.

By the time they reached Rome, the appendages on the end of his legs would probably resemble actual feet again instead of the bloody lumps of raw meat that they had been turning into.

Rome was not as impressive as Denny had expected it to be. It seemed, to his modern eyes, to be little more than an overgrown village. But still large and busy enough to be bewildering to the eyes of a stranger. However, Tamar appeared to know her way around well enough.

'Petreius's place is over this way.' She pointed west. 'Come on, if we're quick we can catch me before I have to fight again.'

~ Chapter Five ~

DENNY HAD DONE his own share of public forum fighting, usually in some hideous seedy bar. But he had never seen anything like this. Bare knuckle was brutal but compared to the gladiatorial arena it was a ballet recital.

Anything was a weapon. The fighters had swords, axes, nets, chains, you name it ... And the point, he knew, was not to beat your opponent into submission, but rather to kill him.

Tamar had, no doubt, killed in this ring. The thought gave him a horrible cold feeling, but she had been a slave at the time, the ultimate guilt had not been hers, he kept telling himself. But what had it done to her? How had this experience contributed to her view of humanity? Especially when she herself had not been human? When he had first met her, he remembered her as having a pretty skewed view of humanity in general. But there had been no hatred there and only a little contempt. In view of what he now knew, he considered this little short of a miracle.

'In there,' she said, as they threaded their way through the crowd. She pointed to a small door. 'Behind that are the cages,' she said. 'God, it all comes back to me now. Horrible. Men locked up in cages, only allowed out to fight. And me in my little bottle.'

'And it's … you're in there too?' he said.

'Yup,' she agreed with rather overdone carelessness.

Down some stone steps, and into a dank looking cellar-like arrangement. This was where the private entrepreneur kept his fighting slaves.

There were indeed cages, some occupied, but search as they might, they could see no sign of Tamar's bottle.

They were heading despondently back up the steps, Tamar having decided that Petreius, must have the bottle with him, which could only mean that she was scheduled to fight, when they heard footsteps coming the other way – *down* the steps.

'That's him,' hissed Tamar. 'He's coming to let me out into the arena.'

'Quick – *hide*,' hissed Denny.

They scrambled down the steps and hid behind one of the cages, breathing heavily.

They did not see the actual moment when Petreius let Tamar out of the bottle. But as soon as he was gone, they both flew to the barred window from where the arena could be seen – if you stood on a crate anyway.

For Denny it was a peculiar experience, with a Tamar behind him and a Tamar in front of him – this last dressed in an armoured breastplate and carrying a sword, oddly she wore no helmet such as the others had worn. It looked dangerous, but of course, Denny knew it was not, not for her.

He watched this other Tamar squaring up to her opponent as he had seen his own Tamar do many times, but never quite like this. She swung the sword a few times as if getting the balance of it, but Denny knew what she was really doing. She was grandstanding – playing for the crowd. He shook his head; he had never thought he would see the day.

Tamar turned her head away. 'I can't watch,' she said. 'Oh, God look at that,' she added, proving herself a liar, as she clearly *was* watching.

'Showing off a bit,' agreed Denny. 'But I suppose you weren't doing anything that wasn't expected of you.'

The crowd seemed to like it anyway.

'I can still be ashamed of it,' she said. 'It really *wasn't* funny, you know. That man wasn't my enemy, I didn't even know him. He was fodder – nothing more. It's horrible.'

Ah! So *that* was it. Denny turned away from the spectacle to look at her. 'It wasn't your fault you know,' he said. 'And *you* don't think you're a good person?' he muttered.

'Does he know?' he asked. 'That man you're fighting now, does he know what he's up against, or does he think that you're just a girl?'

'What?' she said, nonplussed. 'What does that matter? – No, they weren't told as far as I know.'

'Then that makes him a pretty big scumbag in my book,' said Denny.

'No, he was a slave too,' she said. 'He had no choice either.'

'There's always a choice,' said Denny. 'Except for you.'

'You're just trying to make me feel better,' she said.

There was no denying this.

There was a loud roar from the crowd and then they began chanting something that Denny did not understand, but a probable translation was: 'KILL, KILL, KILL.'

'It's almost over,' Tamar confirmed. 'Petreius will be back soon with the bottle. Better get ready.'

There was a wild cheering.

'I just killed him.' said Tamar in a hollow voice.

'Well, look at it this way,' said Denny. 'In a hundred years, who's going to care?' As far as reassurance went this was probably the worst example of a sympathetic statement that anyone in the history of the world ever came up with, and Tamar made him feel it. '*I* still care,' she snapped. 'And as far as I'm concerned, it happened over two *thousand* years ago.'

'Look sharp,' she added. 'Here he comes.'

Petreius entered the dungeon-like cellar holding the bottle in one hand and a bag of coins in the other. He looked extremely pleased with himself.

He put the bottle down and opened the bag, chuckling to himself in a manner that, under the circumstances, Denny found completely nauseating.

He then counted and recounted his loot for an interminable length of time chuckling the whole time. Denny's fingers itched to get around his throat, but he restrained himself. Eventually Petreius rose and tucked the bag into his robes, and then he turned and picked up the bottle and tucked that away too before heading toward the steps.

'Oh, no you don't,' muttered Denny and he slid out of his hiding place and grabbed a training staff that was hanging up on the wall and felled Petreius with one blow. He grabbed the bottle, and he and Tamar fled up the steps.

'This is getting to be a bad habit,' Denny observed.

'Yes,' said a tall figure in a hooded robe (who had been watching the whole thing unobserved) to their fleeing backs. 'It certainly is.'

* * *

Petreius had a stable – for some reason this seemed appropriate, they ran inside.

Denny opened the bottle, and Tamar appeared with a yawn. She realised that she had a new master and began the spiel in a bored tone.

Denny held up a hand. 'That's okay, I know the drill,' he said.

Tamar Djinn sighed. 'Here comes the new master,' she drawled, 'same as the old master. What can I do for *you*?'

'Ehm, I'm not *exactly* the same,' said Denny. 'Tamar!' he called.

'You know my name?' she said, surprised.

'No, he knows *my* name.' said Tamar appearing from behind the door.

'I do not think I can help you,' she said, after they had explained the situation as well as they themselves understood it.

'It isn't that I don't *want* to, you understand? I *can't*. Oh, I can take you both back to Olympus, and I could have killed the gods for you if you could wish for it. But I cannot return powers to you that you never had in the first place, and I do not think that you fully comprehend your situation. You are not who you think you are.' She addressed Tamar. 'You are *not* what the future holds for me. *I* will *never* be *you*.' She turned to Denny. 'And you and I are *not* destined to meet sometime in the future, which is a shame really.' And she winked at him.

'What are you talking about?' said Denny, knowing that she would be compelled to answer him since he was technically her master.

'Nice try,' she said. 'But since you aren't real, I don't have to do what you say if I don't like, so don't try it. However, I like you, so I will try to explain.

'You two, as you are *now*, no longer exist. Any fool can see that. If I understand your explanation properly, it clearly happened when the old gods returned and everything changed. Obviously, for some reason, you two will never meet, which means that, as a part of *this* version of the world, I will never have that particular future and if I don't, then you *can't* be the future incarnation of me. The me from your time is probably still a slave and always will be. God, I'm depressing myself now.'

'You certainly are,' agreed Tamar.

'Are you saying we *really* don't exist?' said Denny. 'And everything we remember never happened to us at all?'

'That's right. Well, yes it did, obviously, but then it didn't. After the world changed, your old lives were deleted and written over. Your powers,' she pointed at Denny, 'and *your* freedom,' she indicated Tamar, 'never happened.'

'Then how is it that we're here at all?'

Djinn Tamar shrugged. 'Beats me,' she said. 'Mind you, you *did* say that some of the deleted files were still running. Maybe that accounts for it.'

'No, we'd be real if that was it,' said Tamar, 'and you say we aren't. I think Clive had something to do with it.'

'You have very strong auras,' said Djinn Tamar suddenly. 'Very powerful, you'd give any psychic a terrible headache, either of you. I think it's possible that you just held on somehow, that you both had such a strong sense of self, of who you are, that it left a footprint in the world, a hole that just fitted your shape and you ...'

Tamar groaned.

Denny was trying not to laugh. 'You were right,' he told Djinn Tamar. 'You definitely aren't her.'

Djinn Tamar pouted. 'You shouldn't mock what you don't understand,' she said.

'But that's just it,' said Denny. 'We *do* understand. We've been inside the mainframe. And it just doesn't work like that. I'm sorry.'

'Well, whatever,' said Tamar briskly. 'If we get rid of the gods as per spec and on schedule, then all of this should just get back to normal shouldn't it. If you help us,' she said to herself. 'All this,' and she waved her arms at Denny like a game show assistant demonstrating the prizes. 'Can be yours.'

Djinn Tamar looked keenly at Denny. A strange longing came into her eyes. 'We-ell,' she said. 'It's tempting, I'll give you that. But ... Oh, hell,' she said irritably. 'I wish I could, I mean I really, *really*, wish I could, you have no *idea* how much I wish I could. But...well it's not going to work you see?'

'Because we aren't real,' said Denny with sudden insight.

'Right. You can't be my master under the circumstances, and I can't do anything really major, like kill a lot of gods without a proper wish.'

'What *can* you do?' asked Denny. 'Can you get us back to Greece?'

'Yes, but to what end?' she asked, puzzled.

'Let's just say, we have nothing left to lose now,' said Tamar. 'And we aren't giving up so easily. At the very least, you can handle the transport for us as long as we are running on empty as far as the power supply goes, and, as long as we have the bottle, you can't be anyone else's slave.'

'Okay, then,' said Djinn Tamar. 'I'll do whatever I can. It'll be a relief to get out of this rat hole anyway. But what about Petreius? Technically, I'm still his Djinn, if you aren't really my masters.'

'Stuff Petreius,' said Tamar, crudely. 'People lose stuff all the time. Let's just say he should have kept a better eye on you.'

'But the rules …' began Djinn Tamar. '

'Ha!' interrupted Tamar. 'The sacred bloody rules. I can't believe I was *ever* that naïve.'

'Don't worry about it,' said Denny to Djinn Tamar. 'We've been down this road before. It'll be all right.'

* * *

'I don't like her,' Djinn Tamar confided to Denny, 'which is odd, don't you think, considering she's me – well sort of.'

Denny thought about it. 'No,' he decided. 'It's not really.'

Djinn Tamar had been as good as her word, and they had appeared suddenly in a small village near the foot of Mount Olympus to the extreme surprise of the locals. All apart from one local sorcerer who claimed he had summoned them and that their arrival had been foreseen in any case.

'She doesn't like me either,' said Djinn Tamar. 'I can tell.'

'It's not that,' said Denny. 'It's just hard for her. You are *her* from a time when she wasn't very happy. I mean that's true isn't it?'

'What's happy?' said Djinn Tamar, shrugging.

The village elders, on the instructions of the sorcerer, had made them welcome and given them a hut to themselves. They were, in a bizarre twist of fate, expected to deal with the village's "god" problem.

According to the sorcerer and his young assistant, the village was under a curse from the gods. Whatever they had done to earn the wrath of the gods was now long forgotten in the depths of time. They had begged and prayed and made sacrifice to the gods for the curse to be lifted but all to no avail. But Arpagius, the self-styled sorcerer, had told them to desist from demeaning themselves, for there was a prophecy that heroes from far away would come and save them from the curse. And he offered to try the summoning at the correct time and lo and behold, it had worked. His young assistant, who went by the unlikely name of Dexius, had been somewhat sceptical about the whole thing until the moment that two Tamars and a Denny had manifested right in front of the magical fire that Arpagius had built (and this seemed like more than a coincidence even to Tamar). Now he seemed mostly terrified. Like many of the other villagers, he was decidedly nervous about the idea of challenging the gods now that it came to it. What if it only made things worse? So far, only the iron will of Arpagius was holding things together.

The village certainly appeared to be under some sort of curse. There was little food – according to Arpagius, every year most of the crops were destroyed by tremendous thunderstorms sent down by Zeus. Their cattle and sheep were taken in the night by wild dogs thought to be the dogs of Ares.

And the village was attacked on a fairly regular basis by various gods – usually Athena. 'And she's a terrible temper on her that Athena,' said Arpagius with a blithe disregard for piety, 'seems to take the whole thing personally.'

'Why don't you all just move away?' asked Denny logically.

'And where would we go?' asked Arpagius severely. 'You can't just uproot an entire village and move it somewhere else you know. The tax collectors wouldn't allow it anyway. Everyone stays put. That's the rules.'*

---

* You may be wondering at this point, how it was that Denny was suddenly able to hold a conversation in ancient Greek. The answer, of course, is that he didn't. This was the power of the Djinn at work. Denny spoke English but he was heard in Greek and vice

'Doesn't *anybody* leave?' asked Tamar.

'Oh, yes, a few more go every year. But where they go and what becomes of them no one knows. They probably end up in the army or in prison.'

'Better than here,' she said. 'Everyone's starving.'

'I can help with that,' piped up Djinn Tamar. 'A feast fit for the … ehm … a magnificent feast every day – no problem.' And she proceeded to prove it.

This was fine – wonderful even – as far as it went. But, unfortunately, it did not really go to the root of the problem.

Curse or no curse, the plan was to kill off the gods and Djinn Tamar had no way of transporting them into the home of the gods, this village had been as close as she was able to get them. (Tamar knew this to be true; the Djinn Tamar could not lie to *her* since she knew everything that the other knew.) And what did they think they were going to do when they got there anyway, as she pointed out. But, sorry as they were for the villagers, they had not, as Denny pointed out, come all this way simply to offer emergency aid.

'Does this prophecy offer any ideas on exactly *how* we are supposed to solve your problem?' asked Denny.

'It is said that you will tackle the gods on Olympus itself,' said Arpagius.

This sounded good to Denny. 'Any clues on how we get there?' he asked hopefully.

'I always assumed you would climb the mountain,' said Arpagius unhelpfully.

'And *then* what?' said Tamar acerbically. 'You *do* realise that no mortal has ever been able to enter the home of the gods. I don't think climbing the ruddy mountain is going to prove very much.'

'I don't know what you expect us to do,' said Denny.

'Ah,' said Arpagius confidently. 'But you *will* find a way. You *are* the ones from the prophecy. If you were not, then why do you stay eh? Why do you look for ways to confront the

versa.

gods? You know as well as I, that you cannot escape this destiny. A way *will* be found. Perhaps you should climb the mountain and see what happens. You are not *ordinary* mortals after all, are you?'

'He's got us there,' said Tamar with a laugh.

Having two Tamars around was giving Denny a headache. They both seemed to have a proprietary feeling about him for one thing, and, for another, they bickered constantly.

It was best when night came, and Djinn Tamar disappeared into her bottle, and he was left with just his *own* Tamar – as he thought of her.

He was sat in front of a meagre fire looking at the Athame and pondering on its possible uses in the killing of gods. Was it still a power stealer? If it was, then the only problem – ha! the *only* problem – was getting close enough to use it.

'Thinking murderous thoughts?' said Tamar, putting her arms around him from behind.

'Pretty much,' he admitted.

'Well, at least this whole fiasco has proved one thing,' she said, indicating the Athame. 'I was right about that thing. It's definitely *not* the reason that magical women like you.'

'What?'

'Remember, you thought it was the power of the Athame that attracted all those magical crazies, and I said it wasn't. It was just you. But you wouldn't have it. Well, *I* was right.'

'How are you right?' he asked her.

Tamar indicated the bottle. 'Her,' she said. 'She's obviously got a crush on you.'

Denny laughed. 'She's *you*,' he said. 'So that doesn't really prove *anything* does it?'

'Oh … shut up,' said Tamar aware that he was right, and she had been outwitted.

But as it turned out, Denny's fatal attraction for magically gifted women was about to be put to the test.

There was a sudden commotion outside – screaming and so on. Denny and Tamar ran outside without considering what they were doing.

By the light of a dying fire, shadowy figures could be seen running to and fro, but most were heading for the shelter of their homes.

Denny caught the arm of one man who almost ran into him. 'What is it?' he demanded.

'Nemesis,' gasped the man. 'The gods have sent her to wipe us out for daring to challenge them.'

'She delivers divine justice.' said Arpagius calmly from behind them, and Denny let the terrified man go. 'Or rather she kills whoever the gods tell her to.'

'Then she's probably here for us, don't you think?' said Denny.

'They say that you don't see her until she is ready to kill you,' Arpagius told him. 'And we have all seen her here tonight. So, you work it out.'

'I'm afraid that's true,' said Tamar.

'Can she be reasoned with?' said Denny.

'Of course not,' scoffed Tamar. 'She's a *god*!'

'Well, I'm going to try,' said Denny. And he stalked determinedly towards the shadowy figure near the fire.

'Is he mad?' asked Arpagius.

'Furious I should say,' said Tamar absently. 'But he's not insane if that's what you mean. You were right about him, you know. He's a bona fide hero.'

The bona fide hero was actually shaking like a leaf by the time he reached the fire. A tiny part of his brain kept saying. *'What are you doing? She'll kill you, and you know what, after she's killed you – you'll be dead.'* But another part of his brain kept insisting. *'What are you afraid of? It's only a god!'*

The figure threw back her hood and raised her bow, the arrow was pointing straight at him.

'I was sent to kill you,' she told him.

Denny nodded. 'I thought as much.' He was feeling a little calmer now. He had a funny feeling that something unexpected

was happening here. Assassins did not usually make small talk
– or did they?

Nemesis lowered the bow. 'I can't do it,' she said.

Denny slouched back into a relaxed pose and went as if to
brush his hair out of his eyes, forgetting for the moment that he
had not got any hair in his eyes anymore. 'I'm glad to hear it,'
he said.

'I have been watching you for some time,' she said. '*I knew
someone was watching us,*' thought Denny in a detached part
of his brain.

'When you returned to my domain,' she continued. 'I had
no more excuses for allowing you to live. But I know now,
from my observations of you, that you do not deserve to die.'

She stepped over the fire and took Denny's chin in her free
hand and tilted his face up toward her own. 'But to tell you the
truth,' she said. 'I do not think I would be able to kill you, even
if you did,' she said.

Tamar slapped her fist into her palm. '*Every* time!' she said.
'I *knew* it. I only wish I'd bet him real money on this. I'd have
cleaned up.'

'She isn't going to kill him?' asked a perplexed Arpagius.

'Looks that way,' said Tamar happily.

'And the village?'

'Oh, I reckon he'll have her eating out of his hand pretty
soon. I don't think you have anything to fear from Nemesis
anymore. And the funny thing is – he doesn't even try.'

'I don't understand it,' admitted Arpagius.

'No, neither does he,' she said. 'But it works anyway.
That's the main thing.'

Denny and Nemesis came over now. She was, of course, as
a goddess, an exceptionally beautiful looking woman, but
Denny was treating her as if she were his younger sister. It was
an attitude that was likely to disappoint, but could hardly
offend her. And Denny was anxious to achieve both of these
effects at the moment.

'Nemesis told me that it was Poseidon who sent her,' he told
Tamar and Arpagius. 'He didn't bother to tell her why, but the

rumour on Olympus – and you'll laugh when you hear this –' He mugged a huge grin. 'The rumour is, that Poseidon has got it into his head that we – *you* and *me*,' he pointed to Tamar and himself, 'have been sent here to *kill the gods*. Can you believe it?'

'But that's …' began Arpagius.

'Ridiculous,' interrupted Denny. 'I know. I mean … we're *mortal*, what are we going to do? Petition them to death?

'Have you met my wife?' he asked Nemesis, bringing Tamar forward.

'Not as such,' said Nemesis with a gracious smile. 'You rival the gods my dear,' she said, to Tamar's considerable confusion. 'Of course the last mortal to do that drew considerable wrath from Aphrodite,' she continued sweetly.

'But Aphrodite forgave Psyche in the end didn't she?' countered Tamar.

I don't know that she actually *forgave* her,' said Nemesis, as if she were trying to remember.

But Tamar was ready for this one. 'Well,' she said. 'At least, she had to accept the situation in the end, didn't she?' she finished pointedly.

'I really can't remember the details,' said Nemesis airily, aware that she had been checkmated.

'All right,' thought Denny. *'That's enough.'*

'Anyway,' he said. 'Nemesis has kindly agreed to help us to take our problem to Zeus himself. Because, obviously the contract on our heads is still active and if *she* doesn't kill us Poseidon will only send someone else after us. There are, apparently, other goddesses of justice.'

'Furies,' muttered Tamar, under her breath.

'Only Zeus himself can help us now,' finished Denny

'You would do that?' asked Tamar narrowing her eyes suspiciously. 'Why?'

'It's as much for my sake as yours,' said Nemesis. 'If I fail in my duty to the gods I *will* be punished for it. The only way around it is to get the contract cancelled.'

'Or you could just kill us anyway,' pointed out Tamar.

'Any more helpful suggestions like that,' put in Denny. 'I think it might be better if you just kept them to yourself.'

'No,' said Nemesis. 'She makes a valid point. But ...' She turned to Tamar. 'Could *you* do it?' she asked. 'Could you kill *him*? Besides, I am sick of doing the dirty work of the gods. They are so arbitrary in their judgements. I never found that easy to accept. Justice is what I am *for*.'

'Okay then,' said Denny. 'Take us to Zeus.'

'It's not that simple,' said Nemesis.

'It never is,' said Tamar.

~ Chapter Six ~

DENNY WOKE UP to his usual hacking cough and, when that was over, he scuttled barefoot to the bathroom cursing the cold on his bare feet and wishing for at least the millionth time that the landlord would get the heating fixed. Then it was downstairs for the first cigarette of the day and the non-delivery of his newspaper before he decided whether or not to go into work today.

He thanked the gods for his job. In no other employment in the world, could he possibly have hoped to have such freedom. The money was crap of course but enough to get by on – supplemented by the sale of all the extraneous crap dropped off by Barry's lads along with his "purchases".

Barry's deliveries had, over the years, become more generous – well he could afford to be generous Denny thought. He had done well for himself over the years – his "redistribution of goods" had taken on the patina of a legitimate business by now – the man had *employees* for gods' sake.

As he wandered back into the bedroom to get dressed, he found himself wondering, not for the first time, who had ended up with that mint condition Millennium Falcon that Barry's lads had delivered to the wrong place so many years ago.

* * *

'Maybe it's just as well,' said Denny. 'I mean it's not as if we have a plan or anything.'

'Maybe you can just make eyes at all the goddesses,' said Tamar. 'I told you so,' she added.

'You've just been dying to say that haven't you?' he said. 'Feel better?'

'Yes, actually. But what about it?'

'What about what?'

'My plan, of course?'

'That's not a plan,' said Denny. 'It's a ... a ... I don't know what you would call *that*. A disaster in the making probably.'

'I don't see why?' she said pettishly. 'I think it could work. Maybe they'll kill each other if you get them riled up enough.'

Okay, *stop* it!' yelled Denny furiously. 'I am *not* the Casanova of the supernatural world okay? And I've had just about enough of this.'

'I was only teasing,' said Tamar meekly. 'I'm sorry.'

Denny subsided.

'But then' she added risking the resurfacing of his wrath. 'How do *you* explain Nemesis?'

'I don't,' he said shortly. 'Maybe she's lonely.'

Tamar raised a sceptical eyebrow.

'Okay so it *looks* like ... whatever. But there *has* to be some other reason,' Denny insisted. He knew in his soul that he was *not* irresistible to women, magical or otherwise, and what was more, he did not want to be. At best it was embarrassing and at worst it could be extremely dangerous.

'I don't know what you're getting all bent out of shape for,' she said suddenly. 'It doesn't bother *me*.'

'Don't you think it's a bit weird though?' he said. 'Suspiciously weird even?'

'No,' she said. 'I can understand it perfectly.'

'Well I can't. Anyway you act as if it happens all the time, and it doesn't. Nemesis was just … a coincidence.'

'Well, there was Cindy…'

'Now she *was* lonely,' said Denny.

'The Faerie Queen …'

'A raving maniac who thought I was the key to her taking over the world.'

'The Succubus …'

'The Succubus *was* Cindy.'

'Oh … right. Yeah … I forgot.'

'And now Nemesis,' she added.

'Three in total,' said Denny. That's a pretty low number compared to say … *your* score.'

'It's been more than that,' said Tamar. She hesitated. 'Hasn't it?'

'Can we please stop talking about this now,' said Denny wearily. 'It's not as if we don't have more important things on hand at the moment.'

'Yeah, how *are* you at climbing mountains?'

'I can't believe we have to climb the damned thing after all,' said Denny.

Tamar shrugged. 'It's always something,' she said.

'Yeah and that *something* is nearly always some stupid rule based in the concept of "free will". Why is it, that every time some bloody bureaucratic mind cites "free will" as the reason for something, I always end up feeling more than ever like a puppet on a string?'

'I know.' she said. 'It drives me crazy too. Do you think that the other me could handle the actual transportation to the summit? I mean that's technically still in this world.'

'Cheat, you mean?'

'We would still have made our own way up there, in a manner of speaking. All the rules say, is that no *god* can bring us there. Well I'm not a god, and I never was so it doesn't count.'

'Hmm, *crafty*,' said Denny. 'I like it. Why don't we put it to her – you?'

'I can take you,' agreed Djinn Tamar. 'But what are you going to do when you get there?'

'Nemesis will petition Zeus to see us,' said Denny. 'If he agrees, there'll be a doorway that opens or something.'

'Yes, I understand that bit,' she said. 'I meant *after* that? – You still don't have a plan do you?'

'We don't do plans,' said Tamar. 'We never have.'

'Well, that may have worked when you had super powers,' said Djinn Tamar, 'but what about now?'

'She's got a point,' said Denny. 'So we bust into the home of the gods. Then what? We don't have the power to do anything about it when we get there.'

'One thing at a time,' said Tamar testily. 'We need to make our minds up now. Are we going or not? Nemesis is returning in the morning for our decision.'

'I think we *have* to go,' said Denny. 'We may never get another chance like this after all.'

'Agreed,' said Tamar. 'But maybe ... we could stall a little. Climb the mountain, but with a *little* magical help. That way, we'll have a little more time to … think of something.'

'That isn't a bad idea,' said Denny. 'Can you do something like that?' he asked Djinn Tamar.

'What do you want from me now?' sniped Djinn Tamar. 'Magic beans?'

Denny choked back a laugh. 'Now that was *very* Tamar,' he thought. Funny how *she* didn't seem very amused.

'It could be a trap you know?' said Djinn Tamar suddenly.

'Funny,' said Tamar sarcastically. 'We never thought of that.'

'Well, we *hadn't* thought of it,' said Denny later.

'I know, but you could have backed me up anyway.'

'Sorry.'

'I don't think Nemesis is trying to lead us into a trap,' said Tamar. 'If she wanted us dead, she would have just killed us there and then. It's not as if we could have stopped her.'

'But maybe she didn't *know* that,' said Denny. 'Or maybe old Zeus wants a word with us for some reason before he crushes us like ants. And it was her job to lure us to him.'

'You'd like that wouldn't you?' said Tamar unreasonably. 'That way our charming Nemesis doesn't have a crush on you at all. She was just the honey trap.'

'Makes a lot more sense that way,' he said defensively. 'But if you really think I'd prefer *that* to the other option, where we *don't* get lured into a trap and killed. You don't know me as well as you think you do,'

'I know,' she said. 'I don't know what's the matter with me lately.' She shook her head. 'I'm a Djinn in the body of a mortal and the truth is, it's driving me crazy. I *hate* being hungry and tired all the time. I never knew a person needed so much sleep just to keep alive. It's terribly inefficient you know. And if I don't get enough sleep I start talking crap all the time because I can't think straight. So I'm going to apologise in advance right now for any more stupid comments that I might come out with over the next few weeks or however long this goes on for. Okay?'

'Okay!' said Denny saluting her.

'Just don't run off with Nemesis and start a little family of demi-vengeance gods,' she said. 'That was a joke, by the way.'

'What would a demi-vengeance god be?' mused Denny 'A sort of lawyer I suppose. You know, they only believe in justice half the time.'

'The half that suits them, you mean?'

'I think I'll stick with you,' he said. 'I wouldn't want to be responsible.'

'Is that the only reason?' she asked flirtatiously.

'What do you think?' he asked.

'I think it's a shame these huts don't have locking doors,' she said.

'Don't think that's going to save you,' he said, his eyes suddenly gleaming. And he pounced.

* * *

They did not use magic beans of course, but Tamar's plan was followed inasmuch as they climbed the mountain or rather they were teleported up the mountain in very short stages and with long and boring periods of inactivity in-between. By nightfall, they were only about half way up and then Tamar suggested they stop for the night. No one wanted to, but it seemed the sensible thing to do. A cautious plan was forming in Denny's mind, well, he had had nothing much to do all day but think. But he did not want to say anything as yet. It was risky – very risky indeed if it did not work. But he figured that, at this point, they really had nothing to lose. The other problem, as he saw it, was that it involved the basest treachery. He was not too happy about that aspect of it. But, after all, considering what they were here for ...

Djinn Tamar had created some sort of shelter by the simple expedient of boring a small cave in the side of the mountain – she was not too concerned with the intricate nuances of blasphemy, nor did she much care if the entire mountain came down. Fortunately it did not – it was only a small cave. Then she obliged them with a fire.

'I remember when *I* could do that,' said Tamar wistfully.

'Yes,' said Djinn Tamar. 'But then again, *you* don't live in a bottle. We all have our problems.'

'I suppose,' said Tamar, too tired to start an argument about it. Denny looked at her in concern. Mortality was really taking a toll on her. He wondered just how much longer she could stand it.

'So,' said Djinn Tamar. 'Just how did you get Nemesis to agree to help you anyway – you never said.'

Denny's face turned a bright red and Djinn Tamar was alert at once. 'Ah,' she said. 'So *that's* it. That's some nice work,' she added, but she was looking at Tamar as she said it.

'Er ... *I* didn't do anything,' said Tamar.

Djinn Tamar raised her eyebrows. 'You didn't?' she said. 'Then ... oh I see. I thought that you ... that Nemesis ... Oh by Allah, you have no idea that you're doing it, do you?'

'Doing what?'

But Denny got it immediately.

It's not *me*,' he said. 'It was *never* me. It's *you*!' And he glared accusingly at her, to her utter mystification.

'You must be doing it subconsciously,' said Djinn Tamar thoughtfully. 'That explains why I felt you trying to do it to *me*. I mean it didn't work obviously. It didn't need to anyway. I *am* you. I was bound to feel the same way as you do in any case. I did wonder why you bothered trying it on me.'

'What the *hell* are you two waffling about?' shouted Tamar.

'You make them see him through *your* eyes,' said Djinn Tamar. 'But I didn't realise that you aren't doing it on purpose. You can't seem to help it.'

'I-I – am *not*!' Tamar stammeringly protested.

'Oh yes you are,' said Denny. 'I see it all now. I *thought* there was something funny going on … and it only ever happens with those women who have met us *both*. It's obvious when you think about it.'

'But … but … I would never …'

'*Think* about it,' said Denny. 'The way you always get so het up when people look right through me or call me ugly to my face. It really bothers you for some reason. You just wanted people to … to …'

'Appreciate you, the way I do,' she finished in a resigned tone.' I guess I took it too far.'

'You didn't *know* you were doing it,' said Djinn Tamar. 'I don't even know *how* you do it. I've never come across anything quite like it.'

'A powerful mind,' said Denny. 'Apparently, even as a mortal, you aren't quite like other people are you?'

'You aren't, strictly speaking, a mortal,' said Djinn Tamar. 'I don't know *what* you are really. But just because you don't have any powers, doesn't mean that you're normal.'

'And it only seems to work on other magical women – not on ordinary women,' said Denny. 'There's some kind of … link there?' he asked.

Djinn Tamar shrugged. 'Maybe,' she said. 'Or maybe she just doesn't have the same impetus to convert an ordinary woman. I mean, on a subconscious level anyway, who cares what they think?'

'But magical people are more susceptible to that sort of thing, aren't they?' Denny persisted. 'Because they can already see things that normal people can't.'

'We may never understand it really,' said Djinn Tamar. 'But it's as good an explanation as any. A goddess or a witch or someone like that *is* in touch with the unseen world on a psychic level.'

'I can see that you're finding all this fascinating,' said Tamar snippily.

'How do we stop it from happening?' said Denny to Djinn Tamar, ignoring this.

'I don't think you can really,' she said. 'Sorry. She isn't conscious of what she's doing you see, so … how can she control it? It's basically an emotional response. Involuntary. And of course, even if there *was* a way to stop it from happening in the future, it's too late for Nemesis.' she added. 'She's hooked now. And that *is* because of you.'

'What do you mean?' said Denny.

'Don't kid yourself,' she said. 'You *are* special. All by yourself. It's just that it can be hard to spot, unless you get a helping hand.' And she looked at Tamar. 'It seems that what she's doing is accelerating the "getting to know you" part. Showing them everything that she sees in you, because she already *knows* you. The rest is up to them. It's not mind control. It's … a quick glimpse inside her head. I guess she thinks so highly of you that that's all it takes. She's showing them who you *really* are, you see, as opposed to just what you *look* like.'

'Stop talking about me as if I'm not here,' snapped Tamar, now thoroughly sick and tired of this.

'But most, no *all*, of them wouldn't look twice at me if she didn't do this?' persisted Denny in spite of Tamar's rising temper.

'It's hard to say for sure, but no, *probably* not. I hate to say it, but at first glance you don't really make a strong impression either way, not good or bad.'

'He did on me,' said Tamar.

'Yes, he did, and now you're spreading the word – everywhere you go,' said Djinn Tamar with a laugh.

'It's not funny,' said Denny. If you knew the trouble it's caused …' He broke off as Tamar finally lost control and burst into tears.

'I think I'll just …' said Djinn Tamar and discreetly retired to her bottle.

'I didn't *mean* to do it,' she wailed.

'I know that,' he said comfortingly. 'It's okay, really it is.'

'But you were right. I mean look at all the trouble it's caused.'

'Nothing we couldn't handle,' he told her. 'It's kept life interesting, hasn't it?'

'I suppose,' she said, sniffing.

'And at least it proves you must trust me,' he added.

'Of course I do,' she said, startled.

'And if it makes you feel any better. From what she said, I would have to say that the whole Cindy fiasco was not your fault. It was definitely mine.'

Tamar said nothing. She was not so sure. Cindy's attitude toward Denny when they had first met had been everything that Tamar found irritating about the way people reacted to Denny when they did not know him, which was basically to ignore him. Had that been the catalyst for this extraordinary manifestation? With Cindy as the first victim? Or had Cindy's opinions of Denny changed naturally as she got to know him better and began to see … what *she* saw?

She realised that she would never know. And it did not matter now anyway. In the end, Cindy's feelings had definitely been real – no matter *how* it had started. As were the feelings of Nemesis according to what her other self had told them. The point was that she had to stop doing this somehow, before it caused any more trouble.

* * *

'So,' said Djinn Tamar brightly as the sun rose and flooded the cave. 'Have you come up with a plan yet?'

'No.' said Denny shortly. 'He did not feel like sharing his idea just yet. He was not even certain that he was going to go through with it.

'You know I've been thinking about this,' she said. 'If you do succeed somehow, the world will go back to how it was before, won't it?'

'Hopefully, yes.'

'So, none of this will have happened,' she said. 'I'll never have met you and all this … you'll just go back to your lives right. Because after you fix it, you won't have to come back in time in the first place in order to fix it. It's a paradox really.'

'I hadn't really thought about it,' said Denny. 'But I suppose you're right.'

'Will that be okay?' she asked in concern. 'Won't you get stuck in the loop?'

Denny thought about it. 'No,' he said eventually. 'Not this time. It'll just be as if it never happened at all. You said it yourself. 'We don't exist at the moment.'

'But it was a good thought,' he added as her face fell. But as it turned out, that was not what was bothering her.

'But I won't remember *any* of this?' she said a little sadly.

'If you did,' he said. 'That *would* create a paradox. I'm afraid that as far as you are concerned, none of this will have happened at all. You will go back to your life too. I wish there was something I could do about it, but I can't.'

'Hmmm,' she said and her face became thoughtful.

* * *

They were greeted by a rather flustered Nemesis at the summit. Djinn Tamar was back in her bottle under the proviso that they understood that it was her decision, and she could chose to come out whenever she wanted to. Since they could not technically be called her masters, this was really just a point of courtesy.

'Well?' said Denny 'What happened, will Zeus see us?'

'Not even after I told him how lovely your wife is,' she apologised. 'I think he's finally getting old. In the old days that would have done it right away.'

'Maybe you should have avoided the use of the word "wife".' said Denny naïvely.

Nemesis laughed. 'Oh, you *are* a treasure,' she said. 'Don't be so silly, as if that matters to *him*.'

'It matters to *me*,' said Denny.

'So, he won't see us?' interrupted Tamar. 'You couldn't get us in?'

'I shall keep trying,' said Nemesis.

'There's no need,' said Denny.

'*What*?' said Tamar in an outraged tone.

Denny ignored her and took Nemesis by the hand and looked steadily at her – it was, he felt, the least he could do under the circumstances. 'I really am very sorry,' he said and plunged the Athame into her heart.

It worked. He had not been one hundred per cent certain that it would – but there was no doubt. He could feel the power flowing. Nemesis fell to her knees as Denny withdrew the blade. She was unhurt but powerless now. A mortal.

Had Denny known it, this was a part of the legend. Although, according to the story, it was the gods who deprived Nemesis of her power for daring to question their "justice". However, this was close enough. She *had* questioned, and now, almost as a direct result, she had lost her power.

She was staring at Denny, a world of pain in her eyes. 'So,' she said. 'It *is* true. You *have* come to destroy us.'

'Yes,' said Denny. There was no point in denying it.

'So, do it then. Finish me.'

'I'm not going to kill you,' he said. 'You are mortal now, that's enough.' He bent down to her. 'You could look at it another way,' he said. 'You may be mortal now, but you are also free. Think about it,' he advised. And he turned away from her, and, taking Tamar's hand, entered the home of the gods.

~ Chapter Seven ~

IT TOOK TAMAR a full five minutes to get her breath back after Denny's stunning performance. She had thought she knew him, but never in a million years would she have imagined that he would do something like *this*. *Her* yes; she would probably not have even hesitated. She had actually thought of doing something like this, but had been certain that he would never agree to it. How wrong can you be?

'I had to,' said Denny as if reading her thoughts. 'And after all, it's what we came here for isn't it? One down,' he added tastelessly.

'I agree,' she said. 'I really do, I would have done it in a heartbeat. I'm just a bit surprised that *you* did it.'

'Well, I had to,' he reiterated. 'It was the only way to get us in.'

'And what the hell have we got ourselves into anyway?' said Tamar looking around in distaste.

'It's like cloud city,' said Denny. 'Not the one in Star Wars obviously,' he added needlessly. Tamar had never seen Star Wars anyway.

So far, all that could be seen was a misty landscape with a lot of pillars rising out of and disappearing into the clouds. There was a faint golden haze over everything like muted sunlight. Here and there shafts of bright golden light shone through thunder headed cloudbanks. Denny thought it was pretty.

'Can you do that to all of them?' asked Tamar. 'Will it really be that easy?'

'I don't know,' he admitted. 'Nemesis wasn't as powerful as most of the other gods and besides ...'

'It won't be as easy to get that close to the others,' Tamar finished for him.

'They're probably expecting us by now,' he said.

'So, where's the reception committee?' said Tamar.

At that moment, a bolt of lightning shot through the clouds and landed at Denny's feet. He never moved a muscle.

'I guess that answers that question,' he said.

'Mmm,' said Tamar. 'Typical gods,' she added, 'always so showy and tasteless. I mean *look* at this place. It's the divine version of a gin palace. All it needs are tasteless cherubs and maybe a few fruit machines.'

'I quite like it,' admitted Denny.

'That's the Athame talking,' she told him. 'The Denny I know would hate all this glitter.'

'Oh, well maybe you're right,' he said. 'Is that it?' he added. 'One lightning bolt? Somehow I was expecting worse.'

Worse was coming. Through the clouds, a female figure appeared. She was scantily clad and had long golden hair. The lady Godiva of the ancient world. Tamar recognised her immediately. She had once taken her face – just for a few minutes – until she found a better one. Because although it was true that Aphrodite was supremely beautiful – the face was somewhat doll-like. It is possible to have features that are *too* perfect. Tamar had never made this mistake. Apart from this, she reminded Denny disturbingly of Cindy. Particularly the way she was looking at him, which was all too familiar.

She smiled at them both and extended her hands in a gesture of welcome. 'Come and play,' she offered.

'They're afraid,' thought Tamar. 'They don't know what we can do to them.'

Denny was rapidly coming to the same conclusion. 'They know what I did to Nemesis,' he was thinking, 'they must do. So they're playing nice now, to see what happens next. They don't know why we've come, but I have the power of a god and Tamar is beautiful enough to be a goddess. They don't know who we are.'

He put on a stern face. 'We want to see Zeus,' he demanded.

'Oh, well,' thought Tamar with an internal sigh. 'In for a penny …'

Aphrodite fluttered.

'Another one,' thought Denny with an internal sigh of his own. He had thought he recognised that look. Still, in this case, it could come in handy. Nevertheless he gave Tamar a look, and she shrugged helplessly. 'What can I do?' she seemed to say.

'But of course,' said Aphrodite. 'We are having a feast. The king of the gods presides. You can ask him whatever you wish.'

Tamar and Denny looked at each other. 'Okay … I mean – very well,' said Denny. 'Take us to him.'

* * *

Aphrodite, clinging firmly to Denny's arm, took them to the feast. It was being held in what they took to be the main throne room or Olympian equivalent. A large space that had clearly been modelled partly on the Elysian Fields and partly on the Parthenon. That is, it looked like a pleasure garden – with pillars. A large crystal clear lake was the central feature and many gods were enjoying a nude swim. Zeus sat on a large marble throne on a dais behind which was a circle of pillars. He looked bored.

They were relieved to see that there was no sign of Poseidon. He was, although they were not to know this, in disgrace at the moment.

They were treated as honoured guests. The whole experience was a little unnerving at first, until they realised that they were apparently not actually suspected of dark designs against the entire pantheon. It seemed to be assumed, from what they could make out, that Nemesis had simply been in their way, or had offended them in some way. And that, given what had happened to her, it was only wisdom to be courteous to their guests, in case the same thing happened to them.

In any case, as soon as Zeus laid eyes on Tamar, he felt the stirring of desires that had been long dormant (and he was not the only one) there were not many mortals – if any – like her. He only had to look at her once to feel like a young god of five hundred again.

Tamar, of course, was shrewdly aware of the effect she was having. It happened all the time. And in any case, Zeus was making no effort to hide it. She wondered how she could use this to her advantage without compromising herself. There was always the jealousy option of course. She was aware of Apollo, in particular, watching her, as she sat at the feet of the king, with smouldering eyes. She could feel his resentment towards Zeus from here.

Meanwhile, Denny was having his own problems. Although, the Athame was protecting him from whatever pheromones or other magical love spells that Aphrodite was using on him shamelessly, and which would, no doubt, have had other mortal men drooling like idiots, she was not to be put off.

However, it could have been worse, he thought. Of the other goddesses present there were only Artemis and Athena who had a high enough caste to challenge Aphrodite and both of them were chaste and, therefore, uninterested in doing so. Thank heaven for small mercies, he thought. However, while Athena was inclined to disdainfully ignore him Artemis challenged him to an archery contest, and he seemed to win her respect at least when he proved himself at least her equal in this art. Thanks, no doubt to the stolen power of Nemesis, who had been a master bow-woman. (Denny had never learned to shoot although he *was* good at knife throwing.)

It was a swinging party. A Bacchanal, in fact. The ambrosia was flowing, and the antics of the gods were getting wilder and wilder. And all the time, Tamar and Denny were wondering what on earth they were going to do. If Denny used the Athame now, on one god, he would certainly never get a chance to go after the others. The rest of them would undoubtedly fall on him as one and that would be the end of him. He knew he was nowhere near a match for all of them. Unless, he went after Zeus himself – perhaps …

No, he decided. Even that would not work. One god could certainly kill another; they knew that. But the whole lot of them? Even the power of Zeus was not going to be enough.

In fact, the more he thought about it, the more he realised that this had been a very, very bad plan. There was nothing they could do here. They just did not have enough power. What they needed, he thought in frustration, was the power of a Djinn, and, unfortunately, that was just what they could not have.

'Come and swim with me,' urged Aphrodite tugging on his arm. He found this side of her particularly repellent. She was like a spoiled child.

'Just take no for an answer, will you?' he said silently.

'I don't like the water,' he said aloud.

Then he looked up and saw that Tamar was being subjected to similar urgings by Zeus, and that Apollo, finally deciding that he had had enough, had stepped in. Of course, Denny thought, they both just wanted to see her naked.

'Over my dead body,' he decided. 'It's time to get the hell out of here anyway.'

He stood up – too late. Apollo was not the only one who had had enough of Zeus's importuning. Tamar had spent the better part of five thousand years with an immovable contempt for gods of all shapes and sizes, and this had been backed by the fact that she herself had had far more power than they. Even as a slave, no god had power over her; that privilege was reserved for humanity. This may have been the reason why she slapped Zeus in the face.

The atmosphere changed immediately. As if a sudden cold wind had blown everyone's laughter away, a deathly silence fell, and no one moved. But the tension in the air was palpable. The gods were angry. Angry but uncertain. It was likely that nothing like this had ever happened before. Denny only had a few seconds while their uncertainly lasted.

As Zeus opened his mouth to roar Denny bounded forward and stood before him.

He said nothing but he forced as much silent threat into his face as it would hold. There was a long moment of uncertainty. And then, for the first time in forever, the unthinkable happened. Denny flinched first.

And that was it. It was over. Zeus roared in triumph and raised a massive fist. Denny grabbed Tamar and dived for cover.

Aphrodite was wringing her hands. 'Daddy, no!' she wailed. 'I *want* him! Leave him alone!'

In his fury, Zeus directed his next lightning bolt straight at Aphrodite. 'Be silent!' he roared. 'Who is the king here anyway?'

Aphrodite rose from the ground with such a look of pure venom on her face that Denny, who happened to catch sight of it, blanched.

Then it was Denny's turn, and he was unlikely to survive it in his current condition.

Tamar acted fast; she scrambled to her feet and interposed herself between the enraged king of the gods and the fallen Denny. What she thought she was doing was anybody's guess.

She stood there waiting for death, there was nothing else she could do, and after he had disposed of her. Denny would also die. Tamar would not have minded so much if she could have taken them all with her. What really annoyed her was that they had failed.

She did not see her Djinn counterpart rising up behind her.

She had come out of the bottle to see what all the commotion was about and was just in time to see Zeus raise his fist ready to throw a lightning bolt and hurl Tamar into oblivion. There was nothing she could do to protect Tamar or Denny, as they were not true masters. But there was something she *could* do, something that might just save them both. No time to think … just do it.

She joined with Tamar. Like a spirit taking over a living body, she simply walked forward into Tamar.

As the familiar power surged through her, Tamar lifted off the ground slightly, and a bright light shone out from the ends of her fingertips, her toes and the top of her head like high beams, they blasted outward and filled the space with a light so bright that the gods had to cover their eyes. Then she floated gently to the ground. 'Ooh,' she said, and there was a slight echo to her voice. 'That's better. I was a bit worried that there might have been a little overload there,'

The lightning struck her full in the chest, but earthed harmlessly at her feet. She did not even seem to notice it. She swept her arm in a wide arc as if swatting the air and Zeus went flying sideways and backwards for quite a distance.

'Now, that's what *I'm* talking about!' she yelled jubilantly. 'Oh, yeah, I'm back!'

Denny bounced to his feet. 'Retreat,' he hissed.

Tamar came to her senses at once. He was right, time to go. Zeus was stunned, but even now, he was getting ponderously to his feet. They needed a new plan.

* * *

'Strike one,' said Tamar as they were getting their bearings back on the ground.

'Could have been worse,' said Denny. 'We could be dead.'

'That's right,' she said cheerfully. 'At least we get to have another go at them.'

'About that,' said Denny. 'What happened?'

Tamar held up the (now empty) bottle. 'You know how she and I are really the same person?' she said. 'Well, it's just a little bit more literal now.'

'She's in there with you?'

'No, she *is* me, and I'm her. It's metaphysical. Don't try to understand it. 'It's like, the power is *my* power, I just needed it back, and she hadn't lost it yet so... Oh Lord, when you try to explain it in regular terms you just can't.'

'So, she's gone? I mean the you from this time, is gone?'

'I *am* the me from this time, the me from *our* time doesn't exist see? Except I'm here somehow, so I'm still *that* me too. I have all my memories and everything. And I'm still free. As in, not a slave.'

'You're *both* of you?' said Denny, his face creasing into a perplexed frown.

'And neither,' she said, which only confused him even more.

Seeing this, she tried to explain. 'Okay,' she said, 'try this on for size. You and I no longer exist in the future, in our own time right? So in order to retrieve the power that I once had, I had to come back in time to a point when I still had that power.'

'But that isn't how it happened,' objected Denny.

'No, but the result is the same,' she said. 'Now, as a Djinn, I had considerable power but no freedom and, therefore, no identity, at least no identity that I could separate from that power. The power was me, and I was the power (no jokes about He-Man please) and that was all. My personality was incidental. And as a mortal I had my freedom, I was *just* me, *all* me, but I had no power. Now, I have both – again. Now, I'm me, and I have the power too. She was the power – in some ways that was *all* she was. All *I* was, I should say.'

'Both and neither,' said Denny. 'I see. Did you know that this would happen if she – if you ...'

'Yes, at least I knew it in an abstract way. That is to say, I hadn't given it a lot of thought. But I *would* have known if I'd thought about it. But it honestly never occurred to me.'

'It occurred to her – obviously. Why do you think she did it?'

'Because it's what *I* would have done. The alternative was watching you die, and that's unacceptable to me. *Any* me apparently.'

A thunderous crash from the top of Olympus brought their minds back to more immediate concerns.

'We should get far away from here,' said Denny.

'Oh, I don't know,' she said. 'It's the last place they'll look for us. And you notice they haven't come after us yet. They're scared.'

'Scared enough to gather a huge army of gods and other … things and come after us and crush us.' Denny said. 'I'd bet my… I'd bet on it.'

'And you would be right,' said someone from behind him.

'Aphrodite?' said Denny turning in surprise. 'What are you doing here?'

'I have come to offer my help to you,' she said, 'if you agree to spare me of course.'

~ Chapter Eight ~

THIS WAS A master that Tamar hated bitterly – of course she never liked any of them much but honestly ...

If you were going to use a Djinn for criminal activity – and many did, she was used to that – at least have the sense to think ... well *bigger*!

All this petty thievery was getting on her nerves. She was capable of so much more. But apparently Barry had no further ambition than to be a biggish fish in a very small pond and not get put behind bars. Tamar could do this standing on her head.

And he was so *stupid*! Not, it had to be said, stupid enough to have made his three wishes and have done with it (she had been stuck here with him for twenty years now) but certainly stupid enough to drive her crazy.

'If I were free ...' She began the familiar train of thought but stopped herself. It was no use – she would *never* be free. She had finally given up on that one about twenty years ago. She had just awoken one day to the cold and absolute realisation that it was never *ever* going to happen. Not in *this* life.

* * *

'But she *can't* be on our side,' said Denny after Aphrodite had withdrawn to let them discuss it. 'She's the enemy.'

'I don't see why not.' said Tamar stubbornly. 'Pitting the gods against each other is a good plan actually and if we can get one god to join us maybe we can get others.' said Tamar.

'You mean we get a lot of them on our side, and then just sit back and let them all kill each other?' Denny gave the idea some thought. 'It's a bit ...' he began. 'Mind you ...' he continued. 'But it'll never work. We'll never get any more of them to join us – or at least not enough of them and anyway ...'

'I know it's a bit morally ambiguous,' she said.

'Actually, I don't have a problem with that,' he told her. 'Any gods that join us will be doing it mostly to save their own skins at the expense of the others. They'll deserve everything they get. Okay,' he said decisively. 'On that basis, she's in.'

Since Tamar had got what she wanted, she forbore to point out that Aphrodite had more than likely decided to join them out of a desire a – for Denny himself, and b – for revenge on Zeus – and who could blame her for that? The bastard *had* thrown a bolt of lightning at her.

Aphrodite took the news with an air of smug satisfaction. 'I knew you'd see it my way,' she seemed to say. 'After all I am the goddess of love. Where would the world be without me? But those other gods ... who needs them?'

Tamar and Denny read these thoughts in her face as clearly as if she had spoken them out loud, which may have been what she intended of course.

But their original problem remained; how to kill the gods? They were beginning to feel as if maybe they were not supposed to manage it at all. It would not be the first time that Clive had sent them on a wild goose chase, or that the clerks had set them up. Because, no matter what, they were trapped here. They might technically have the power to go home now, but they had nothing to go home *to*. Not until the gods were dead and history was set back on course.

'You weren't exactly what we were expecting,' Aphrodite confided. 'I mean no wonder Prometheus would rather have stayed chained to a rock than try to tell the gods that two mortals, and one of them a *girl* too, were the ones who would finish us all off. They wouldn't have believed him anyway.'

'*What* was that?' demanded Denny. 'I thought Prometheus was chained to that rock for stealing fire from the gods.'

'Oh yes, he was. But Zeus found out that he knew the name of the one who would eventually destroy the gods and he offered to let him go if he would tell. But he wouldn't. Said they'd just have to wait and see. At least that's what I heard.'

'That's interesting,' said Tamar noting Aphrodite's use of the word "they".

'Titans,' said Denny. 'Now there's an idea.'

'He's the only one left,' said Tamar. 'But he certainly hates the gods. And a Titan is always impressive.'

'He'd scare the sandals off Zeus,' chipped in Aphrodite. 'I'd love to see his face if you unchained Prometheus. Can you do that?'

'I thought Heracles had already freed him.' said Denny.

'P.R. job,' said Tamar dismissively.

'That's *right*,' said Aphrodite in surprise. 'But how did *you* know that?'

'I must have read it somewhere,' said Tamar.

'*Read* it somewhere?' said Aphrodite. 'Mortals can *read*?'

'I can whistle and chew gum at the same time too,' said Tamar acerbically. 'There's really no end to my talents.'

'We could probably free Prometheus somehow,' said Denny. 'If we knew where he was?' he looked at Aphrodite.

'He's in the underworld somewhere,' she said.

'I thought he was on a mountain,'

'Oh, he is. There are many worlds within the underworld.'

'I can vouch for that,' said Tamar mysteriously. 'And we'll never find him without some sort of guide.' She did not seem terribly surprised to discover that Prometheus was in the underworld. 'Isn't he chained up with the chains of Hephaestus?' she asked.

'Yes, but Heph doesn't know ... Oh all right, I suppose I could ask him. We don't get on,' she confided to Denny in an aside. 'Arranged marriage. Total disaster.'

'Your fault,' muttered Tamar. '*I* thought he was a pretty nice bloke.'

Aphrodite heard this. 'Oh, he's nice enough, but he's so dull.' she sighed. 'And bitter too. After Hera threw him off Olympus for being too ugly, he never got over it. Said marrying him to *me* was the final insult.'

'Why?' said Denny.

'The goddess of love *and* beauty,' supplied Tamar. 'Zeus did it for a joke.'

'Yes,' agreed Aphrodite. 'Funny sense of humour if you ask me. Anyway Heph was pretty awful about it. Acted like it was all *my* fault. So I left him.'

'I thought he chucked you out after he caught you with Ares,' said Tamar tactlessly.

'What do you think I was doing with Ares in the first place?' said Aphrodite. 'You seem to know an awful lot about it,' she added. 'Who *are* you anyway?'

'It sounds as if Hephaestus has got no reason to like the gods on Olympus either,' said Denny. 'Maybe you two could bury your differences on this one ...?'

'I would think he'd be only too glad to help us free Prometheus,' added Tamar, 'if it was going to upset Zeus.'

'And I'm sure that if anyone can get around him, it's *you*,' put in Denny smoothly.

Aphrodite preened. 'I'm sure I can,' she said. 'But why do you care about freeing Prometheus anyway?' she asked suddenly. 'What does that have to do with anything anyway? Surely you don't *need* him?'

'That's *our* business,' said Tamar curtly. Aphrodite really was not as empty headed as she appeared. 'We don't need *you* either if it comes to that, so I'd stop asking questions if I were you. We have our own plans, and if you want to be involved you'll do as you're told, or we might as well just kill you now.'

'All right, all right.' Aphrodite backed down immediately. 'I was just asking ... but I won't anymore.'

'Why *don't* we just kill her?' said Tamar later. 'Two down?'

'No,' said Denny. 'Not yet anyway. She might come in handy. It was *you* that said so in the first place. And it's beginning to look like you were right.'

'Prometheus and hopefully Hephaestus too,' said Tamar. 'If she can deliver them, we'll be on our way to an army. We've been down this road before.'

'Not quite like this, though,' he said. 'We don't want *either* side to win this time.'

'And just *how* are we going to free Prometheus anyway?' said Tamar. '*I* can't do it. At least, I'm not certain, but I couldn't break the chains of Hephaestus when Askphrit used them on Hecaté and we know that the Athame is no use on them either.'

This was, unfortunately, true.

'Anyway,' she resumed. 'One thing at a time, we have to find him first. And I think maybe *I* should be the one to talk to Hephaestus. Just at first anyway. I mean, when Aphrodite said they didn't get on she wasn't telling the half of it. And if she's still mooning over *you* ... Well that's just going to get his back up even more.'

'She seems to be over that,' said Denny.

'I wouldn't count on it,' said Tamar. 'We thought Cindy was over it – several times. And look how *that* turned out.'

'Don't remind me,' said Denny with a shudder. 'Okay, *you* talk to him. I think you're right. But we still need her to tell us where to find him.'

'You don't ... *like* her do you?' asked Tamar, narrowing her eyes at him.

'No, not exactly *like* her,' he said. 'But she's all right compared to some of the others I suppose.'

'You *do* like her,' accused Tamar her temper flaring suddenly.

'What's the matter with you?' he said defensively. 'Bringing her on board was *your* idea not mine.' he reminded her again.

'Well, you didn't exactly put up much of a fight about it,' she said sullenly.

'Because you were right,' he said. 'What's all this about? You can't possibly be jealous. Not of *her* surely. You have no reason to be jealous of anyone in any case. Not on my account. You never get jealous anyway.'

'Oh, yes I do,' she admitted calming down a little. 'I was terribly jealous of Cindy at one time you know. I wanted to kill her.'

'You *were*?' Denny was startled. 'I never knew you had it in you.'

'It's ... hard sometimes,' she said.

'No kidding,' he said dryly. 'What do you think it's like for *me*? If there's a straight man in the whole world who can resist *you* ...' He left the sentence hanging.

Tamar pulled a face. 'I thought it didn't bother you,' she said.

'Yeah, well ...' He shrugged. There was a long awkward silence. Then a twinkle came into Denny's eye. 'Still, It makes life interesting,' he said with a sudden grin.

'I guess I asked for that,' she said.

* * *

'This was *not* the plan. They were not supposed to get so far.'

'I told you they were resourceful,' said Clive.

'But at this rate, they might actually succeed. I mean, who could have foreseen that they would find a way to get their power back?'

'I could have,' said Clive, 'if anybody had bothered to ask me.'

'And this plan to pit god against god. It's ... innovative. I confess, we did not see it coming. It could even work.'

'Don't we *want* them to succeed?' came another voice.

'It's not that simple,' said the first voice. 'The fact is *we* don't need them to succeed. Only *they* need that. As far as we are concerned, it's taken care of.'

'And if they do succeed?'

'Well, we won't need to do anything in that case. History will be restored, and there will be nothing to sort out.'

'And if they fail?'

'If they fail? Then they will never have existed, and this problem will never have happened in the first place. It *was* them who caused it.'

'Then why send them back?'

'To punish them,' said Clive bitterly.

'No,' said the first voice. 'That was not the reason. They were sent back because of the historical imperative. They themselves had become a paradox. Had they not done what they did, then they would not have changed their own history to the point where they no longer existed to be able to do what they did. However, they *did* do it, therefore, they could not have possibly done it, therefore, they didn't do it, and because they didn't do it, they did and so on.' he summarised for the benefit of the second speaker who he knew to be easily confused.

'A paradox goes round and round on itself forever,' said Clive. 'The only way to break it was to send them back to the point where the paradox began. I see.'

'And whether they succeed or fail in their quest is now immaterial to us.' said the first voice.

'But not to them,' said Clive.

'No, not to them.' agreed the first voice. 'But from our point of view, it would be better if they were to fail. And none of this ever happens in the first place.'

How can you say that?' said Clive. 'If they fail then surely *everything* they have done will be undone and they have not exactly been spectators you will admit. Their actions have affected many lives over the years.'

'Wrong again,' said the first voice. 'Only the actions that caused the paradox will be undone. All the rest ... Well you should know this stuff by now. Everything else that has happened will stay happened because of the paradox. Do *they* not still exist in spite of the fact that they have destroyed their own history? That's the paradox at work. They exist and yet they do not. Or, I should say, they *did* exist but from the moment that history changed they *no longer* existed. I should not have to explain this to you as if you were an infant. This is what happens to a mind when its owner spends too much time in the company of humans, is it?'

'So, it really is only they who will be destroyed if they fail?' said Clive.

'Not destroyed as such,' said the first speaker, 'just stuck in the past because they no longer exist. There are worse fates.'

'Not for them,' said Clive. 'Trust me on this one. There's no way they'll give up until they've succeeded. And I know this much – as long as there's a chance that they will succeed. The paradox will continue.'

'You are, unfortunately, correct,' said the first voice. 'I had hoped it would all be over by now. But they simply will not give up.'

'More than that,' said Clive. 'I think they'll do it.'

'You are *not* to interfere,' warned the first voice.

'I won't have to,' said Clive in a smug voice. 'But, just for the record, I hope they do it and to hell with the lot of you. You're a bunch of conniving, cold blooded bastards, and I'm sick of the lot of you. And you can make that official if you like, I couldn't give a toss.' And he switched off his communicator.

'Touchy isn't he?' said the second voice.

* * *

They found Hephaestus in his forge as expected. This was in a place called Lemnos, which was, unsurprisingly, a volcanic region in those days, although it is not now. He was not inclined to be helpful. One part of the story of Prometheus that Aphrodite had conveniently missed out was that the fire that he had stolen had come from the forge of Hephaestus, and as they had reason to know, Hephaestus was prone to holding a grudge.

He was not very pleased to see Aphrodite either, who had insisted, despite Tamar's disapproval, on being involved, and all in all it was going pretty badly until Tamar took a hand.

She shooed Aphrodite and Denny outside and turned on the charm.

'Why should I?' he asked. 'I've got no reason to help that thieving Titan. And you can stop batting your eyes at me. *Look* at me? Do you think I'm likely to fall for that, with a face like mine? No woman as beautiful as you is going to want *me*.'

'You don't remember me, do you?' she asked. 'We only met briefly, but ...'

'Oh, I remember you all right,' he said. 'And I'm not saying that you weren't quite nice as far as it goes, but you never pretended that I was handsome, now did you?'

'You aren't as ugly as you think you are,' she told him.

'Hmm, that was quite convincing,' he said with a short laugh. 'Suppose you tell me what's really going on. And what that wife of mine has got to do with it? I warn you, she's treacherous. I wouldn't trust her as far as I could throw her. She's got her eye on that man of yours too.' he added. 'Not that that's a big surprise.'

'I know,' said Tamar. 'But it won't do her any good.'

'Aha!' said Hephaestus. 'So he *is* with you. I thought as much. What are you flirting with me for then, eh? Or is that a stupid question?'

Tamar shook her head as if to clear it. 'You know what,' she said, 'we only came to ask for your help against Zeus. Tell us where Prometheus is and ...'

'It won't do you any good,' he interrupted her. 'You can't break *my* chains. No one can. Not the gods nor mortals nor even you, little Djinn.'

'That's *our* problem,' she said. 'You needn't be involved if you don't like. But I warn you, I've tried to be nice about this, but if you aren't with us, then we *will* come after you when we go after the rest of the gods.'

'So *you're* the one,' he said, his eyes round with wonder. 'It didn't take long for Aphrodite to join your side I see. But I wonder … what do you want with Prometheus? And if you *are* here to destroy the gods, as was foretold, why should I believe you will spare me in the end?'

'How do you know, *what* was foretold?' she said. 'Not *all* the gods have to die,' she said truthfully enough.

'But Zeus definitely does?' he said.

'Oh, yes,' she said. 'Definitely.'

'You aren't telling me everything,' he said, 'not by a long way, but ... very well. I shall accompany you to the underworld and take you to Prometheus. And then we shall see ... whatever we shall see.'

'Thank you,' said Tamar.

'Just keep that wife of mine out of my sight will you. Or else I won't be responsible.'

* * *

'Back in the underworld again,' said Denny with a sigh and to Aphrodite's profound astonishment. 'Who *are* you?' she asked again.

'They haven't added Hell yet,' said Tamar. 'But Charon's still here with his little ferryboat. What fun.'

'You speak for yourself,' said Denny. 'He always gives me a hard time about not paying and the fact that I'm still breathing and so on.'

At this Hephaestus roared with laughter. It quite transformed his pitted, scarred and, above all, sour face.

'You leave Charon to me,' he said. 'I'll brand his ugly head if he gives us any trouble.'

'Sounds painful,' agreed Denny. 'It'd convince me.'

'Ah, I doubt that,' said Hephaestus. 'But Charon's an old coward.'

'I told you he was a nice bloke,' said Tamar. 'Once you get past his grumpy exterior anyway.'

Whatever he said to Charon apparently worked. Denny had never seen him so cooperative. He practically bustled in his efforts to get them comfortably seated, and he punted them across the Styx in record time.

They were greeted in Tartarus, not by Hades, but by a disconcertingly familiar face.

'Hecaté!' This was Denny. He was staring at her in an uncouth manner, mainly because he had never seen her dressed in so little. The costume was – well to call it revealing was to assume that there was at least slightly more clothing than person on display, and this simply was not the case. For Denny it was like finding out that your favourite aunt used to be a pole dancer

'Hecate,' Tamar told him. 'Heh – Kate.' she pronounced slowly as she reached over and gently closed his mouth for him.

'I know why you have come,' said Hecate. 'The time of our destruction is at hand. I shall not fight it.'

'Er ...' began Denny awkwardly.

'You know about that do you?' asked Tamar.

'From here I see all that passes in the upper world,' she said. 'I knew you were coming, and I know why.'

'I'm not so sure about that,' muttered Denny.

'We aren't going to kill *you*,' said Tamar bluntly.

'Why not?' asked Hecate with equal bluntness.

'It's not your time yet,' said Denny. 'We're absolutely certain.'

'Positive in fact,' added Tamar.

Hecate frowned. 'It is not that I would wish to dissuade you,' she said. 'But, I am wondering, how is it that you can be so certain.'

Tamar and Denny looked at each other and grinned. 'You'll understand one day,' said Denny. 'I *know* you will.'

'Then you *are* here to fulfil a destiny?' she asked. 'And not, as it is rumoured among the gods, to manifest vengeance.'

'Are we?' said Denny blankly. 'Well, if you say so.'

Hecate nodded. 'I see,' she said. 'You would bid me mind my own business and let you mind yours. I shall ask no more. But beware Hades. If you have come for him, he will not go easily.'

'Then he'll go the hard way,' said Tamar. 'But you don't seem too bothered about it either way. You don't like him?'

'If Hades dies and she lives then she'll rule in the underworld,' put in Hephaestus.

'Ah, Hephaestus,' said Hecate. 'I did not see you hiding there in the shadows.' She addressed Tamar. 'I have no wish to rule here, I only wish to escape. I am the prisoner of Hades. A fact that is little known and even less likely to be believed, I am aware. But the truth nevertheless.'

'*I* believe you,' said Denny. 'Why don't you come with us? We won't hurt you, I promise.'

'I believe *you*,' she said. 'Although I have no reason to, since I know nothing of you except that you are the god slayers whose coming was foreseen. Because of this, I should fear you, and yet I do not. In some extraordinary way, you engender trust.'

'Good,' said Tamar, 'because it's not easy being the "god slayers". Right now we could use all the friends we can get. As you can imagine we have most of the gods baying for our blood and, foreseen or not, this thing could still go either way.'

'You want my help?' asked Hecate in considerable surprise.

'If you don't have anything better to do,' said Denny.

'I ... am uncertain,' she said. 'To betray one's kind and kin simply to save oneself.' And here she gave Aphrodite and Hephaestus a scornful look. 'It seems like treachery to me.'

'Suit yourself,' said Tamar. 'But you know we aren't going to hurt you, no matter what you decide. I tell you what, why don't we give you a few minutes to think about it?'

What's the matter with her?' hissed Denny. 'I thought she'd remember us. I mean – sort of. Doesn't her memory work both ways or something?'

'This isn't the Hecaté that we know,' said Tamar. 'She's only a very minor deity at the moment. Nothing like the power she will eventually become when the witches start to venerate her. But even so, she does seem as if she vaguely knows us, don't you think? It's like she knows we are her friends, even if she doesn't remember us. It's like intuition. I reckon she'll say yes.'

'Are we sure that's a good idea?' said Denny. 'We don't want her to get hurt.'

'Better keep her where we can keep an eye on her then,' said Tamar.

'Can we persuade her to put a coat on or something do you think?' asked Denny.

Apparently persuading Hecate to join them was as far as Tamar was prepared to go. Denny was just going to have to get used to seeing far more of her than he had ever expected to.

Now that she was with them, Hecate was surprised to be told that they were actually here not for Hades (although they would happily deal with him if they happened to run across him) but to free Prometheus.

Like Hephaestus, she wondered how they were planning on freeing him. 'No one can break those chains,' she told them, much as he had.

'Be glad that's not exactly true,' muttered Denny. In the future, it was actually Jack Stiles who had managed (no one knew how) to break the chains around Hecaté in what was clearly a manifestation of destiny. They were counting on this concept in the present case. They did not have anything else and, after all, Hecate herself had said that they were here to fulfil a destiny. It was a vain hope, and they knew it.

It was a bloody high cliff and, unfortunately, they would have to climb it. There was no astral plane in the underworld and, therefore, no teleporting. It was, as Denny put it, a damned nuisance.

Aphrodite was pouting. She had not wanted to make the climb and declared that it was pointless for her to do so in any case. "What could she do up there anyway?" she said. "*She* could not free him."

But Denny put his foot down. 'We *all* go,' he said. And he meant it too, as she could plainly see.

Hecate had made no such protests, neither had Hephaestus. In fact, he had been quite helpful. There were caves, he told them. Passages inside the cliff that wound upwards and would take them almost to the top with relative ease. Hades had had them made in order to make it easier for himself to check on Prometheus's progress, as ordered by Zeus, who liked to hear of his prisoner's sufferings occasionally.

'I should have thought of that,' said Tamar. 'I'm only surprised he never got around to having a lift put in.'

But Hephaestus did not know what she meant by this.

Hecate had not known about the caves. In fact, she had never seen Prometheus personally, and she was quite curious about him. Having heard nothing but bad things about him from the other gods, she was sure she was going to like him. It was her immovable contempt for the gods, Zeus most of all, that had been a strong contributing factor in her decision to join Tamar and Denny.

In the final cave there was a shaft leading up to the top. It looked pretty straightforward to Tamar and Denny; they had certainly done harder things. But Aphrodite baulked at it, and even Denny could not make her agree to try it. Neither threats (Tamar) nor gentle persuasion (Denny) nor contemptuous needling (Hecate) would change her mind; she simply refused.

There was no way that Hecate was staying behind with her so it was up to Hephaestus, a tactless choice at best, but there was no one else and they could not leave her on her own. When it was suggested, she almost wailed like a baby about it and, for once, they could hardly blame her. There was something horrible inside these cliffs. They had heard the distant feral cries of some sort of creature as they had made their way up. No doubt Hades had the place guarded by some hideous creation, and no one particularly wanted to speculate on what it might be.

Climbing the shaft was pretty easy; there were a number of useful handholds and the three of them went up quickly. Denny first, followed by Tamar, and then Hecate last.

The fresh air was invigorating after so long in the stuffy caves below. But of course, they were not interested in that for long.

Prometheus was forty feet long – and I say long instead of high, because he was lying down, stretched out, in fact, in a most uncomfortable fashion on an extremely large rock and, of course, chained down. Despite the chains, he did manage to heave himself up a little way, into a half sitting position from where he fixed Tamar with a glaring eye. 'You took your bloody time, didn't you?' he said.

* * *

'Come on, he said. 'Get on with it then, my little feathered nemesis is due any minute,' Denny was sure he put a slight emphasis on the word "nemesis".

It was hardly a surprise that Prometheus had been expecting them so Tamar did not bother to pretend that it was. 'Get on with what?' she said with deliberate obtuseness.

'Ah,' said Prometheus knowingly. 'It's like that is it? You're going to bargain with me. All right, so what do you want then?'

'A big heap of dead gods?' said Denny shrugging his shoulders.

'Is that right?' said Prometheus addressing himself sarcastically to Tamar. 'Well,' he added with heavy scorn. 'I knew *that*!'

He looked from one to the other to the other, his eyes ranging across the three of them from Tamar to Denny to Hecate and back until his gaze fell upon Tamar again. 'By Zeus,' he said. 'You don't know what to do, do you? You can't break the chains?'

'We were sort of hoping that something would come to us?' admitted Denny, and Tamar glared at him.

'What?' he said. 'He deserves to know.'

Tamar rolled her eyes, 'The gods save us from heroes,' she said.

'He's a *hero*?' said Prometheus in a voice somewhere between disbelief and disdain. 'He looks like a ...'

'Don't say it,' warned Tamar. 'Whatever you were going to say, just don't. You aren't too big for a good hiding.'

'I'm not?' he asked in surprise. 'I must say I always thought that was the one thing I ...'

'Let me try,' said Hecate suddenly coming forward and grasping the chains.

'More destiny?' said Denny to Tamar out of the side of his mouth.

'Could be,' she said. 'After all she *is* the only god ever to escape the chains.'

'But that hasn't happened yet,' said Denny. 'No what I meant was ...'

'It's happened as far as *we* are concerned,' she said. 'You're the one that told me that time isn't necessarily linear.'

'If she manages to do it, he'll still have escaped them before she did,' said Denny.

'Ah, but not until it happens,' said Tamar obscurely.

Meanwhile, Hecate was not pulling ineffectually at the chains as another might have done, she was examining them carefully – microscopically carefully.

'Iron of course,' she muttered. 'Some copper, only a trace – probably got in there accidentally. Gold ore, very flashy but soft ... The weak link, in fact ...'

Ninety nine per cent of magic consists of knowing one extra fact. There is a whole universe of quantum dimensions out there that most of us know nothing about. Hecate did – she could *see* the magic in the way that a biologist can see the microbes. Most of the people who use magic, including Tamar and Denny, do not really know how it works, any more than most normal people really know how a computer or even a television works. They can make it work – but they could not invent one. But Hecate knew. Her natural gift was to see the nuts and bolts of the paranormal and render it no more than a series of equations to be solved.

There was a bright flash of light and Hecate had done her very first ever magic spell. The chains had not merely broken; they had gone up in smoke.

'That puts a slight crimp in the future,' said Tamar.

'If she could do that,' said Denny. 'Then why didn't she just ... I mean the future her, why didn't – won't ...'

'I know what you mean,' said Tamar impatiently. 'And the simple answer is, I don't know. But I do know that *this* wasn't supposed to happen. We're changing things.'

'I suppose it was inevitable,' said Denny. 'We were bound to change a few things that we shouldn't. How could we not?'

'But it's a part of our *own* future that we just changed,' said Tamar. 'I don't think that we're going to get away with this whatever we do.'

'We'll discuss this later,' said Denny. 'Right now, we have bigger fish to fry – so to speak.'

He was right about this. Prometheus was rising slowly and stiffly; a massive figure etched darkly against the skyline. It was all very... mythic. Especially the part where he reached out a twelve foot arm, snatched the soaring eagle out of the sky and ate it in revenge for all his suffering.

Then he reached down and plucked Hecate off the ground, she stood on his palm, and they looked at each other.

'Like King Kong and Fay Wray,' said Denny with a laugh.

'He's not going to eat *her*, is he?' said Tamar in a worried tone.

Denny gave her a look of disbelief. 'Don't be so damned silly,' he said eventually when he realised she was serious. 'He wouldn't dare,' he added as it hit him that they were dealing with people who did not necessarily follow what he would consider the "normal" rules of behaviour. Tamar's anxious query had not been quite as daft as it had sounded when you put it this context.

In fact, there seemed to be something else going on.

Denny spotted it first. 'Oh, no,' he said. 'They've gone all soppy on each other. That's all we need. I think I'd rather he *had* eaten her,' he added.

'It might come to that,' said Tamar. 'These people are not known for resolving their emotional conflicts amicably.'

'Speaking of which,' said Denny. 'Is that a shrieking I hear from below?'

Tamar listened. 'It's Aphrodite,' she confirmed. 'Do you think they're fighting?'

'I don't want to get in the middle of it if they are,' said Denny decisively.

Tamar put her head in her hands. 'I miss our proper friends,' she said. 'This lot just aren't the same. It's like babysitting a lot of Big Brother contestants.'

'The tantrums,' said Denny

'The massive egos,' said Tamar.

'The drama,' said Denny.

'The short lived fame ending in ultimate disaster?' said Tamar.

'Well, that's the idea anyway,' he said grinning.

There was another shriek and this time it contained the unmistakeable sound of a cry for help.

They scrambled down the shaft, leaving Prometheus and Hecate, for the time being, gazing at each other in the sickliest manner imaginable.

Aphrodite was being terrorized by two of the most unusual creatures they had ever seen. One was definitely a large boar of some kind but massively oversized, and the other ... well there was no telling what the hell it was, apart from hideously ugly. But they did not look like creatures at all, apart from the stamping and snorting and generally threatening behaviour.

But metal statues, even of hideous beasts of unknown etymology, were normally found sitting on plinths behaving themselves, not indulging in the above offensive behaviour.

'Call them off Hephaestus,' ordered Tamar.

'I can't,' he said. 'They were a gift to Hades, they only obey him now.'

'Bugger!' said Tamar. 'Well, you made them, how do I get rid of them?'

'What the hell are they?' asked Denny – who thought he had seen everything.

'Automotones,' she told him. 'Hephaestus made a lot of them. What are these ones though?' she asked. 'I don't remember a boar or a ... a ... What the hell is that one supposed to be anyway?'

'It was *supposed* to be a horse,' he said slightly huffily. 'Came out a bit ... I was young when I did them,' he added defensively.

Tamar laughed and clapped her hands in delighted mirth. 'Rejects,' she said. 'Damaged stock. And you gave them to Hades. That's priceless.'

'Well, they *work* all right, they just *look* a bit ... Even Hades agreed that it didn't really matter what they looked like down here where no one would ever see them.'

'I don't think Aphrodite's amused,' said Denny. 'Perhaps we should *do* something, before she gets hurt.'

'Oh, right, right,' said Hephaestus. 'Only there's not a lot to be done. They can't be killed or hurt or anything. They aren't alive you see. You might as well punch a rock. Hurts you far more than it hurts the rock.'

The putative "horse" chose that moment to take a large bite out of Aphrodite's dress, causing her to scream in terror as it then spat this out and began snapping at her heels. She was backed into a corner. No more choices.

Denny grabbed it round the neck and flung it over in a wrestling type move. Of course, it was unhurt; it merely rolled over until it was upright again, however, it did give Aphrodite the chance to escape. But what to do with it now?

Denny kicked it down the passage, but it did not go very far before it turned and headed back, and there was still the other one to deal with too.

Aphrodite was staring at Denny with a mixture of awe and longing, as he squared up to the metal monster.

Tamar, however, was less than impressed with his tactics so far. 'What's that in your hand,' she called to him, 'a butter knife? Are you a god slayer, or aren't you? It shouldn't be too hard to deal with a couple of oversized money boxes! Especially with a blade that can cut through *any metal in the world*. Come on, it's not like they're made of the same stuff as the chains.' she hinted encouragingly.

'Ah!' thought Denny. 'Right then!' he said.

She was right; the Athame sheared through the metal hide of the creature as if it were cutting paper. The head bounced off and landed at his feet to general cheering, which was cut short, when it was noted that it had not exactly slowed the creature down.

'Get its legs,' called Hephaestus.

'Yes, thank you, Socrates. I hadn't thought of that,' said Denny sarcastically. 'Any time you want to join in,' he added to Tamar.

'But you were doing so well,' she said. 'Oh, all right then.' Tamar rolled up her sleeves and prepared a quick fireball and aimed it at the boar. It scorched the creature but no permanent damage was done. She had been too hasty. 'Oh, well,' she thought, 'up a few degrees then.' The next one melted it into a puddle.

'Now, why couldn't you have done that in the first place?' asked Denny as he sheathed the Athame. The "horse" was now scrabbling uselessly on the floor of the cave without its legs.

'What, and deprive you of the chance to show off to your new girlfriend?' said Tamar sarcastically.

'What's *that* supposed to mean?' he asked, suddenly angry.

'N-nothing,' she backed down confusedly. 'It was just a joke.'

'Well, it wasn't funny,' snapped Denny, still angry.'

'I-I know,' she said with a frown. 'I don't know what made me say it.'

'Maybe bickering is catching,' said Denny with a sudden grin.

They both looked at Aphrodite.

'Don't look at *me*,' she said. '*I* didn't do anything.'

Tamar didn't believe her. 'Trust me,' she said. 'Denny's the last person you want to put in a bad mood. He might seem pretty sweet and nice, but when he loses his temper, *everybody* suffers.'

'But I *didn't*.' Aphrodite insisted. 'Why would I?'

'Arguing with me?' said Tamar. 'That'd suit you down to the ground wouldn't it? But it won't do you any good.'

'*Him*?' said Hephaestus incredulously looking at Denny. He turned to Aphrodite. 'Him? *Really*? But he isn't any handsomer than *I* am.'

'*Hey*!' said Tamar indignantly. But no one took any notice of her. Denny was snorting with laughter, and the other two were getting into a heated argument.

'Looks aren't everything,' said Aphrodite. 'You were always far more worried about your ugly face than *I* was. Anyway, he's *not* ugly.'

'But *I* am?'

'I never thought you were all that ugly, it was *you* that made such an issue of it, until I just couldn't stand it anymore. Huh! And people say that *I'm* vain.'

'*You're* calling *me* vain?' Hephaestus roared indignantly.

'All I'm saying is, you worry too much about the way you look, when it really isn't as bad as you think it is. Take him,' she pointed rudely at Denny. 'Maybe he *isn't* Adonis, but at least he doesn't moan about it all the time. It's such a refreshing change. Why can't you just accept who you are?'

'My mother threw me off Olympus for being too ugly to be a god,' said Hephaestus in a subdued voice. 'That sort of thing can affect a person. A face even my own mother reviled.'

'Hera?' said Aphrodite in a scornful tone. 'What does *she* know? She's horrible to *everyone*. Get over it. It could be worse. You could look like Proteus.'

'By Zeus,' said Hephaestus, who seemed struck by this idea. 'That's the truth. I never thought of that.'

There was a silence. Then Aphrodite, falling back on the old standby of, "when in an awkward situation, throw a cliché at it" said. 'Well, no one's perfect, anyway.'

'You are,' said Hephaestus. Causing Tamar to poke her fingers down her throat and make gagging noises.

'Grow up,' said Denny. 'If it stops them from arguing all time ...'

'That's so sweet,' said Aphrodite.

'But you'd still rather have *him*, wouldn't you?' he said.

'Okay,' said Denny deciding to take hand here before the whole thing fell apart again. 'You might as well tell him,' he said to Aphrodite taking her arm and gripping it so hard that she winced. 'She was just trying to make you jealous. Women do that you know,' he added confidentially. Then he gave Aphrodite a hard look that said: "*Go along or it'll be the worse for you.*"

This was patently ludicrous, as Tamar was on the verge of pointing out, but incredibly, Hephaestus seemed to be falling for it. Perhaps because he wanted to.

'Well,' said Tamar later as they talked over the campfire. 'I still can't believe it worked. I mean, the look on your face alone would have given the game away to an infant. You've always been a terrible liar. Still, I suppose it's better that they aren't fighting any more. If we're going to have to stop for a row every five minutes, we'll never get *anything* done.'

'It seems a shame really,' said Denny. 'I mean, they've only just sorted everything out, and they'll be dead soon. If that was us ...'

'Well, it's not,' said Tamar shortly. 'Don't get too involved. We have a job to do. Besides, they've had an eternity to sort it out. It's their own fault if they didn't. *We* wouldn't have been so stupid in the first place.

'And Hecate and Prometheus?'

'Well, we have to split that up anyway,' she said. 'It only happened because of the proximity of Aphrodite anyway,' she added. 'She tends to have that effect. Even on gods apparently.'

'I don't see how that would work anyway,' said Denny. I mean he's … *huge* and she's just a normal human size so ... well the logistics of it are a bit ...'

'She can be any size she likes. The gods are descended from the Titans. It's all very incestuous. But it's not our problem anyway.'

'Has he said anything about the prophecy to you?' asked Denny, who did not want to follow this line of discussion any further. 'He doesn't talk to me. I think *you* are the one he was expecting. I'm just the sidekick.'

'Not yet,' she said. 'He's not very communicative at the best of times I think. But it was nice of him to carry us all down the cliff like that.'

'Yeah, I suppose so, but it kind of made me feel like a gnome or something.'

'Four gods,' she mused. 'Well, three gods and a Titan. It's not going to be enough is it?'

'No, it is not.' It was not Denny who made this negative statement.

Tamar jumped to her feet. 'It's still two against one, right here,' she threatened.

'You might try hearing me out before you gut me,' said Artemis sitting down by the fire placidly. She gave Denny a curt nod. 'You were not expecting me,' she said.

Since this was not a question, Denny did not answer it. 'What do you want?' he said.

'I was debating whether I should come myself,' she continued as if he had not spoken. 'It is plain to me that you do not intend to spare any of us. You cannot afford to − or so I have heard.' She laughed at their stunned faces. 'Prometheus is not the only prophet among us,' she said. 'My own twin brother is Apollo. The time of the gods has come. I know there is nothing I can do to prevent this destiny, but for you, it will be a formidable challenge. You may lose your own lives in its execution. That, at least, is not clear as yet, but by that time, it will be too late for us. You are here to begin the final days, the great war of the gods, in which we shall all be destroyed. If not by you, then by one another.'

She leaned in toward Denny. 'Make me mortal,' she said. 'Do not kill me outright, I beg you. Show me the same mercy that you showed to Nemesis. And, with my power, you will have a greater chance of defeating Zeus and maybe ensuring your own survival. Promise me you will show him no mercy and that is all I will ask. I'll even make it easy for you. I won't fight.' And she threw down her bow.

'You *want* to be mortal?' asked Denny incredulously.

'I do not *want* to be mortal,' she said. 'But considering the alternative ...'

Tamar beckoned Denny to one side.

'There's something hinky here,' she said. 'She's up to something. It *has* to be. What will happen if you use the Athame on her? And how the hell does she know about that anyway?'

'I don't know about the second one,' said Denny. 'But as to the first – the same as always happens, surely? Her power will go into the blade and be my power from then on – just like Askphrit's and Nemesis's power did.'

'All I know is, gods do not willingly give up their power like that,' said Tamar.

'She's right about her power, though,' he said. 'She has a *lot* more power than Nemesis did. It could tip the balance in our favour quite a bit, if I take it.'

'But you said yourself that even the power of Zeus himself wouldn't be enough to defeat them all. So in the end, what difference does it make? We're here to make them kill *each other* – she even said so. We need to ask ourselves, what's in it for her?'

---

* Tamar didn't believe in prophecies despite seeing a few come true in her time. She believed in making your own luck and if it happened to fit into a pre-ordained destiny – well, that was just a coincidence. *

*Not that she believed in coincidence either.

'Apart from not dying in a horrible war between the gods, I can't think of a thing,' said Denny.

'And that's another thing,' said Tamar. 'Who says we're going to start a war, even *we* don't know that for sure, not yet.'*

'It's a bloody good idea, though,' he said. 'Even if we do die, it's not going to matter, 'cause as soon as they're all dead, everything goes back to normal, doesn't it?'

'Whatever,' said Tamar. 'And maybe that's just what she *wants* us to think. I'm telling, you, you can't trust gods. She took a hell of a risk coming here. How did she know that you or I wouldn't just kill her right away – no questions asked? And then she gives us this cock and bull story, but then again, it could all be the truth, and she just doesn't want us to believe her. If we think she's lying and do the opposite of what she says, then maybe that's what she really wants us to do ...'

'Black is white,' he said. 'But then again maybe it really is black.'

'That's what I mean,' she said. 'When you're dealing with a god, you never know *what* to think.'

'Hmm,' said Denny. 'Know what *I* think? Power good – not dying good. Take chance – take power. Kill Zeus – go home – see friends – see daughter – have a rest – maybe have a curry – and a beer – two beers – a *case* of beer.'

'And if it backfires?' she said.

'When doesn't it?' he said in his normal voice.

'That's true.'

Denny took Artemis aside. 'You don't want anyone to see this,' he told her. 'You're quite likely to scream – everyone does.'

'I am not afraid,' she said stoutly.

'You will be,' he said. And before she could change her mind he plunged the Athame into her chest.

He had been right. She screamed a lot.

After it was over and she was on her knees and shaking, Denny looked curiously at the Athame. 'Very clever,' he said. 'I guess Tamar was right after all. You lied to us.'

'What do you mean?' she said.

'I don't know how you did it,' he said. 'You can get up now, by the way, stop pretending. I *know* you see. The Athame talks to me. It's telling me that this isn't *your* power at all. What power is it? I don't recognise it?' He kept his voice light and conversational, but he was tensed and ready for the spring when it came. Artemis was getting slowly to her feet.

'Whatever it is,' he continued. 'I guess it was supposed to hurt me in some way. It won't. It doesn't work that way with the Athame. But you didn't know that, did you? You were expecting a direct power transfer of some kind, weren't you? but the power is in the Athame, not me.'

'How did you do it?' he asked. 'I really want to know, it was very clever. I honestly didn't see it coming.

'I suppose you carried another power within you, like a virus,' he answered his own question. 'But how could you be sure I would get *that* power and not your own – or even both?' Artemis was glaring furiously at him.

'You won't tell me,' he said.

'It's not a terribly strong power,' he said. 'Was it just supposed to replace the power of Nemesis instead of yours? And then, when I was weak and vulnerable because I believed that you were powerless and that I had *your* power, were you going to kill me? I hate to tell you this, but it doesn't work like that either. *Both* powers are in the Athame now. It stores them all … like, like ... oh you'd never understand anyway. Never mind.

'I suppose it was Zeus that sent you. You were to be his Trojan horse.' He shook his head sadly. 'He should do his own dirty work. But never mind, he'll pay for this sooner or later. He'll run out of lieutenants eventually. I wouldn't want to be him when Tamar gets her hands on him, not after this. For some unfathomable reason, you see, she takes it badly when people try to hurt me. No, I don't understand it either.'

'She loves you,' said Artemis with a slight smile. She was calming down now – accepting the inevitable, 'and I am beginning to see why. All right,' she shrugged her shoulders.

'You win – this time. It was worth trying. You understand we do not intend to just lie down and take it.'

'I wouldn't either,' he said.

She bowed her head. They were dancing now; she wanting to slip away and he desperate to stop her. 'We will not meet again,' she said, backing slowly away from him, 'until the end.'

She walked backwards straight into Tamar's waiting arms.

Denny gave her a rueful smile. He had seen Tamar waiting in the shadows, and he had just hoped that she would catch Artemis before she teleported away. Only a Djinn had the power to hold a god.

'I'm sorry,' he said. 'But a promise is a promise. I promised to make you mortal ...'

He walked forward and plunged the Athame into a furiously struggling Artemis for the second time. 'And I intend to keep my word,' he finished.

~ Chapter Nine ~

PROMETHEUS STROKED his beard thoughtfully. 'A war?' he said. 'I don't know about any war as such. There will be fighting I dare say of course. But really all *I* ever knew was the name of the one who would come and bring the doom of the gods upon them. You are that one,' he said to Tamar. 'But I suppose a war is as good a way as any to get the job done. I was expecting more of a quest, though.'

Both Tamar and Denny groaned at this. They knew about quests and it never went well. They had got up at dawn for *this*? The gods were all still asleep though, so it had seemed an opportune time to talk in private. Well, Tamar had. Denny had not actually been invited to this little party, but he had got up earlier than expected and joined them without being asked. Prometheus made no objections and Tamar had been planning on telling him all about it anyway.

'Why a quest?' asked Tamar. 'A quest for what?'

'Well, legend has it that if you wanted to kill all the gods off in one go, which I had assumed you would, you need to find the Terastu.'

'Sounds like a Mexican dish,' said Denny.

'Wouldn't this Terastu kill you too?' asked Tamar. 'If it does what it's supposed to do.'

'I have no idea,' said Prometheus. 'I have no idea what it is, let alone how it works.'

'So, why would you be willing to help us then?' she said. 'It's a bit of a risk, isn't it?'

'I know,' said Denny. 'Let's just stay here and wait for them to come after us. We can pick them off one by one, like Artemis.'

'They won't risk that again,' said Tamar.

'You are wrong,' said Prometheus. 'Zeus will send more gods after you, but in unexpected ways. You may not always know them when you see them.' And he glanced over, his eyes twinkling, at a large pig taking a rest in the shade under a lime tree.

As they both turned to look, Prometheus picked Denny up between his finger and thumb.

'Hey,' Denny objected, struggling indignantly. 'Let me down you big ape. What do you think you are doing?'

This was pretty clear diction for Denny – there was a reason for this.

'What's going on then?' said Denny walking upon the scene. 'Why's he dangling that – hey that's me! What the ...'

'This is Proteus,' said Prometheus. 'He arrived this morning, as a chicken, but I knew him all right. Say hello Proteus.'

Proteus growled at him.

'But he sounded just like Denny,' said Tamar. I mean he even groaned about the quest and that remark about the Mexican food ...'

'Mexican food?' said Denny puzzled.

'Prometheus was telling us about the Terastu and you – I mean *he* said it sounded like Mexican food,' Tamar explained.

'It does,' said Denny. 'So what? What's a Terastu?'

'How does he even *know* about Mexican food? Did *you* understand what he meant?' Tamar demanded of Prometheus.

'No,' he admitted. 'But I have been chained to a rock for a thousand years. You miss things.'

'Put me down and I will explain everything,' said Proteus. 'I was not sent by Zeus. I came on my own.'

'Actually, I believe him,' said Prometheus, nevertheless holding on firmly. 'He hates Zeus even more than I do, and that's saying something. In fact, Proteus hates *all* the gods.'

'That's right, that's right,' said Proteus. 'I do, I'm on your side.'

'So why disguise yourself as me?' asked Denny. 'Why not be straight up about it?'

A sly look came over the face of Proteus – which was currently also the face of Denny – but he shook his head.

'You have a lovely wife,' said Prometheus. 'He wanted to be you for that reason I imagine. It's an old trick of the gods.'

'Ugh,' said Tamar, 'as if I wouldn't have known.'

'You *didn't* know,' pointed out Prometheus.

'No, but that was just talking, I mean if he'd tried anything ...'

'You would not have known the difference I assure you,' said Proteus. 'I become the person whose face I take – I even find myself saying things I do not know the meaning of. It is a gift, really. Other gods can take a form other than their own, but only I can take on the form of their mind also.'

'Hard to see why we shouldn't just kill you now then really, isn't it?' said Denny, who, for obvious reasons, was not happy with this idea at all.

'It sounds like a handy power to me too,' he added.

'You would not be able to handle it,' asserted Proteus. 'It takes a lot of practice and even then it can be very confusing. You wouldn't like it at all.'

'Well, you would say that now, wouldn't you?' said Tamar. 'All right, you can let him down now,' she added to Prometheus. Who dropped him on his head making Tamar wince involuntarily. '*He's not Denny, he's not Denny,*' she repeated in her head like a mantra.

'Can't you wear your *own* face?' she pleaded. 'You're freaking me out.'

'How do you think *I* feel?' said Denny.

'Trust me, it's worse from where I'm standing,' she said. 'You're used to seeing someone else wearing your face, but it's usually me. From where I'm standing, there are two of you.'

'And one is bad enough,' he said with a laugh.

'One is *just* enough,' she corrected him. 'Unless the other one is me.'

'I cannot remember my own face,' said Proteus. It has been a long, long time since I wore it. But I will change it to someone else if you prefer.'

'Cannot remember your own face?' said Prometheus. 'How is that possible when your reflection in a pool or a mirror is always that of your own face, no matter what face you appear to wear?'

'Know it all,' muttered Proteus.

'He does not wish to wear his own face because he does not want you to see how ugly he really is,' said Prometheus.

'That's enough Prometheus!' said Denny sharply. 'Leave him alone now. He can wear any face he likes, as long as it's not mine.'

Proteus gave him a look of wonder at this unexpected support followed by a tremulous nod, by which his face transformed into that of a young man who looked faintly familiar.

'This is my all-purpose face,' said Proteus. 'I always look like someone you think you might have known with this face. Very useful for building trust. But you see I'm being completely honest with you. I did not wear your face in order to seduce your wife,' he said, giving Prometheus a dirty look. 'I merely wanted to observe you all in the character of one of you, so that you would talk freely before me. I wanted to know what manner of people you were and if it would be wise to reveal myself and my purpose.'

'And what purpose would that be?' asked Tamar.

'I wish to join you,' he said simply. 'I do not wish to die. I make no excuses. I am afraid. And I do not owe the other gods any loyalty. I can be useful,' he added.

'If you are afraid of my playing tricks on you,' he said, seeing that they were uncertain, 'I will not give you empty guarantees. You would not know that they were worth anything anyway. But Prometheus told the truth. A mirror will always reveal my real face to you if you are ever uncertain.'

'Useful how?' said Tamar bluntly.

'Well, I am a god,' he said. 'Aren't you collecting gods?'

'You could put it that way,' said Denny, amused. 'All right, you make yourself useful, and we won't hurt you. Now clear off, we need to talk about you.'

They did not, however, talk about Proteus after he had gone away; they talked about the legend of the Terastu and speculated on what it might be and whether it was worth looking for.

'Sounds like some kind of weapon,' said Denny. 'Maybe it releases something fatal to gods (like the blood of the Golden Hind) but which is harmless to humans.'

'Biological warfare?' said Tamar. 'Sounds good to me, but if that's what it is ... what about Hecate, how do we protect her?'

'She'd probably be safe in the underworld,' said Denny.

'"Probably" isn't good enough,' said Tamar. 'But then again it might not be anything like that.'

'It couldn't *be* the Golden Hind could it?' said Denny. 'Isn't that supposed to be ...?'

'There was more than just *one* of them, said Tamar. 'But they're all gone now anyway. Ares finished them off. Anyway, we already kicked that idea to the curb right at the start, when you brought up the Purple Hart it would be as hard as trying to get them all one by one with the Athame. Not to mention that to try and kill all the gods would take every drop of blood in one animal, if not more than that. It *can't* be that. Prometheus said, whatever it is, it would kill them all at once.'

'Oh, yeah, right. He did say that, didn't he? Are you sure he isn't just making it all up?'

'No, I'm not sure at all. But we have to consider the possibility at least.'

'It just sounds a bit too good to be true,' he said. 'It's just what we happen to need, you know.'

'That's mythology for you.'

'I suppose.'

'But you don't believe it?' she said.

'I just don't know,' he said. 'I think maybe I have a problem with the whole thing really.'

'Explain.'

'Well, we *are* here to commit genocide, I mean, let's not sugar-coat it. For some strange reason, that just doesn't sit well with me. And you can't tell me that *you're* happy about it either, I just won't believe it.'

'I try not to think about it,' she said, which was as good as an admission that he was right.

'So, we have to be sure,' he said. 'If we go on this damn quest, is it because we truly believe in it, or is it just to waste some time, to put off the inevitable? Because, let's face it, we know what we have to do, we just don't want to do it. If we believe Prometheus, is it because we want to, because believing in his story helps us to put off our decision? If we decide to go, it has to be because we are bound and determined to fulfil our mission here. So which is it?'

'Oh, hell,' she said. 'I don't know.'

'Or maybe we're just second guessing ourselves because we don't want to go on another dammed quest. I mean we hate quests.'

'You speak for yourself,' she said. 'I love a good quest. So many exciting things can go wrong.'

'And we never did get an answer from Prometheus about why he would be willing to help us find it,' said Denny choosing to ignore this piece of sarcasm.

'There is one thing we haven't considered,' she said. 'For now anyway, plan A is a bust. The plain fact is, we don't have nearly enough gods on our side to start anything like an actual *war*.'

Denny thought about this.

'The quest it is,' he said resignedly. 'I hope we don't regret this.'

'Quests are our lot in life,' she said. 'We might as well just get on with it.'

'It doesn't mean I have to like it.'

* * *

Artemis was running from him through the dense forest, but she had no chance of escape – she was mortal now. Denny felt like a serial killer; he hated feeling like this, but it had to be done. Even as a mortal she was a threat to their plans, she would go back to Zeus, maybe he would give her the ambrosia, and she would become a god again. But there was just something about this that felt terribly, terribly wrong. Killing a god was one thing, a bad thing but not as heinous as killing a helpless mortal. If Tamar had not let go of her before it was over ... but there was no use blaming her. She would be all too easy to catch up to now, and the end result would be the same. It was his fault too; he had hesitated, hung back from crossing that line from warrior into murderer. A fine line, but one that he had never crossed – yet.

As he had predicted, he had run her to earth – like a frightened animal – the comparison disturbed him. She was terrified but proud, too proud to show her fear. Somehow this made it worse.

He had her trapped and still he hesitated. He didn't want to be this person. But this was not about what he wanted. And putting it off was only making it harder for both of them. She was tensed and waiting, knowing there was no escape unless he let her go. But he *couldn't* let her go. He closed his eyes and struck. Brave and proud to the end she died without a sound. And Denny felt like killing himself too.

He woke up, as he had too many times in his life, sweating and shaking.

Ever since he had taken her power from her, this nightmare about that night had haunted even his waking hours, but it was worse when he slept. In the night, the nightmare became real and even more vivid than it had been in reality. His conscience was torturing him.

He was not fooling himself this time about Tamar's awareness of his feelings. Although he was certain that he had not given the slightest indication of his feelings, he knew that she knew. She *always* knew. She was probably just waiting for him to say something and if *he* did not, *she* would – eventually.

In the meantime, he was just going to have to get over it. There was a whole Pantheon to deal with and a quest (bloody quests!) to go on.

The only problem with that was they had no idea where to start. (Well, there was that, and then there was the fact that they had no idea what they were looking for either – but one problem at a time as Tamar would say.) Prometheus had been vague at best about the meaning of his premonition.

'It is in a hidden place,' he said, which surprised no one. 'Defended by a hideous guardian.' Again, not exactly a shock. 'Oh, and it would only exist for a limited time.'

'What the hell does that mean?' asked Tamar.

'I don't know,' said Prometheus. 'That's just what I know about it.'

'Do you actually know anything *useful*?' she said. 'Like where to start looking for it.'

'You'll just have to work that out for yourselves,' he said.

'It's like talking to Clive,' groaned Denny. 'If you dare to mention "free will" I will start exercising my own free will to pummel you into a giant pile of mush.'

'Oooh,' said Aphrodite. She nudged Hephaestus. 'I think he means it,' she said.

'Of course he means it,' he replied testily. 'He *is* the god slayer.'

'*A* god slayer,' corrected Denny. 'And don't call me that.'

'Can we get back to the point?' said Tamar. 'Thank you.' She addressed Prometheus. 'There must be more you can tell us,' she said.

'Ask the Fates,' said Hecate. 'They will know.'

'That's not a bad idea,' said Denny. Hecate inclined her head.

'What are you smiling at?' snapped Tamar at Prometheus who was indeed smiling and gently shaking his head.

'The Fates will tell you nothing,' he said. 'They are under the rule of Zeus himself, they will, at best, tell you nothing, and at worst, so obfuscate the truth that they will lead you down completely the wrong path.'

'There's Arachne,' said Aphrodite. 'She answers to no one, that one. And she is the keeper of the wheel.'

'Brilliant,' said Denny, genuinely surprised at this good idea considering where it had come from.

'You do not have to sound so surprised,' said Aphrodite. 'I am a goddess, you know. I am not a fool.'

'Arachne is a devil,' said Prometheus, 'with a temper as bad as that of Ares. Are you sure you want to tackle her? Her lair is a dangerous place for men, even the god slayers, for Arachne is a monster and not a god.'

'Really?' said Denny. 'I didn't think she was all that bad. I quite liked her really – the last time we met.'

Prometheus's mouth fell open.

'She called you an upended broomstick,' said Tamar.

'Yeah, but not, like, nastily or anything,' he said. 'Anyway, she had a point didn't she?'

'I suppose so,' said Tamar, and Denny scowled.

'She's just like anyone else,' he said to Prometheus. 'She doesn't like being judged on what she looks like. So as long as you don't call her a monster to her face, I reckon it'll be all right.'

'Or a demon,' added Tamar. 'Well, in the absence of any better plan, I think that's what we'll do then.'

Denny was stomping out the fire when he was approached by Aphrodite. Her attitude toward him had not changed since her reconciliation with Hephaestus, a fact which did not seem to bother her husband at all. Perhaps he was under the impression that she was merely continuing her campaign to make him jealous and, after all, who was he to question the methods of Aphrodite herself when it came to the tactics of promoting love? Or perhaps he just had not noticed.

'Are we really going back to the underworld?' she asked him.

'Yes,' he said. He straightened up and looked at her. 'You know, sometimes I think I spend more time down there than all the dead people.'

'Oh, I don't think so,' she said seriously. Then she smiled. 'Oh, I see, that was a jest.

'Not very good eh?' said Denny with a grin. He did not like Aphrodite much, but she was so pretty that he found it hard to be unfriendly to her – even though it was clearly annoying Tamar.

She moved closer to him and laid a hand on his arm. He shook her off and frowned. 'Look,' he said. 'You have to stop doing that. If you don't then, deal or no deal, Tamar *is* going to kill you.'

She stepped back. 'I can't seem to help it,' she said. 'It's strange really. Heph was right. You aren't handsome at all ...'

'Or witty either apparently,' he said before he could stop himself.

'Have you really met Arachne before?' she said, changing the subject abruptly.

'Yes,' he said. 'But she won't remember us, it hasn't happened yet for her.'

'Like Hecate?' said Aphrodite shrewdly. 'I saw that right away. You know her, but she doesn't know you – at least not yet. Have *we* met before, in *your* life I mean?'

Denny looked at her, taking in the bright blonde hair, the doll like features, the soft doe-like expression. 'You *are* sort of familiar,' he said.

* * *

'What was all that about?' said Tamar suspiciously, after Aphrodite had sloped off.

'What was all *what* about?' asked Denny, genuinely mystified.

'Her!' snapped Tamar. 'What did she want *this* time?'

'Oh, that. She just wanted to know if we'd really met Arachne before.'

'And that's all, is it?' Tamar looked as if she did not believe it.

'Well, *yes*, actually,' he said a little testily. 'What's up?'

'She's always hanging around you,' she said. 'It's really getting on my nerves.'

'Why?' he said. 'It doesn't mean anything, she's just bored. And besides, it's your doing anyway. I certainly didn't ask for it.'

'But you can't deny that you're flattered by the attention, she *is* Aphrodite after all. That'd turn any man's head.'

'Not mine,' he said. 'I've got you.' He faltered. 'Haven't I?'

'Of course,' she said, but not very convincingly.

Suddenly Denny understood. Or thought he did. 'This is about Cindy, isn't it?' he said abruptly. 'About what I did?'

Tamar scowled. 'That was a long time ago,' she said. 'I'm over it.'

'No,' he said. 'You don't trust me anymore.'

'It's not that exactly ...' she began, realising that she had started all this, and there was no getting out of it now, so she might as well talk about it.

'Not that I blame you,' he said. 'It was a betrayal. I've never tried to deny that. But ... why now? You seemed to be okay for years and then ... You weren't really okay at all, is that it?'

'I was,' she said. 'I was fine when I didn't know. I mean I knew *something* had happened, but I swore I would never ask. Not ever, and then ...'

'I went and told you anyway,' he finished for her. 'My big mouth. But I thought it was for the best.'

'Why did it have to be *her*?' Tamar burst out. 'You didn't even like her all that much. At least that's what I thought.'

'And that's what makes what I did to her so terrible,' he said, 'because she knew it too.'

'What you did to *her*?' snapped Tamar indignantly.

'Yes,' he said gently. 'Think about it. *She's* the one who really got hurt. Just witness what she did afterwards.'

Tamar shuddered. 'I see what you mean,' she said.

'Yes,' he said sombrely. 'I reached out to her and used her shamefully, or I tried to, because I was breaking my heart over *you*. It was a selfish, cruel, unforgivable thing to do. Because she knew, you see. It was all about you. It's always been you, not her. You asked, why her? It was because *she* wanted me, and it seemed at the time as if *you* didn't. But that's no excuse, I know it. I was a bastard.

'And everything she did afterwards, everything she brought her son up to do, all the terrible things he did too, that was all *my* fault.' He sighed. 'And then you stepped in,' he continued. 'And you forgave her and then you forgave him and because you did that, you redeemed what I had done. That's like miracle to me. How can you possibly believe that I could ever want anyone else but you? You're wonderful, don't you see that?

'You wiped out my sin, but I know you didn't do it for me. Because you haven't forgiven *me*, have you?'

Tamar had tears in her eyes. *If only she had known all this before.*

'I never blamed you in the first place,' she told him. 'This was never about forgiving you. And I *would*, if I had ever thought you needed it. I'd forgive you for just about anything. But what did you do that was so terrible? You made a mistake, that's all. And I don't think you could be more sorry if you tried. And you were definitely punished for it – more than you deserved.'

'Then what?' he said. 'Why can't you trust me anymore ?'

'It's not you I don't trust,' she said. 'I'm afraid, that's all.'

'Afraid of what?'

'That someone will come along and take you from me.'

'Impossible.'

'That's what I used to think,' she said. 'But then I realised I was being arrogant.'

'Arrogant?' Denny shook his head. 'I don't understand.'

'I used to think ... this is embarrassing,' she admitted. 'I used to think, that my beauty was enough to hold you. It had to be, what else have I got ...?'

'We've been over this,' he said.

'I know, and I see now that I was wrong about that. But that's what I thought. And then ... Cindy happened and I sort of lost faith in that idea. But you're the only one, you know, who sees me that way. You talk about all the admirers *I* get, but with them, it's not love, they only see *this*.' She gestured to her face. 'And I don't care for that. But with you, when *you* get admirers, it's not like that ...'

'Not unless they've got really bad taste,' he supplied wryly.

Tamar gestured impatiently. 'You are *not* ugly,' she said. 'Once and for all, will you just accept that? What was I saying ...?'

'That my admirers don't go for my looks,' said Denny. 'Which we already knew, let's face it.'

'Right, they see what I see in you.'

'*Exactly* what you see actually,' he pointed out. 'It's *you* that makes them see it. It's not exactly flattering when you look at it that way. If it wasn't for you, I'd still be the invisible man.'

'It doesn't *matter*,' she wailed. 'Anyway, that's not what *keeps* them interested. That's *you*. In any case, what if one of them turns out to be better than me?'

'There *is* no one better than you,' he asserted. 'And ... I don't think it works that way,' he added thoughtfully. 'I love you, that's all. It won't stop. And as long as I do, no one else has a chance.'

'I don't always treat you right,' she said. 'I can be ...'

'That's just what it's like,' he said. 'People fight. For God's sake, don't turn into a "yes woman" I don't think I could stand it. I like you the way you are, sarcastic comments and all. It's not as if I didn't always know who you are, what you're like. I'm not perfect either, as I think we've established.'

'*I* know that,' said Tamar and she was smiling again. 'But it's not so easy to convince others. And I think I thought that if anyone could turn your head it would be the goddess of love. I mean, she's the expert.'

'She hasn't yet,' he said.

'Just let her try it,' said Tamar, but without venom.

'I'll tell you what,' he said. 'If she really starts to bug you, why don't you just kill her?'

'You wouldn't have a problem with that?' asked Tamar, startled.

'Well, it's not very nice I suppose. But isn't that what we're here for?'

'Well, yes, but ... you really mean it don't you? You *don't* like her.'

'I don't hate her either,' he pointed out. 'But I think you need to know whose side I'm on.'

'I think she's safe for now,' said Tamar. 'She's very like her, isn't she?' she added.

'Cindy you mean?' he asked. 'Yeah, I noticed that. Weird, isn't it?'

'I think that's what dredged all this up really,' said Tamar. 'I mean before Cindy, I would have bet my immortality that no blonde airhead could tempt *you*. But I understand all that better now,' she added hurriedly. 'If I had been there, it never would have happened, would it?'

'Didn't you already *know* that?'

'I guess I wasn't sure. I mean, I drive you crazy sometimes, I know I do.'

'But in a good way,' he said. 'I'd rather fight with you, than have all my own way with someone else. It's more fun.'

'Especially the making up part,' she said slyly.

'Oh, yes,' he agreed, 'Especially that.'

'And if I looked like a warthog?' she challenged him.

'I should have seen that coming,' he said. 'You never give up do you? Did I ever tell you about Mandy Carlson?'

'I don't think so ... no I don't remember that name, who was she?'

'Before I met you, she was the prettiest girl who ever agreed to go out with me. She was nothing compared to you, but at the time, I was ecstatic. We lasted three weeks, and I was the one who ended it. God she was boring. I've never met anyone so egocentric. She was self-centred and self-absorbed to a degree that was unbearable. I have no idea what made her agree to date *me*. She probably thought I'd make a willing slave – she was wrong. I think I hated her.'

'I can be pretty egocentric,' said Tamar.

'Not like her,' he said. 'Trust me, compared to Mandy, you're Mother Teresa. I guess my point is, you could look like a baboon's backside, and I'd still rather have you.'

'Okay, okay,' Tamar held her hands up. 'I surrender, you've convinced me.'

'Does this count as a fight then?' he asked hopefully, putting an arm around her waist.

'Down tiger,' she said. 'We haven't got time for all that. We have a quest to begin.'

'Bloody hell,' he said in a chagrined tone.

* * *

'Well, said Hephaestus. 'It looks as if you were right.'

'I am *always* right when it comes to matters of the heart,' said Aphrodite smugly. 'I knew there was some unresolved issue festering between those two. It was so strong that I could practically see it. A betrayal of some kind was most likely, but I have to admit, I thought it more likely to have been her. He doesn't seem the type, which only goes to show, even I don't know everything.'

'You knew enough to interfere though,' he said.

'I can't seem to help myself,' she admitted. 'They needed to talk about it. They had been avoiding doing so for many years until they no longer knew how to.'

'So you stepped in.'

'I may have stirred things up a little,' she admitted. 'And it could have gone either way. They may have ended up in a permanent estrangement. But I thought it unlikely. And if that had been the case, well then they wouldn't have been likely to last much longer anyway in such a state of doubt.'

'You are a better person than you are given credit for, I think,' he said. 'You had no reason to help them. In fact, I think you have a personal reason *not* to. Yet you did. And they will never know.'

'No, they will never know. And I have no personal reason not to help them, why would you think so?'

'You don't need to pretend to me,' he said. 'He matters to you far more than he ought to I think. There's no point in denying it.'

'You don't seem unduly upset by the fact,' she said, not even attempting to deny it. 'I hadn't even realised that you knew.'

'I can't pretend I like it,' he told her. 'I admit I was hoping for a different answer, although hardly expecting one. But now, at least I think I understand why you did this. It was for him, wasn't it?'

'I am a god,' she said. 'Sometimes we are able to rise above our petty emotions and do the right thing. I want him to be happy.'

'He came here to kill us.' Hephaestus thought this was worth pointing out.

'They both did,' she said. 'And yet here we are. Rise above it,' she told him. 'I have. Besides, no one knows what the future may hold.'

'Arachne does,' he said.

'Usually yes,' she agreed. 'But in this case, I suspect that even to her, things may not be so clear.'

'Either way, she'll never tell us,' he said sourly.

~ Chapter Ten ~

THE GODDESS HECATÉ wandered through the interesting graveyard. She had been summoned here of course. This was her job now. Hades had demoted her – a final humiliation – collecting the souls of the dead. What a come down.

Of course, slapping his silly face had probably been a mistake in retrospect, but he had deserved it. Him and that silly simpering wife of his. The fool would not know a real woman if she bit him on the ...

She stopped by the grave. "Jack Stiles" she read, and a cold hand reached out and grabbed her heart and squeezed it hard.

She felt an inexplicable sense of loss wash over her as she stared at the gravestone and its irrevocable truth carved in the granite. Jack Stiles was dead it told her, and she wanted to sob her heart out and had no idea why.

She shook herself. "I must be going soft" she told herself. "Why, he's only a *human*! Millions of them die every day"

'Have you come to take me to the other side?' a deep voice asked her.

She turned and looked him.

'Wow!' said Stiles's spirit. 'You're Hecaté, aren't you? I always wanted to meet you. This *is* an honour.'

And Hecaté just stared at him in wonder and disbelief until he began to feel quite nervous.

* * *

Arachne was disinclined to be helpful. She gave them a stony, disinterested stare and turned away without a word.

So, with a heavy sigh of resignation, Denny took a personal hand again. However, it did not seem to be working. Denny looked at Tamar who shrugged. It had worked on Arachne before, that is to say, in the future.

'You had to get control of it now?' hissed Denny. 'Just when it might actually come in handy?'

'Actually,' she whispered back. 'I'm quite certain I *don't* have control of it at all. It's *her*. She's ... different, harder. In the future, she was – will be softer – more human.'

'Well, we'll just have to threaten her then,' he said.

'I wouldn't,' put in Hecate. Prometheus had declined to revisit the underworld and no one had been able to think of a practical way to force him to come, so he was waiting on the surface; however the other gods had been given no such latitude.

'You cannot frighten her,' continued Hecate. 'And threatening her is only likely to make her angry.' She glanced at the glowering face of Arachne. 'Angrier,' she amended.

'Then what?' said Tamar. 'Should we have brought her a gift?'

'You!' snapped Arachne, pointing at Denny. 'I will talk to you. The others must leave.'

'I *told* you it was working,' said Tamar. 'It just took a bit longer this time.'

'I don't think so,' said Denny, looking at Arachne's face. 'This is something else.'

'You cannot leave him alone with her,' said Hecate. 'He will die.'

Tamar tossed her head impatiently. 'Rubbish,' she said. 'This sort of thing happens all the time, she's just ...'

'No,' said Hecate. 'Look at her face.'

Tamar looked. 'Oh!' she said. The expression was one of pure malice.

'But ... he'll be all right,' she faltered. 'If anyone can take care of himself ...'

'Even the gods fear Arachne,' said Hecate and she indicated Aphrodite, Hephaestus and Proteus huddled together and shuddering. 'In her domain, only she has power. His will be useless to him – we should leave now, before it is too late.'

'Er, I think she's right Denny,' said Tamar. 'C'mon let's go.' she tugged at his arm. But he refused to move, it was like trying to tug a mountain.

'I'm going to stay,' he said in a curious monotone. 'You leave, I'll join you soon.' He was gazing into Arachne's hypnotic stare like a man bewitched.

'Oh, no,' said Tamar. 'I'm not leaving you here – no way.' And she tugged futilely on his arm again. 'Come *on*!' she shrieked as panic descended on her. She reached around and slapped his face. 'Snap out of it.' and she pulled so hard on his arm that she was sure it loosened in the socket. But still he could not be moved.

Tamar turned to the others. '*Help* me!' she ordered.

But they hung back. Proteus was actually already half way out of the cave and backing up fast.

'He's already gone,' said Hephaestus. 'There's nothing we can do for him now.' He too was backing out of the cave taking a reluctant Aphrodite with him.

'No!' snapped Tamar, and with one last momentous effort, she managed to turn him round to face her. 'Look at *me*,' she ordered.

He did so, but he was like a man in a trance. 'Leave,' he said to her in the horrible robotic voice and then, just for a second, barely long enough for it to register, his face relaxed and he gave her a conspiratorial wink, before resuming the mask and sending her flying out of the cave. The cave mouth sealed up behind him immediately with a dense spider web material.

'Oh *shit*!' wailed Tamar. 'Denny! *Denny*!' She hammered on the springy doorway without making either a sound or a dent.

'We should go now,' said Hecate gently. 'It is over.' she shook her head sadly.

'It's *not* over,' said Tamar fiercely. 'He winked at me, I'm *sure* he did.'

'He could not have done,' said Hecate. 'I have seen this before. He no longer has a will of his own.'

There was a terrible shrieking from within the cave. Aphrodite went white, and even Hecate looked concerned, but Tamar just smiled. 'That's not him,' she said confidently. 'I've heard him yelling, that's too high pitched for him.'

'Depends on what he's yelling about,' said Hephaestus grimly.

'Don't be so gruesome,' said Aphrodite sharply.

'*Aieeee*... ugh.' then a silence fell broken suddenly by a tearing sound as a blade appeared through the web across the cave mouth and sliced through to reveal a grinning Denny. 'I think she's ready to talk now,' he said.

'I *told* you he winked at me,' said Tamar triumphantly. 'I'm always right,' she added.

They re-entered the cave in some trepidation wondering what they were going to see. Well, Tamar had a good idea already, she had seen Denny's handiwork before; it was similar to her own. But the others had not and so seeing Arachne tied up in a corner with her own legs was something of a surprise to them, not an unpleasant surprise though. In fact, the only person who seemed a little chagrined, apart from Arachne herself of course, was Tamar. 'Oh well, that's just great,' she said. 'She's going to be *delighted* to see us in the future now, isn't she? Oh well, I suppose it couldn't be helped.'

'I'm fine, by the way,' said Denny a little testily.

'Well, of course you are,' she said in surprise. 'I never doubted it.'

'How did you do it?' asked Hecate. 'I have never seen anyone escape the clutches of Arachne.'

Denny nodded at Tamar. 'We make a pretty good team,' he said, as if this was an explanation, which it was not really but Hecate accepted it as such for the time being. They had other business to deal with at the moment.

Arachne was glaring at them with such a look of fury on her face that it was a wonder that they did not all turn to stone. But it seemed that she knew when she was beaten.

'All right,' she said. 'You want to know your future I take it. You are looking for the Terastu. Well, I suppose I don't have a problem with that in principle. But I can't help you to find it. However,' she continued hurriedly. 'I will tell you this. You are not all here yet. There is one more you need. Find him and have him join your cause and the quest for the Terastu can begin. When you find him, it will all become clear to you. But I warn you, you will not find him easy to handle. He will need ... taming.'

'Taming?' said Denny. 'Oh gods, it's going to be the three headed dog, isn't it?' he added with a flash of insight. 'It's always something like that,' he added in explanation to the assembled gods.

'*Why* would we need a three headed dog?' said Tamar. 'That's ridiculous. What possible use ...? You know, you're probably right.'

'*Is* he right?' demanded Hecate emboldened by Arachne's current condition.

Arachne just hissed viciously at her.

'I used to pull the legs off spiders when I was a child,' said Denny inconsequentially.

There was an awkward silence; even Tamar was a little taken aback. But surely he did not *mean* it.

Arachne seemed to think he did, which, given her particular arena of expertise, could only mean that ... he *did*.

'Cerberus is the one,' she muttered.

'What was that?' said Tamar cruelly. I didn't quite hear ...'

'I *said* Cerberus is the one. Not that it matters. You would have found out sooner or later anyway. That's fate for you – it happens anyway, whether you know about it or not.'

'And just exactly how is that going to help us?' said Tamar.

'All will be revealed,' said Arachne mysteriously.

'Bollocks,' said Tamar to assorted gasps of shock from her deific audience.

Denny laughed. 'It's always the same,' he said shaking his head. He brought his face close to that of the spider demon. 'I know you're not telling us everything,' he said. 'But as that's pretty much par for the course I'm going to give you one more chance ...' He stopped while he tried to decide how to frame the question. How would Jack have put it? Ah yes, of course ... 'Tell us everything we need to know about the quest for the Terastu, or I'll pull all your legs off and make you eat them.'

'Nice,' said Tamar. 'Subtle.'

'All I can tell you is that the dog is with you when you begin your quest. This much I can see clearly,' said Arachne.

'That's not the same as saying it's *all you know is*, is it?' said Denny.

'Are we going to find the damn thing or not?' snapped Tamar losing patience.

'Oh, yes, you will find it.' said Arachne.

'Oh, right then ...' Tamar faltered. 'Good, then ...'

'Where?' asked Denny. 'When? How? Come on, give us *something*.'

Arachne did. She gave them a warning. 'You search for the Terastu to kill the gods,' she told Denny. 'And what do you think *you* are now? Are you sure this is what you want to do? But then, fate is fate and cannot be avoided.'

'You're telling me, I'm going to die?' asked Denny.

'Everyone dies,' said Arachne. 'It is only a question of when and how.'

'You know,' said Denny. 'You *are* a monster. But you'll change. I *know* you will.'

'Despite everything,' she said. 'I like you. You are brave, and you are no hypocrite. Beware the treachery of the gods.

They *are* hypocrites. I should know. A monster I may be, but I am not a liar.'

'Then tell us the truth,' challenged Denny.

'I have,' she said. 'Tame Cerberus, it is the first challenge. The others will be harder.'

* * *

'Well that was a complete waste of time,' said Tamar.

'Not entirely,' said Denny.

'Oh, you don't think so?' she said tartly. 'She told we had to tame a great smelly three headed dog, that we *will* find the Terastu but that when we do, it'll probably kill you, and she kept it all vague enough that it's entirely possible that that's not what she meant at all. Big help!'

'She said that taming Cerberus was the first challenge,' he said. 'And we know from experience that one clue leads to another. So when she said that it would become clear after that, that's probably what she meant.'

'But that's not how a quest works,' argued Tamar. 'We should never have gone to her. Now we're all muddled up. Were we *supposed* to go to her first? Has she given us the first clue, is that what that was? Or ...'

'From what I can tell,' he said. 'We were destined to run into Cerberus anyway, and then ... well, we'll see won't we?'

'See, a waste of time,' she said. 'She only told us what's going to happen anyway.'

'Well, when you put it that way ... Still at least we'll be ready for him now – Cerberus I mean.'

'I hate quests,' she said mutinously.

'Damn straight!' agreed Denny. 'They never make any sense.'

'So where is he anyway?' asked Tamar. 'We might as well get it over with, and, by the way, *you're* doing it. You have a way with vicious animals.'

'What makes you say that?'

'You tamed Fulk didn't you?'

'Fulk? He was just a big softie.'

'Not until you got your hands on him, he wasn't. Anyway, I'm just not a dog person.'

'I think you will find that the only way to tame Cerberus to your will is to kill Hades,' said Hecate. 'Hades is his master. He answers only to his commands. Only death can break that tie.'

'Where do we find Hades?' said Tamar.

'He has a palace down here,' she said. But it *is* guarded.'

'Let me guess,' said Tamar. 'Harpies.'

Hecate inclined her head.

'I'm not facing any Harpies,' said Aphrodite resolutely. 'I don't care what you say, *any* of you.'

'Coward!' sneered Hecate.

'*You* go then,' said Aphrodite. 'And I hope they rip you apart.'

'We'll split up,' said Tamar, coming to a decision. 'And *you*,' she pointed at Aphrodite, 'will either come with me to face Cerberus. I mean *someone's* got to,' she addressed Denny for a moment, 'or else the moment the tie with Hades is broken, he'll be off, and we'll *never* catch him.' She returned to Aphrodite. '*Or* you can ... no, on second thoughts. You come with *me*. Hecate can go with Denny to face Hades. There's a few unresolved issues there I think. Proteus, you go with them too. I hardly think your shape shifting talents will be useful against a big dog. That just leaves you.' She turned to Hephaestus. 'What do you want to do?'

'Er, whatever you say I want to do?' he said to general laughter.

'Fine,' said Tamar, looking thoroughly unamused. 'You probably want to come with us and keep an eye on your wife, don't you?'

'If you say so,' he said.

'I thought you wanted *me* to face the big ugly dog,' said Denny.

'I'm going to have to do it now though,' she said. 'Unless you want to give *me* the Athame and I'll go after Hades.'

Denny drew her aside. 'What are you doing?' he hissed in her ear. 'You can't tame Cerberus until Hades is already dead, so what's the point in splitting up? We should stick together.'

'All right,' she said. '*You* talk Aphrodite into facing the Harpies and waste even more time. She won't come, not even for you. Remember the shaft in the cliff? And *one* of us has got to keep an eye on her. We can't just leave her behind on her own. And I'd, quite frankly, rather it was me.'

'And ...?' asked Denny who knew damn well that this was not the real reason.

'*And*, I *told* you, I think it's more than likely that when Hades dies Cerberus will become his own boss, so to speak. And if that *is* the case, then *I'm* probably the only one who'll be able to handle him. We don't want him running off before we can stop him. And wreaking all sorts of havoc too I'll bet. So I think I should be on the spot when it happens to try to contain him.'

'You make a good point,' Denny conceded.

'Of course, there really isn't any easy way to tell the difference between a large vicious dog attacking you because it's under a command to do so and a large vicious dog attacking you because it just wants to,' she said, 'so I suppose I'm just going to have to get it under control until you come back and tell me we're all clear.'

Denny saluted. 'Sir, yes Sir,' he barked.

'Oh ... shut up,' she said. 'I'm not *that* bad.'

'If you say so,' said Denny with a grin.

* * *

Hecate led the way. They threaded their way through the shades of men, milling around the underworld like so many waifs and strays down at the unemployment offices. Denny shuddered. How horrible to be dead in this place. An eternity of unending and absolute boredom seemed to be the basic package. Denny rather thought he would prefer the punishments of Hell than this. Or maybe this was Hell, or rather Tartarus.

The palace of Hades was not exactly hard to find. Hades evidently believed in advertising, and it loomed over the underworld like a ... great big looming thing, Denny thought. (Denny had many excellent qualities but a strong imagination was not one of them.) 'I can see you,' it seemed to be saying. But Denny rather doubted that they were actually being watched as they approached.

'No sign of the Harpies yet,' he commented.

No,' said Hecate. 'We will not see them coming. Be ready.'

Denny patted the Athame in his belt and tensed up, looking around him for signs of attack.

Hecate seemed relaxed though; she might have been on an evening stroll. And Denny realised, with a start, that she was on her own ground here. It was funny; he had known, in an abstract way, for as long as he had known her, that she had once lived down here, but he had never really *realised* it before. The Hecate that he knew did not belong in this miserable place. But this was not the Hecate that he knew. The Hecate he knew wore more clothes for one thing.

Proteus was neither relaxed nor tensed for battle; he was poised to run, and he skulked rather than walked along the path that led to the palace. Denny was not sure that he was going to be a lot of use to him. He felt he could rely on Hecate, even this unknown Hecate, but Proteus seemed likely to run at the first sign of trouble. Even Cindy... *Aphrodite* would have been more use. But if he could not have Tamar at his back, he wished he could at least have Stiles. Good old Jack who could always be relied on to back him up no matter how crazy the undertaking. Who would, no doubt, had he been here, have been tunelessly singing some silly song about the impending danger before them and somehow making it all seem like a funny adventure rather than the life and death mission that it was.

He was musing on this and not paying attention when the Harpies swooped. Before he could react, a claw raked across his head drawing a deep gash and making him stagger dizzily.

'You were not paying attention,' admonished Hecate sharply as she drew back from a similar attack.

'Run!' shouted Proteus.

'Fight!' countermanded Denny, drawing the Athame. 'There's no way we can outrun *them*.' He suspected that trying to run was the mistake most people would make in this situation. But running away from an enemy that could fly was a pointless exercise. The key was to stand still and make them come at you. Then you would have them exactly where they wanted you – or something like that.

The Harpy that had gouged open his head had circled round and was making its second attack, this time head on. Well he was ready for it this time. Nothing – but nothing survived the Athame. It flew at his face screaming like a banshee and beating its wings like a butterfly caught in a net. But these were enormous and heavy wings; one blow could cause a serious concussion. However, it was the claws that were the main problem. Not fast enough again, Denny was caught across the face, and as he staggered backwards, he was vaguely aware of Hecate going down under a storm of beating wings. He wiped the blood from his face and snarled. He slashed at the relentless wings and managed, by sheer luck probably, to shear one wing right off. The Harpy wheeled haphazardly, completely off balance, and crashed inelegantly to the ground where Denny fell on it and sliced the head off. So much for that one, he turned his attention to Hecate's problem.

This one was easier in that the Harpy was already on the ground and fully occupied. Unfortunately, what it was occupied in doing was trying to turn Hecate into kibble.

'Get the hell off my *friend*, you bitch,' yelled Denny furiously and grabbed at the neck, dragging the Harpy away. One sharp twist and the neck was broken.

More were coming, but at a distance.

'Okay, said Denny, '*Now* we run.' He looked around. 'Where the hell is Proteus?' he said.

'Hiding,' gasped Hecate. 'Forget him, he takes care of himself.'

Denny gave up; grabbing Hecate by the hand he took off towards the entrance.

The Athame made short work of the lock; he simply sliced it off and threw his weight against the heavy door. It opened but painfully slowly, and two Harpies were now bearing down on them. But, as it is written in the laws of narrative, the door swung open just, as they say, in the nick of time, and they tumbled inside and fought against the counterweight of the Harpies on the other side of the door for a few moments before managing to shut them out. Then they slid down the door together with a sigh of relief.

They were both bleeding and weary, but Hecate was in far worse shape than he was.

'Are you all right?' asked Denny awkwardly. Hecate's clothing had been torn, and there had not been that much of it to begin with – Denny was not used to seeing women (apart from Tamar) so exposed. He was trying to assess the extent of her injuries, therefore, without actually looking at her.

'I am well enough,' she told him. 'Nothing that will not heal. You called me your friend,' she added.

'I did? Oh, er ... well, aren't you? I mean sort of. We're on the same side anyway,' he temporised.

'Indeed,' she said. 'And that is what you meant?'

'I suppose so, look do you want to borrow my cloak? You haven't got much of an outfit left.'

'Thank you,' she said in surprise, accepting the gift and wrapping it around her shoulders to Denny's immense relief.

'So, what the hell happened to Proteus?' said Denny.

Hecate pointed to the bottom of the door. A small rodent was working its way under the gap, as soon as it had squeezed through it grew rapidly into Proteus as they had last seen him.

'I see,' said Denny sourly. 'Well, since we're all here, where to now, where's Hades?'

'Follow me,' said Hecate. 'And keep that dagger handy. Hades has guards stationed throughout this place.'

'He would have,' sighed Denny.

* * *

Tamar had fought a lot of monsters in her time, but even for her, a giant three headed dog was a bit of a challenge.

Finding the damn thing was challenge number one. Hecate had said that Cerberus was usually to be found guarding the entrance to the underworld, but they certainly had not seen him on their way in – either time. Tamar thought this was suspicious. 'It's almost as if Hades was expecting us, and doesn't care either.' she said. 'Do you think he's up to something?'

'I doubt it,' Hephaestus said. 'He never was all that bright. I expect he's just letting things get a little slack around here. I mean who on earth would want to break into the underworld anyway? Apart from Heracles, who's gone now anyway, you're the first, as far as I know.'

'So, if Cerberus isn't here,' said Tamar. 'Then where is he?'

'Who says he isn't here?' said Hephaestus.

'Well, *I* can't see him,' said Tamar impatiently. 'It's a dirty great three headed hound of hell, you couldn't exactly miss it.'

'There!' shrieked Aphrodite suddenly and ran to hide behind Hephaestus.

'Was that there all the time?' said Tamar.

Cerberus was approaching slowly and silently on huge padded paws. Where the hell he had come from was anybody's guess. There were no shadowy caves or tunnels that he could have been hiding in, as far as they could see. It looked as if he had simply appeared out of thin air. This was a bit of a worrying development as far as Tamar was concerned. No one had told her he could do *that*. And if he could appear, then presumably he could also disappear.

'Will those chains of yours hold him?' Tamar asked Hephaestus.

'If you can get them on him,' was the doubtful reply.

'You leave that to me,' she said confidently. 'You just give me the chains and get back. 'I'll deal with this.'

'Bossy isn't she?' said Aphrodite.

'But fearless,' Hephaestus said. 'Just look at her.'

Tamar had looped the chains into a lasso and was whirling it around her head ready to throw. Cerberus was shaking his heads from side to side in confusion, watching the progress of the chains as they swung back and forth. He kept up a steady deep growl – which was usually more than enough to scare anybody away, but it was not working this time. He bared three sets of impossible teeth and Tamar knew her time was up. She threw the lasso at the middle head. It caught – naturally – and Tamar pulled hard. The lasso tightened, and she dragged Cerberus to the ground.

'By Zeus, exclaimed Hephaestus. 'Would you look at that? How strong *is* that woman?'

Of course, there were two other heads still snapping and snarling, to deal with. Still there was plenty of chain left. With horrendous, reckless disregard to her personal safety, Tamar leaped onto the right hand head and brought a fist wrapped in chains crashing down on the beast's forehead. The eyes crossed comically and then closed.

'Pretty damn strong,' said Aphrodite. 'Stronger even than Heracles maybe. She knocked him out.'

Tamar wrapped the loose chain around the right hand head, thus attaching it to the middle head. But now she had run out of chains, and there was still the left hand head to deal with. And Cerberus was getting to his feet again.

'Right!' she thought. 'I made a mistake there.' She would never, under any conditions, have admitted this out loud. She looked up and saw... Yes, that ought to do it. Unwrapping the chains swiftly from the unconscious head ignoring the cries of protest from Aphrodite, and kicking desperately at the other head, she swung the loose end of the chain high and prayed it would catch. It did, sort of, but although it caught on the ropes and chains above, (the gods knew what they were there for, but they could not have been handier at the moment) it tangled up and did not go right over. Damn it, she would have to climb. She went up the chain swiftly with Cerberus snapping at her heels, and untangled the chain, then, still hanging on, she dropped. As she went down, Cerberus went up and over. Then she tied off the end leaving Cerberus dangling from a complicated arrangement of chains, ropes and what appeared to be nets.

'Got him!' she said standing back and breathing heavily.

'You certainly did,' said Hephaestus. 'Do you always work like that?'

'Like what?' she said.

'So ... impromptu?' he said. 'Just making it up as you go along?'

'You noticed that did you?' she said with a grin. 'I find it works for me.'

'Unfortunately,' said Hephaestus, 'Those other chains are not of my construction. I don't know how long they will hold him.'

Tamar looked at the furiously struggling Cerberus. 'Denny, will be in Hades palace by now,' she said. 'We'll just have to hope they'll hold him for long enough.'

'If he managed to get past the Harpies,' said Hephaestus.

'Oh, he will have,' said Tamar authoritatively. 'You don't know him like I do.'

Aphrodite looked at the fiercely angry animal fighting to extricate himself from the impromptu prison that Tamar had fashioned. 'I hope you are right,' she said.

* * *

'What can we expect then?' said Denny as Hecate led them along the dark passages of Hades' palace. 'Skeletal warriors?' he said hopefully, 'those ones that spring from the dragon's teeth. I've *always* wanted to see those.'

Hecate gave him an indulgent smile. 'You are like a small boy,' she said. 'You think of this as an adventure. Yet you fight like a hero – although you do not *look* like one. I do not understand you at all.'

'Never judge a book by its cover,' said Denny absently.

'And you say the strangest things,' she said. 'Sometimes it is as if you are speaking a different language, although I understand the words.'

'It's best not to take too much notice of me sometimes,' he said evasively. I can talk a lot of nonsense at times.'

'I do not believe this is the case,' she said firmly. 'But I will get to the heart of the enigma that you represent in time.'

Since Denny personally knew this to be true he could not stop himself from saying so. 'I know you will,' he said. 'In time.'

Hecate stopped short. 'All right,' she said. 'You know *this* about me, and you know *that*. Who *are* you?'

Denny bit his lip. *Ooops!*

'I feel as I ought to know you,' she said, 'but I do not. So tell me.'

'Is this really the time for this?' said Denny hopelessly. He knew from experience that this ploy never worked. By the look on Hecate's face, it was not working now. She raised an interrogative eyebrow.

'We could be attacked by Hades' guards any second,' he tried.

'Then tell me quickly,' she countered.

'I couldn't tell you all that quickly if I tried,' he said. 'It's a bit of a long story.

'All right, all right.' He ran his long thin fingers nervously through his hair, which, although it was still short, was beginning to look untidy again. 'Short version, Tamar and I have met you before, but a long time in the future. That's where we've come from.'

'I see,' she said. 'There would indeed seem to be a long story behind that statement. You can tell it to me later. We have, as you say, pressing business at the moment.'

'I can't tell you too much,' he said. 'It could change the future.'

'Tell me whatever you can,' she said. 'And I will try to be satisfied with that. I trust you at, least, not to lie to me.'

'You see,' he said. 'You know me too. You just don't remember it.'

'I cannot remember a thing that has not yet happened,' she said.

'Not yet anyway,' said Denny. 'But things change.'

'Did you know me too?' asked Proteus who had been listening to all this with avid interest.

'No,' said Denny shortly.

'Oh.'

'I knew someone a bit like you once,' he said seeing that Proteus was disappointed by this answer for some reason. 'Knew someone like Aphrodite too. Very like her, in fact.' he added thoughtfully. 'Practically the same person. It's enough to make you believe in reincarnation.'

But immortals don't understand the concept of reincarnation so all he got for his trouble was a blank stare.

'Yeah well ...' he said. 'So, where are all these guards then?'

'Ah,' he said, turning at the sounds of scuffling, 'ask and ye shall receive,'

Behind him were seven of the standard "empty suit of armour" type magical warriors lurching towards them in a threatening manner. Denny was disappointed. He knew he could dispatch these without breaking a sweat. They were hardly impressive, or particularly fast moving. For a moment he had a vision of himself as he had been before the Athame, before Tamar. He would have been terrified, back then, of these lurching monsters. But now ... What the hell had happened to his life, to *him*, that this sort of thing was commonplace? He began to laugh.

'What is so funny?' demanded Hecate. But Denny just continued to laugh.

'Is he all right?' asked Proteus in a worried voice. If Denny had gone off the deep end, then they were all in very big trouble.

'Perhaps the stress ...?' said Hecate. 'The danger ...?' she shrugged helplessly.

'*What* danger?' snorted Denny, apparently hearing this. 'These guys aren't dangerous. That's what's funny.'

'*Oh god, when did I become so arrogant?*'

'Stand back,' he heard himself say. '*I'll* deal with this.'

'*I've finally turned into Tamar,*' he thought. '*Maybe it was bound to happen eventually.*'

He had fun. He twirled his sword (the Athame in disguise) he swung from the chandeliers (he had always wanted to try this) – after all, there was no point in taking a fight like this *too* seriously.

'Are you having fun?' said Hecate dryly as he slid past her backwards dragging a warrior along with him and catapulting it into the hangings.

Denny grinned at her.

'A small boy,' she said. 'Just like a small boy. I said so. Just *look* at him!'

'If that's the best old Hades has got,' he said when it was over (all too soon) 'Then this is going to be easy.'

'It's usually more than enough for most people,' said Hecate. 'But you are *not* most people are you? I wonder if you realise ...'

'Realise what?' said Denny sheathing the Athame.

'Never mind,' she said.

'That won't be the last of them,' said Proteus in a slightly peeved voice. He was a god after all; he did not like being outshone so completely by a mortal. It was humiliating. This guy was worse than Heracles. At least the son of Zeus had taken this sort of thing *seriously*. *Old* Hades indeed! He might show a *bit* of respect.

'Okay,' said Denny to Hecate, ignoring Proteus, 'which way?'

'Actually, we are here,' she said. 'Just beyond that door, is the throne room of Hades.'

'Do you want me to go in alone?' Denny asked.

'No, not at all.' A spiteful look slid onto her face. 'I want to see this.'

Denny raised an eyebrow but said nothing. He opened the door.

As Hades rose from his throne, several warriors hastened into place before him and raised their weapons.

Denny ignored them; he was staring at Hades in utter bewilderment and shock. Now *that* was a familiar face. He looked at Hecate in confusion. She hated *this* man? Then how was it possible that, in the future, she could ...

He grabbed Hecate by the collar of his cloak that she was still wearing and demanded angrily. 'What's going on?'

'Let me go!' she said haughtily.

'Not until you explain yourself,' he told her. There was something wrong here; he just knew it. He pointed to Hades. 'Who is *that*?' he snapped.

Hecate looked at him as if he was insane. 'That is Hades,' she said. 'Lord of the Dead. Who...?'

'*That's* Hades?' said Denny in disbelief. 'But ... but ... it *can't* be.'

The guards of Hades had been standing to attention awaiting orders, and now, Hades clicked his fingers, and three of them attacked. Denny swatted them away absently, still holding on to Hecate with one hand. He had a preoccupied look on his face. Upon seeing this, Hades fled from the throne room through a back exit.

'He's escaping,' shrieked Hecate. 'Go after him.'

'All right,' agreed Denny, releasing her. 'I want some answers.'

'Wait,' said Hecate. 'What is it you think you are seeing?' she asked him.

'What?' he said.

'It is a power of the gods to take an image from your mind and project it on to their own appearance. A talent Zeus often employed in the seduction of young maidens.'

'That wouldn't work on me,' said Denny. 'The Athame protects me from glamours.'

'Are you certain?' she said. 'Do not let Hades fool you. He is cunning, the face you see, does it belong to one whom you would not wish to come to harm?'

'Er, yes, yes it does. You mean ... it was a *trick*?'

'Of course. Hades is a coward. He hides behind guards and behind the faces of other men. It is inconceivable that he did not know of your arrival. He was prepared. But, you must not let him escape, you *must* kill him.'

'If he's still wearing that face, I don't know if I can,' said Denny. 'Why do *you* care so much anyway?' he added. 'It's not as it makes any difference to you. Why do you hate him so much?'

Then suddenly Denny got it, unrequited love. Hadn't he himself been the victim of this very thing, didn't he know the symptoms? How such a love could turn to bitter hate. So, that *was* Hades real face. He had known that no mere glamour could blind him. But Hades was only the forerunner, a preview, as it were, of the *real* love of her life. She would find out one day, he *knew* she would.

Knowing all this made it easier. Hades was Hades, no matter what he *looked* like. Denny was now ready to do what he had to do.

He took Hecate gently by the shoulders. 'Thanks,' he said. 'Let's do this so we can get out of here.'

'Er, where would he go?' he asked.

Hecate thought for a moment then a slow smile came over her face.

'His seat of judgment,' she said. 'It is where he feels most powerful.'

'Seat of judgment?' asked Denny. 'Does he by any chance carry out interrogations there?'

'You could call it that,' she replied, looking puzzled.

'Innocent or guilty sort of thing?' asked Denny.

'Yes, Elysian Fields or Tartarus, reward or punishment. It is for him to decide.'

'And he never gets it wrong?' said Denny, knowing already what the answer would be.

Of course not. He can see into men's souls. You cannot lie to Hades. He does not listen to the words you say aloud anyway'

'I should have known,' said Denny. 'The same but different.'

He did not bother to explain this remark. She would understand one day in any case, if she even remembered this conversation.

'Where is this seat of judgement then?' he asked.

'I will show you,' she said. 'But it is unfortunate.'

'Why?'

'I believe I mentioned that he is at his most powerful there,' she said.

'I can handle it,' said Denny.

'I believe you,' she said.

Denny bowed before Hades at the seat of Judgement. He could not help it; he was being crushed under the weight of his own guilty conscience. He saw himself betraying Tamar with Cindy, murdering Artemis, the whole Nemesis thing; in fact, every horrible thing he had ever been ashamed of doing was now passing before him to torture him.

'Fight it,' hissed Hecate. 'He's using your conscience against you. If you were a bad person, you would not feel guilty.'

'Uh, huh,' grunted Denny.

'Oh ... *hell*!' Hecate tasted the unfamiliar word and found that it helped release a little frustration. 'If you want a thing doing,' she said. 'You must it yourself.' And she took the Athame from Denny's belt. It was a sign of his complete and utter prostration that he made no protest when she did this. He barely seemed to notice.

Hades, his attention focussed entirely on Denny's suffering, never saw her coming as she crept up behind him.

'I just hope this thing works,' she thought to herself. She had no clear idea of what the Athame was nor what it was supposed to do, but she had become aware that Denny intended to use it against Hades in some manner. She could only improvise and hope.

She rose up before him like an avenging angel and thrust the Athame into his heart.

'*You?*' Hades managed to gasp as his power was drained away. 'Betrayer,' he accused.

Denny leapt to his feet, released suddenly from his prison of shame.

'Hecate!' he cried out in horror. She turned to him, withdrawing the Athame as she did so. Hades fell to the floor twitching. 'He is still alive,' she said in a voice tinged with disappointment. And then, to Denny's immense relief she handed him the Athame. 'Finish it,' she said.

He took it from her and walked slowly and hesitantly over to the prostrate body of the former Lord of The Dead.

It was a bad moment to have to commit yet another murder, with the horrible memory of the guilt of the last time still lingering in his mind. Still, there really was nothing else for it. Denny bent down and quickly and painlessly snapped the neck of the man who looked for all the world exactly like his friend Jack Stiles.

While Denny was still shaking, a strange transformation was taking place before the eyes of Tamar, Hephaestus and Aphrodite.

Cerberus suddenly stopped struggling, snarling and growling and looked straight at Tamar (with all his heads) and said – actually spoke the words – 'Hades is dead. You can let me down now.'

Tamar's eyes widened. 'You can *talk*?'

'Yes, I can talk, at least, I can now and I'm really not dangerous, not now that Hades is no more. Please let me down.'

'You can see where I might have a problem with that idea,' said Tamar. 'You *were* trying to kill me a little while ago.'

'But I didn't want to,' said Cerberus. 'I had no choice in the matter. In actual fact, I find myself in your debt. I take it you had something to do with the current reversal of my fortunes. The death of Hades,' he explained.

'You seem quite intelligent enough to be laying a trap for me,' Tamar noted. 'So I think not, at least for now.'

'Oh, dear,' said Cerberus. 'This is what happens when one gains a reputation for violence.'

'You speak for yourself,' he told himself (with another head of course) 'I never hurt a fly,' Tamar raised her eyebrows in amusement.

'Only because you weren't quick enough,' said the middle head.

'I take offence at that remark,' was the reply.

'Well, I think you are *both* wrong,' he added. 'This charming young lady is only being cautious in the face of danger. We *all* attacked her after all. How would you feel in her place?'

Then the heads began to argue at such a pace that it was impossible to keep up. Tamar was laughing hysterically. Then Denny appeared with Hecate and Proteus in tow.

'How did you do that?' asked Tamar startled out of her amusement.

'The power of Hades,' he said holding up the Athame. 'He was the only one who could use his power in the underworld. Well it'd be a bit pointless him being in charge down here if he couldn't.'

'Then you *have* done it?' she said. 'Good, perhaps you can tell me what to do about the Three Stooges over here.'

Denny looked at Cerberus arguing vehemently with himself and laughed much as Tamar had done. 'Let him down,' he said. 'It'll be okay. I think he's got enough on his mind at the moment, don't you?'

'He says he's free now that Hades is dead,' she said. 'I was kind of hoping you'd be in charge of him instead.'

'I didn't know he could talk,' said Denny.

'It happened when Hades died ... What's up? You look all squinky. You *did* kill him didn't you?'

'Oh, yes,' said Denny suddenly sombre. 'I certainly did.'

'You want to talk about it?'

'Not now,' he said. 'Maybe later. Hey Cerberus,' he called.

Three heads swivelled comically to look at him.

'What?' they said in unison.

'Ever heard of the Terastu?'

'No, I never heard of it, did you?'

'No.'

'No.'

'Well, I suppose it was never going to be that easy,' said Tamar. 'All right, let's cut him down.'

'*Thank* you,' said Cerberus just a little snippily.

'Oh, god,' said Denny. 'I've just realised. A bunch of meddling kids and a talking dog. We're the Scooby gang.'

'We aren't meddling kids,' said Tamar. 'Although we *do* meddle I suppose. And you do look a bit like Shaggy. You eat like him too.'

'Scooby Dooby doo-oo,' said Denny.

'What *are* you talking about *now*?' said Hecate impatiently.

~ Chapter Eleven ~

CINDY ROSE LATE off satin sheets and began the slow process of getting herself ready for ... What? Yet another day of shopping and lunching and charity endeavours.

She had never thought it could happen, hadn't she got what she had always wanted, a rich, powerful, influential husband and more money than she could ever hope to spend in several lifetimes? But the truth was she was finally starting to wonder if this was all there was to life.

She was actually bored.

The other day she had seen a long legged scruffy man with hair that might once have been blonde but was now a sort of yellowish grey colour and not at all attractive. But he had been loping down the street with a sort of carefree stride whistling to himself and grinning happily and she had found herself wondering about him. Was he happier than her? Did he like his life? Did he do more exciting things, day by day, than she could even imagine?

Was he in love? Was that the secret of his happy smile? What would that be like, to be in love? What would it be like to be in love with a man like that? Would he be more exciting to be with than Richard? Who was nice but extremely dull. Cindy had never kidded herself that she was in any way in love with Richard. She had married him for his money. Could she have married for love? Was that was she was craving, or was it something else?

Some women in unhappy marriages have affairs (and Cindy was having some outrageous fantasies about the scruffy man it had to be said – she thought about dragging him off to her satin flounced bedroom and letting him make a terrible mess of the sheets)

Some women shoplift – what Cindy did was unusual, to say the least.

She began to save people.

It began simply enough. A quick binding spell on a purse snatcher so that he fell over his own feet and was unable to get up again until the police arrived. But the sense of satisfaction that she got from this one simple act spurred her on to more and more acts of silent heroism.

Pretty soon she was stalking the streets at night, looking for trouble to help people out of.

And she was happy. *This* was right; *this* was what she should have been doing for years.

But for some reason she could not forget the scruffy man she had seen on that day that had started it all.

Eventually she decided that the only thing to do was to track him down.

* * *

It was nice to breathe the real air again. They had made camp again outside the village at the foot of Mount Olympus, there being nowhere in particular to go at the moment. They had managed to free Cerberus (who was promising to be an interesting companion when he was not arguing with himself) and Denny had killed another god, but they did not feel as if they were really much further forward.

Cerberus had, as he had said, never heard of the Terastu. But he did add that if Arachne had said he was integral to the quest in some way then it was undoubtedly the truth. Arachne was unable to lie. 'She is the very embodiment of fate,' he said. 'And fate does not lie.'

'So we're just going to have to wait and see?' said Tamar. 'Is that what you're saying?'

'Didn't she tell you that you would find this object?' he said.

'Well, yes, she did,' admitted Tamar. 'But she never said it would be in time, or that it would be any use to us. I just wish she had given us a bit more to go on.'

'Everybody has path that they must travel,' said Cerberus sententiously.

'Well we did the first task,' said Tamar. 'And usually in a quest that leads us to the second and so on, but it hasn't. So what are we supposed to do now? We're stuck.'

'Unless anybody else has any bright ideas.' She threw the floor open. No one had.

'Typical,' she snorted.

Denny was standing a few feet away from the rest of them staring out at nothing with a blank look in his eyes.

'I think this has been hard on him,' Hecate said to Tamar following her gaze. 'He does not like to kill, I think.'

'No, you're right there,' said Tamar with a sigh. 'And so far I haven't really helped out much in that department.'

'I do not think that he really wants you to,' said Hecate shrewdly. 'He would rather take it all upon himself, despite his distaste, if that were possible.'

'Neither of us *wants* to do this, you know,' said Tamar. 'It isn't like that.'

'Of course not,' said Hecate. 'Great movers of destiny are always reluctant, always the victims of a fate that has been thrust upon them. It is the way of things. You do this thing, not because you desire it, but because you must.'

'I doubt that putting it that way is going to make him feel any better about it,' said Tamar. 'It doesn't make *me* feel any better.

'Still it's our own fault I suppose.' she added morosely. 'But, I have to admit, I'm not altogether sorry that the quest seems to have ground to a halt. And I don't think Denny is either.'

'Something will happen,' said Hecate. 'Something unexpected that will put you back on the path. You will see.'

'That's what I'm afraid of,' said Tamar.

Suddenly Denny pitched forward with a movement that was almost balletic and landed with a thud on his face and never moved again. He had an arrow in his back. Tamar sped over to him and crashed to her knees beside him in horror. She knew before she even touched him – he was dead. Were he alive he would have bounced straight up again.

She plucked out the arrow with shaking hands and turned him over and held him helplessly on her lap. Too stunned even to cry.

It was Hecate who picked up arrow and she turned it over in her hands curiously. 'This is an arrow of Nemesis,' she said.

'He's dead,' said Tamar in a horrible toneless voice. 'How? He's been shot a hundred times before. Burned, drowned ... How can he be dead from one arrow?'

'The arrows of Nemesis can kill gods,' said Hecate.

'We ... we ... didn't know,' said Tamar shakily and then she did begin to cry.

'You can kill me now,' came a voice from behind her. 'I no longer care, I have had my revenge.'

Tamar did not even look up at Nemesis. 'It doesn't matter,' she said in a hollow voice as if she really did *not* care. 'It won't bring him back, only the death of the *all* the gods will do that now. Once that is accomplished, all this will never have happened. I was so uncertain. I didn't want to, it seemed so wrong. But now I have no choice. If I have to slaughter them all with my own hands one by one, I'll do it.'

She leaned down and whispered in Denny's unhearing ear. 'I *will* bring you back. Whatever it takes, I promise. I'll bring you back. My love, my love. Oh god.'

She stood up and pointed to Nemesis. 'Hold her,' she ordered. And Hecate and Hephaestus darted forward and took an unresisting Nemesis by the arms. 'Take her arrows,' said Tamar, 'and let her go.'

'Let her go?' said Hephaestus. 'Are you sure?'

'Death is what she wants,' said Tamar. 'And I am in no mood to grant her any favours.'

She bent down again and gently retrieved the Athame from Denny's belt. She held it for a moment – all she had left of him now. 'I'll keep it safe for you,' she said.

'Thanks,' said Denny's voice from behind her.

Tamar spun. 'What?'

Denny was standing before her; she turned again. *And* he was also lying on the grass with a hole in him.

'What the ...?'

'I'm a spirit,' he explained. He nodded to the Athame. 'Power over the dead,' he said. 'Remember? From Hades. You called me here.'

This, at least, made sense. Tamar nodded uncertainly. 'So you're ... you really are ...?

'Dead?' he said. 'Fraid so, but it's not too bad. Didn't even hurt. She's a good shot. Aren't you going to bury me then?'

Tamar's face crumpled, and she began to sob in earnest.

'Oh god, I'm sorry,' he said. 'What a *stupid* tactless thing to say.' And he held his hands out helplessly – he could not even comfort her. He was dead.

'I-I'm okay,' she said contrary to all the evidence.

'Who is she talking to?' asked Proteus.

'Him, I imagine,' said Aphrodite, pointing at Denny's body.

'But he isn't here,' said Proteus obtusely. 'I mean obviously he is, but I doubt he's got a lot to say any more.'

'Oh, I don't know,' said Hecate. 'In my experience the dead can be quite talkative. She has the power of Hades, fool. In that dagger of his. I expect she summoned his spirit. It's what I would have done in her place.'

'So, why can't we *all* see him?' said Proteus.

'Have *you* got the power of Hades?' snapped Hecate. 'No. I thought not. *You* will only be able to see him if he wills it so, and I cannot imagine for a second why he would. Now be silent, I want to hear what she is saying.'

'Hey, Denny was saying, 'it could be worse. At least, thanks to you, I'm not stuck in the underworld. I really hate it there, you know.'

'I know.' The others heard her say, apparently to thin air. She was still sniffing, but she did seem to be calming down.

'I wonder what he's saying to her,' said Aphrodite. 'I wish we could at least *hear* him.'

'It's my own fault really,' he said. 'If I hadn't been so gutless and I'd killed Nemesis when I had the chance, this wouldn't have happened. I really didn't think it would matter, though. I figured as a mortal she'd have maybe fifty years tops – well within the time frame. I should have known better. That's not what we're here for.'

'You weren't being gutless,' said Tamar vehemently. 'Mercy is never gutless.'

'It is when killing someone would be kinder in the long run,' he said. 'I didn't want to be a murderer. It was selfish.'

Tamar was silent; this was pretty pointed. The others crowded round – but at a respectful distance – to see what would happen next.

'Anyway, bright side,' said Denny. I can see things from a different perspective now, you might say. Arachne was right, in a manner of speaking.'

'What are you talking about?' asked Tamar.

'That's what I would like to know,' said Aphrodite *sotto voce*.

'The quest,' said Denny. 'I know what to do next. And if Arachne hadn't sent us to tame Cerberus I never would have killed Hades and then, when I died, you wouldn't have been able to summon me here with the power over the dead that I took from him and ... Anyway, this was how it was supposed to go I think.'

'You know what to do next?' said Tamar flabbergasted. 'How?'

'It's ... it's hard to explain,' he said. 'I just do.'

'And you had to *die* to find this out?' she wailed suddenly. 'It's not *fair*.'

'It was the only way,' he said.

'But I *need* you.'

'I'm still here,' he said, 'as long as you don't let go of me.'

'I'll never, never ...'

'I know.' he said, and he came forward again as if to put his arms around her, then he dropped them helplessly again. 'This really blows,' he said in chagrin.

Tamar gave a weak smile. 'Okay,' she said briskly. 'So what *do* we have to do next then? The quicker we get on with this, the quicker it'll all be over.'

'You need to kill Nemesis,' said Denny.

'And what's that going to prove? All right, all right, I was going to have to do it anyway, wasn't I?'

'I'm sorry,' he said. 'I wish now, that *I* had done it. But this was the way it was meant to happen. You were supposed to kill her in revenge for me, I think, but you always did defy destiny.'

'What aren't you telling me?' she said suddenly. 'Don't go all "Clive" on me now.'

'You know, I think I understand that guy a little better now,' he said. 'But you trust *me,* don't you?'

'All right,' she said. 'Keep your secrets.' She turned to Hephaestus. 'Where did Nemesis go?' she asked. 'I've decided to kill her after all.'

'I am still here,' said Nemesis, stepping forward from behind Prometheus. 'I knew you would change your mind.'

'Why do you want to die anyway?' said Tamar curiously.

'Why do you care?' said Nemesis. 'Just do it.'

'You could kill yourself,' said Tamar, 'if you're that keen to die. Why have *me* do it? I just want to understand,' she said to the shade of Denny who was shaking his head at her.

'It is justice that it be you,' said Nemesis. 'It cannot be any other way. It's all that I understand. I killed him in revenge, now you must do the same.'

'Destiny,' said Tamar. 'You really don't have a choice do you? And neither do I,' she added, finally understanding. 'I'll make it quick, like you did for him.'

Nemesis nodded and closed her eyes. And Tamar twisted her neck as Denny had done to Hades. A quick and bloodless death. The only kind Tamar felt able to deal out even in her grief.

Denny came up behind her and made her jump. 'Sorry,' he said. 'Are you all right?' she was shaking all over. 'It does take you that way for a bit,' he sympathised. 'Deep breaths,' he added. 'You'll be okay in a minute.'

'It's different,' she said. 'Not like in a fight, when it's you or them.'

'I know,' he said.

After a few minutes Tamar started to calm down again. 'Better?' asked Denny. No one else had said a word since Tamar had declared her intention to kill Nemesis. No one knew what to say.

'I'm okay,' she said. 'I'm fine now.'

'Sure?' he said. 'You can take as much time as you need. You need a clear head for this next bit.'

'There's a next bit?'

'Yes, you have to summon her spirit the way you did mine. But it's going to be harder. With me you did it on instinct and anyway, I *wanted* to come. *She's* probably going to resist. You'll have to concentrate.'

'I can do that,' said Tamar with grim determination. 'Aren't you going to tell me why?'

'I don't know yet,' he said. 'I didn't know that you would have to summon her until after you killed her. It's coming to me in stages. Cause and effect.'

Tamar concentrated. 'I don't think it's working ...' she began and was interrupted by a petulant voice. 'Can't you even let me rest in peace?'

'No,' said Denny and Nemesis turned in surprise.

'You?' she said. 'You're dead.'

'Much as you are,' he agreed.

'So you are a spirit too?' she said. 'Can't you let *anyone* rest in peace?' she said to Tamar.

'Shut up,' snapped Tamar and Nemesis did – immediately.

'Like a Djinn and its master,' said Denny. 'She has to do whatever you tell her to. Well, so do I, I suppose. You have complete control over the dead.'

'So what are we going to do with her then?' asked Tamar.

'*Her*?' hissed Aphrodite. 'What's going on *now*?'

Denny smiled. 'I see it all now,' he said. 'She will be leading you on the quest.'

* * *

Of course, when Denny said that he could see it all, he was exaggerating somewhat. But he had become aware of a few interesting facts. Nemesis, for example, was the founder – or one of the founders – of the quest. She would never have agreed to help them as a living god or even as a living mortal, but now she literally had no choice – no will of her own at all, in fact.

And how was Denny gathering all this interesting information? Quite simply, since he had died he was seeing things from the point of view of eternity. Similarly to the way he had seen things inside the mainframe but in a more limited fashion. In practice, what this meant was that Denny could see the future. Because he was no longer in the streams of time, he was able to view the present from the point of view of the future. Like a memory of something that has not quite happened yet. But it had to be *about* to happen for him to see it.

'I wish you could see further,' said Tamar as they sat together by the light of the dying fire. 'Like how it's all going to end.'

She had let Nemesis drift back to the underworld for a while, on Denny's advice. She would call her back when they were ready for her. The others had backed away to a safe distance where they could watch the strange proceedings without getting in the way. It was just the two of them; it almost felt normal. Almost.

'That's still uncertain,' he said, 'from the point of view of the universe anyway. I can't see what are still only possibilities. There are too many of them for me to separate out and make sense of. It takes a special kind of mind I think.'

'Like Arachne,' she said.

'Yes, but the past is easy to see,' he said, 'for the most part anyway. It's static, it's already happened, fixed points. Unless someone like us comes along and buggers it all up of course.'

'Of course,' she said.

'The Terastu isn't quite what we thought it was,' he said. 'It's not a weapon as such. I'm not quite sure, but basically, it was Apollo who was behind it in the first place. You see he knew that the time of the gods was going to end sometime, and the Terastu was their only chance to cheat destiny in some way. It could work either way, you see.'

'I don't understand,' she said.

'No, neither do I,' he admitted. 'You see, he set up the quest with the help of his sister Artemis and Nemesis. Because he thought it was the only way that the gods might have a chance. It doesn't make any sense to me at all. But that's what happened.'

'But we know for a fact that the gods *will* survive unless *we* make sure that they don't,' she said.

'But that wasn't their original destiny,' said Denny thoughtfully. '*We* changed it – that's why we're here.'

'So, what does that prove?'

'Well, at least it proves that Apollo was right when he saw the demise of the gods.'

'But their original destiny has *already* changed,' she said. 'Are you saying that we now have to find this Terastu to change it *back*? Or are we now stuck in some hideous paradox where *we're* going to be the ones who change their destiny in the first bloody place – again. This could be how it happened.'

'We're second guessing ourselves again,' warned Denny. 'It never gets us anywhere when we do that.'

'But it *could* be,' she insisted.

'I don't think it's that simple,' he said.

'*Simple*!' said Tamar. 'You must be kidding! My brain's going cross-eyed just thinking about it.'

Denny grinned. What a way to put it. Very Tamar

He had to admit, though, it was easier to think clearly now that he was dead. His own brain was coping with the conundrum much better. But there were disadvantages too. Now that he could not touch Tamar he found he had never wanted to so much – not since the last time he had not been able to. Her skin had never looked so satiny to him, her hair so silky, her mouth so inviting. It was driving him crazy.

'Awful, isn't it?' she said, divining his thoughts. 'And it's only been a few hours.

'Anyway,' he said to distract himself, 'I think ... I *think* ... we went back along the timeline where the gods survived. Right to the point or thereabouts that history changed, so we have to find this Terastu to change their destiny back to what it ought to be.'

'But you aren't sure?' she said. 'I mean, if we're in the timeline where the gods survive, then why would Apollo set up the quest in the first place?'

'It could go either way,' said Denny. 'That's the point. Even now, since we came back, the future is uncertain again. Just coming here changed things again, set us back on the path where the gods *will* die unless ...'

'Unless we fail,' she said. 'What a bloody mess we made. Clive was right. We really cocked it up this time.'

'We have to find this Terastu,' she decided. 'If only to find out what the blasted thing *is*.'

'I agree,' he said.

'It's so strange,' said Aphrodite to Hephaestus, 'don't you think? Watching her sitting there arguing with herself.'

'She isn't arguing with *herself*,' he said. 'We know that *he's* there. At least, Hecate seemed certain of it.'

'Well, they've been talking for hours and hours,' she said. 'What's going on do you think?'

'I have no idea.'

'Poor boy,' she said. 'He was young to die.'

'Well, he doesn't seem to have let it slow him down too much,' said Hephaestus tastelessly.

'Don't be crass,' she admonished him.

'Well it hasn't,' he said defensively.

'You don't like him, do you?' she said. 'You never use his name.'

'Stop going on about him, will you?' snapped Hephaestus. 'How is a man supposed to feel about the man his wife is in love with?'

And he stalked away in high dudgeon.

'There's going to be trouble there sooner or later,' said Hecate to Prometheus.

'What's old Hephaestus going to do about it?' he replied. 'It's too late to have the boy killed.' And he laughed like a drain at his own wit.

But Hecate had been growing fond of Denny in a sisterly sort of way and did not think this was very funny. She swept away haughtily without another word.

'You'll pay for that later,' said Proteus.

'I know I will,' said Prometheus gloomily. 'Women!'

* * *

Nemesis was looking sulky and defiant, but to no purpose whatsoever – she might as well have been gracious about it for all the difference it made. If anything, Tamar had more control over the dead than even Hades had had. She had a very strong will and was prepared to exploit her new power shamelessly to get what she wanted.

'Where do we go first?' she demanded.

'It's not like that,' said Nemesis. 'I was not made privy to the secrets behind the quest, I was not considered important enough. Apollo and Artemis set up the quest. I only hold the clues.'

'Good enough,' said Tamar. 'I suppose you were meant to lead the quest then?'

'In the name of Apollo,' she said. 'But he has not chosen you.'

'Fate chose us,' said Tamar, 'literally. Now get on with it.'

Nemesis looked at Denny. 'Well, she said, I suppose anything's better than having to spend eternity with him. And it's not as if I have any choice is it?'

Tamar made a squeezing gesture with her hand causing the spirit of Nemesis to let out a scream. 'No choice at all,' she confirmed. 'That was nothing,' she added. 'Don't piss me about, or you'll see what I can really do to you.'

'Tasks,' said Nemesis. 'You have to perform tasks. That's how he did it. Each task ... no, no, I have to explain this, *please.*'

'Tam,' put in Denny. 'Give her a chance.'

'Each task leads to the next.' she finished hurriedly.

'How many?' said Tamar.

'Seven,' said Nemesis. 'Seven tasks to complete.'

'Seven tasks,' repeated Tamar. 'And what's the first one?'

'An impossible one, even for you,' said Nemesis with a nasty smile.

'I'll be the judge of that,' said Tamar. 'I don't see why Apollo would have made the task impossible. He meant for *someone* to succeed, didn't he?'

'The world has changed since then,' said Nemesis. 'You are to retrieve the belt of Orion,'

'Retrieve the belt of Orion?' Tamar repeated for the benefit of those who could neither see nor hear Nemesis.

'But ... Orion has been placed in the firmament,' gasped Hecate. 'It's impossible.'

'I'll be the judge of that,' repeated Tamar. Denny was grinning. He knew his Tamar.

'Okay,' she said. 'This shouldn't take long.' and she vanished.

'It occurs to me,' said Prometheus, 'that even had Orion *not* been placed among the stars, this would have been a difficult task for a mortal to complete. Orion was a mighty man indeed, a son of Poseidon. I cannot see how Apollo expected anyone not of immortal descent to capture his belt or any other thing of his.'

'He would have helped them of course,' said Aphrodite cuttingly. 'If he deemed them worthy, which he hardly ever does. I don't suppose he ever expected a Djinn to take up the quest and throw all his plans out in this way.'

Nemesis threw a startled glance at Denny. 'She is *Djinn*?' she asked.

'Oh, yeah – yes. Didn't we mention that?'

'Who then is her master?'

'She's pretty much her own master,' said Denny. 'She's free.'

'Free? A free Djinn. I never heard of such a thing.'

'There are probably a lot of things you never heard of,' he said. 'Doesn't mean they aren't true.'

'Apollo should have made the tasks harder,' said Nemesis.

'I don't suppose he ever thought of this,' said Denny.

'But ... she could *succeed*!'

'Oh, believe me,' said Denny, 'she *will*. I've never seen her beaten.'

'What, *never*?'

'Never,' affirmed Denny. 'You think this is the first time I've been dead? She never gives up.'

'You've been dead before?' said Nemesis in utter disbelief. 'How is that even possible? It makes no sense.'

'I know,' he said. 'Believe me, I know.'

* * *

Tamar was – well, among the stars. It was peaceful up here – quiet. It had been easy enough to get here, but now she had another problem.

Orion really was just a constellation. Nothing more. How the hell was she supposed to get the belt, when all it was, was a line of stars? Did that even matter?

'Having trouble?'

Tamar floated round. 'What are you doing here?' she said.

'You called me,' said Denny. 'You really have an incredibly powerful mind, just not a lot of self-control.'

'That explains a lot,' she said. 'But I'm glad you're here. I don't know what to do.' She gestured to the constellation. 'You know, it really shouldn't even *look* like this up close,' she said. 'But that's mythology for you.'

'So?' said Denny. 'It's not just a lot of stars then, is it? It's more than that.'

'I realise that,' she said snippily. 'But how do I use that fact?'

Denny shrugged. 'I don't know everything,' he said. 'Omniscience, that's *your* department.'

'It's just symbolic,' she said. 'You can't *do* a lot with symbolic.'

'I've had enough of this,' she said suddenly sitting down cross legged in the complete lack of air. 'What's the point of all this anyway? Why don't I just take Nemesis's arrows up to Olympia and start shooting? Why does it always have to be so hard? You know, I don't think I can do this anymore.'

'What?' asked Denny, alarmed.

Tamar waved her arms. 'This! All this ... crap. The price is too high. After I get you back, I'm packing it in. I mean it. Enough is enough. The world can save itself from now on.'

'You know you don't mean that,' he said.

'I believe I said I *did* mean it,' she said. 'You're dead. *Dead*! I can't keep doing this.'

'I'm not more important than the whole world,' he said. 'And you ...'

'You are to me,' she said.

Denny would have taken a deep breath, except for there being no air and the fact that he was dead anyway. 'But ...' he began.

'No, Denny,' she cut him off. 'I'm sick of it. Sick of almost losing you and everyone else I care about. Of *actually* losing you. Sick of always fighting. All we wanted was a little break – just once – haven't we earned it? And look what happens. What *always* happens.'

'Are you done?' he said.

'Yes.'

'Feel better?'

'Much better.'

'And ...?

'I know what to do,' she admitted. 'I think maybe I always did.'

'Well, don't keep me in suspense. What is it?'

Tamar vanished. And reappeared as a constellation of stars.

'Wow!' exclaimed Denny. 'I never saw *that* coming.'

The constellation Tamar winked at him.

From Tamar's point of view, it looked rather different. It was like entering another world. Everything looked normal – for a given value of normal– like the world below. There was Orion, and the Pleiades fleeing from him. And Scorpio chasing *him*.

But it all looked like the real world. A sort of still life cameo of the real world. Tamar though it was creepy. She grabbed the belt and got the hell out of there.

~ Chapter Twelve ~

IT WAS NOT SO MUCH that the job was boring; it was that it was *so* boring that Denny often found himself contemplating digging out his own eyes just for something to do.

But at least he could go for a kip in the back whenever he wanted to; it was not as if there were ever any customers.

So it was a bit of a surprise when the bell over the door – well it did not tinkle; it had not tinkled for many years, but it did make a sort of grinding noise that made Denny look up as the door opened.

A gorgeous blonde stood in the doorway. Denny straightened up automatically. 'Can I help you?' he said dredging up the phrase from the recesses of his memory.

The blonde smiled. 'Maybe,' she said. 'I want to know all about you.'

This was actually far from the strangest request Denny had ever heard – at one time the store had been the general hang out of all the local stoners and street dwellers in the area. Denny had been asked some pretty peculiar questions during that period. So he smiled and not just with his mouth – it reached to his eyes – and said. 'Okay then.'

Well it beat being bored senseless, he thought and wondered if she would feel the same way after he had finished telling his absurdly tedious life story to her. She had evidently mistaken him for someone with a life.

The blonde seized on what Denny had considered she would find perhaps the least interesting part of his ramblings.

He only mentioned it because it was so much on his mind lately.

'I bet I can find out what happened to your Miltonian Fulcrum thingy,' she said suddenly as he was just in the middle of telling her about his nasty tooth infection of a few years ago.

'Millennium Falcon,' he said.

'Yeah that thing,' she said. 'After all I found *you* didn't I?'

'You *found* me?' said Denny perplexed. 'Why were you *looking* for me?'

The blonde blushed. 'It's not important,' she said dismissively. 'The thing is ... if you want me too, I bet I could find out what happened to it. It seems very important to you.' She leaned seductively over the counter as she said this – it had the desired effect. That is, it confused Denny enough to make him forget his original query.

'It's a collector's item,' said Denny. 'I really, really wanted it at the time. But now...'

'Now you just want to know what happened to it?' she finished.

She looked thoughtful for a moment. 'Sounds fateful to me,' she said without bothering to explain this remark. 'Leave it with me.' she added. 'You know you might turn out to be quite interesting after all.' And blowing him a flirty kiss, she stalked out of the shop.

Denny went back to thinking about the best way to dig out his eyes.

A sharpened spoon was submitted to his brain for consideration.

It was a pretty ordinary belt really, apart from the stars still twinkling along its length.

Tamar put it on. It seemed the thing to do. Nothing happened, except her chiton bunched unflatteringly.

She would have to ask Nemesis.

'I'm not sure it suits me,' she said landing back on the earth and giving a twirl. 'What do you think?'

'Is that ...?' began Aphrodite. 'Is that really it? You really did it?'

'Piece of ca... Er, it was easy,' Tamar amended.

'Amazing!' said Hecate.

And then suddenly she was getting a round of applause. Nemesis was looking sour.

'I *told* you she'd do it,' said Denny.

'Shame it's not working,' said Nemesis.

Tamar whipped round. 'What's not working?' she demanded, before Denny could even open his mouth.

'Er ...' Denny pointed with his mouth open. 'I think actually it *is* working.'

Tamar was being transformed. Into a hunter. The greatest hunter in the world as it goes.

Gone was the flowing chiton, and in its place was a short toga-like arrangement, in a supple soft suede-like material that draped like silk. The costume of the Amazon warriors. The bow arm was bare. On her head was a silver helmet adorned with wings at either side. Leather gauntlets covered her arms to the elbow. A quiver full of arrows was hung across her back, and a large hunting knife was in the belt. She looked fearsome. And very, very sexy – to Denny anyway.

'I had to be dead,' he mourned. 'I had to be dead *now*.'

'*What's* the matter with you?' asked Nemesis. 'Why is being dead *now*, suddenly any worse than it was before?'

'She didn't look like *that* before,' said Denny plaintively.

'She looks the same as she always did to me,' sniffed Nemesis. 'Fierce.'

Tamar was indeed looking fierce. Frighteningly so. She stalked over to Nemesis and barked. 'What do I have to kill?'

'The Manticore,' said Nemesis backing away involuntarily.'

'And that's it?' said Tamar, looking disappointed.

'The Manticore has the reputation of being the fiercest and most dangerous ...'

'Yeah, yeah, yeah,' Tamar cut her off. 'Whatever. The Manticore it is then. So, that'd be Persia right?'

'So rumour has it,' said Nemesis.

'You've never actually seen one, have you?' said Tamar.

'No, I have not.'

'Have *you*?' Denny asked Tamar.

'Yes,' she said. 'And so have you.'

'I have?' Denny scratched his (technically) nonexistent head. 'I don't remember that.'

'They're doing it again,' said Aphrodite.

'Yes,' replied Hephaestus. 'But it's getting easier to fill in the empty parts of the conversation, don't you think?'

'Not really,' Aphrodite sniffed. 'Harder really, since Nemesis joined them.'

'It is perfectly obvious that Tamar has become a hunter with the donning of the belt of Orion, and the next part of her task is to hunt down the Manticore of terrible reputation,' said Hecate.

'Oh, yes, I got that much,' said Aphrodite.

Hecate rolled her eyes. 'What more do you need to know?' she asked.

'You'll know it when you see it,' said Tamar to the empty air. 'I guarantee it.'

The empty air shrugged.

'Hey, did you see that?' cried Aphrodite.

'See what?' said Proteus.

'I thought I saw... I saw... something,' she said lamely.

'There,' said Hecate suddenly. 'It's looking at me.'

'*What* is?' said Hephaestus.

'I – I don't know,' she admitted. 'I think it's him.'

They all peered hard at the empty space where she was looking.

'*I* can't see anything,' said Proteus eventually.

'No, nor can I, now,' said Hecate. 'But it *was* there. Just a suggestion in the air. He was smiling, I'm certain of it.'

'Grinning,' corrected Aphrodite. 'I think he's amused by us.'

'Well, I wouldn't be surprised if he was,' said Hephaestus. 'All straining our eyes at nothing but empty air.'

'Boo!' said Denny into his ear and Hephaestus jumped suddenly.

Tamar covered her mouth to hide a smile.

Then she was all business again. 'Right.' She snapped her fingers. 'Persia it is then. Come along then, hurry up last train leaving now.'

'Surely we don't all have to go?' said Aphrodite.

Tamar looked at her sternly. 'If you think I'm letting *any* of you out of my sight – Denny, stop pulling faces – then you've got another think coming.'

Denny stuck his tongue out at her.

'*What?*' she snapped.

'You're being a bit ...'

A bit *what?*'

'Keen?' he tried. 'Bossy? Try and calm down, will you. You'll have an aneurysm.'

'Unlikely,' muttered Nemesis.

'I just want to get this *over* with,' stormed Tamar. 'And if you ...'

She stopped. 'Have I been making a fool of myself?' she asked.

'No, not ... exactly. You just seem a bit... I was getting a bit worried that's all,' he said.

'I'm, fine,' she said.

'You're not exactly yourself, though, are you?' he said quietly. 'That's more than a costume, isn't it?'

Either Tamar didn't hear him, or she chose to ignore this.

She was not worried. She was fine. Absolutely fine. Absolutely.

Next stop Persia.

* * *

It was hot and stinking in the jungle, but Tamar walked coolly through the trees as if she were on an afternoon stroll. She looked alert but relaxed.

'We should be careful,' said Aphrodite, apparently forgetting that she was a god and therefore, immortal. 'There could be something dangerous in here.'

'There is,' said Tamar. 'Me.'

'We need a kid,' she added.

'Why?' said Denny. 'Whose kid?'

'As in a baby goat,' said Tamar, who was sure he knew this and was just being silly, 'to tether to a tree.'

'And that's how we hunt a Manticore is it?' he said.

'That's how we hunt anything,' she said. 'No point chasing it all over the place when we can get it to come to us.'

'Well,' said Denny taking in her new attire. 'I guess you know what you're doing.'

'I hope so,' she said curtly. 'We need to be downwind,' she added. 'Well, I don't suppose it matters in your case, but the *rest* of us, need to be downwind. All right you lot – move it, over here.'

'And now what?' asked Proteus.

Tamar gave him an evil smile. 'I'm glad you asked,' she said.

Proteus, in the form of a kid, allowed himself, under heavy protest, to be tethered to the tree. And the rest of them moved downwind to wait.

'How long is this going to take?' said Aphrodite grumpily.

'It'll take as long as it takes,' said Tamar calmly. 'Keep quiet.'

Aphrodite shifted restlessly, and Tamar glared at her. Aphrodite froze. 'Sorry,' she whispered.

Several hours went by. Apparently the Manticore was busy elsewhere and had not had time to fit them into his schedule yet. The gods found this extremely irritating. They were used to people waiting on them, not the other way around.

'*Do them good,*' thought Tamar callously. She was not bored at all. The suspense was building in her; the longer they waited, the more excited she became. She was tensed, ready to spring, and she knew that she was invisible, blended into the jungle in a way that had nothing to do with magic and everything to do with the hunter's instinct for camouflage.

It happened suddenly. One minute nothing but the rustling of some trees and the next, it seemed, Tamar threw her spear with unerring accuracy at the movement There was a howl in the bushes and Tamar leapt into the undergrowth and emerged carrying the hide of a ...

'That's a tiger,' said Denny in disappointment.

'That's right,' said Tamar tipping him a wink and feeling extremely grateful that only she could hear him.

'*That's* the Manticore?' said Denny aghast. 'But it hasn't got spikes on its tail or anything.'

'Oh, all that stuff about spiked missiles on its tail and scorpion stings on its head and all that, was just exaggeration,' she said. 'I *told* you you'd seen one before,' she added.

'The body of a lion and the head of man,' mused Denny. 'I can sort of see that I guess.'

'So, you have captured the Manticore,' said Hephaestus trying not to seem too impressed. 'What is the next task?'

'Good point,' said Tamar. 'Nemesis?'

'You must go to the kingdom of ----- in Arabia.'

'And do what?' asked Tamar, who did not like the sound of this.'

'Steal the Djinn from the sultan, who is not a true sultan but only an ordinary thief who has become a tyrant overlord.'

Tamar was silent for a moment. 'His name isn't Aladdin is it?' she said. 'That'd be just typical.'

'It is,' said Nemesis.

'It would be,' sighed Tamar. 'It bloody well, would be.'

* * *

'I know who that Djinn is,' said Tamar gloomily to Denny. 'I mean it just *would* be, wouldn't it? A bloody Djinn. The one thing I'll have a real problem with.'

Denny said nothing. It was better just to let her rant.

'I mean, technically, he'll have a lot more power than me. If Aladdin tells him to kill me, he will.'

'Then that'll make two of us,' said Denny.

Tamar ignored him. 'And Old Jham Bhutti's got more power than I ever had anyway,' she resumed. 'He's one of the old ones.'

'Jam butty?' said Denny in disbelief. Then he shook his head. After Slammer Lung, he was prepared to believe just about anything. He realised to the full for the first time that they were both lucky that Tamar had kept her real name – more or less. Imagine being married to a girl named ... He hesitated. Well something really silly anyway.

'What do you mean – old ones?' he asked.

'In the olden times, before humanity reigned, the Djinn were free,' she said. 'And they used to take each other's powers. There were epic battles. Jham Bhutti took the power of a lot of Djinn. Much more than Askphrit.'

'Well, he's not free now,' said Denny comfortingly. 'And *you* are.'

'How is that going to help?' said Tamar testily. 'Aladdin's not just going to hand him over, is he?'

'Steal the bottle ...'

'Lamp.'

'Lamp then – *really*? I thought that was just in the stories. I've never come across a real Djinn in a lamp.'

'Lamps are metal,' said Tamar as if this was some kind of explanation.

'And ...?' queried Denny patiently.

'Metal is stronger than glass,' she said. 'More powerful Djinn need stronger prisons. It's all symbolic really.'

'How come you've never told me all this before?' he asked.

'Before my time,' she said vaguely. She was clearly fretting; her mind was miles away.

'I've never seen you beaten by anything,' he said encouragingly.

'Well, you're about to have a front row seat to the first time,' she said. 'I can't beat Jham, and that's flat.'

'But ...' he began.

'Just ... leave me alone for a while,' she said. 'Please.'

Of course, she did not have to say please. He had to obey anyway. But when she had been his slave, he had always been careful not to give orders to her. Some things were important. Denny drifted away into the ether.

'Denny's right,' she thought. There had to be a way. There was *always* a way. She began to think about possible strategies.

'Well, whatever I do, I'm not dressing up as a harem girl again,' she decided. 'This isn't a bloody "Carry On" film.'

The trouble was it was beginning to *feel* like a "Carry On" film.

'My whole bloody life is a "Carry On film",' she thought. 'Or at least a right carry on.'

* * *

'He isn't really a tyrant,' said Tamar as they approached a palace of unparalleled tastelessness. 'It's just that the gods don't like people getting above their station. What if one of them suddenly decided to try for a godhood? It's pretty crowded up there already.'

'It's very ... glittery, isn't it?' said Denny.

'Yes,' she said. 'You can see what the gods mean really. He's already thinking like they do.'

'What's wrong with it?' said Aphrodite who had detected the criticism in the tone, if not the words.'

Denny and Tamar laughed, although the others could only hear her laughing, of course.

'Okay, shhh now,' hissed Tamar as they got nearer. But it was pointless. A gargantuan Djinn manifested at the palace gates.

'Tamar the Black?' said Jham Bhutti peering down at her in surprise. 'Is that you?'

Tamar sighed. 'Hey,' she said, and gave a languid wave.

'So it is *you*?' he said and roared with unflattering laughter.

'What is me?' she said with rather overdone innocence.

Jham roared with laughter again. If only they had a human handy, she thought. A bunch of gods and two spirits. You would think they could have picked up at least one human along the way somewhere; the world was teeming with them after all. One human to trap the Djinn in a handy lamp and this would be so easy. Was it really too much to ask?

Apparently.

'If it was easy, we wouldn't have to do it,' said Denny divining her thoughts.

'I don't suppose we could borrow you for a while?' Tamar tried. 'We'd bring you back, when we were finished.'

'Now, now Tamar the Black,' Jham shook his head. 'It's no skin off my nose you know that. But it's not my choice to make. And you know that very well too. I don't *want* to pound you into mush, but I have to.'

Tamar sighed. You do, don't you?' she said.

Tamar matched her height to his – about twelve feet – and rolled her head as if loosening up. 'Let's get on with it then,' she said.

She held a hand up suddenly. 'Just one thing,' she said. 'How did you know we were coming?'

'My master has me on constant alert,' said Jham. 'I'm under standing orders to scan for threats to the kingdom and the king himself. You did come here to steal his Djinn didn't you? Can't say I'd be sorry if you did,' he muttered. 'Do this do that ... An extra wing on the palace please Djinn. A feast for a thousand nobles ... I don't know ...'

Tamar was nodding sympathetically as a great fist suddenly slammed down on her head.

'Damn!' she said bouncing back up again. 'That *hurt*!'

'Sorry, said Jham and he sounded as if he meant it too. It did not stop him from doing it again, though, but Tamar was too quick for him this time.

This was the Denny school of fighting, keep dodging until you get a chance to stick the knife in. Tamar had learned a lot from watching him over the years. Speed was her only advantage here anyway.

Speed and – she threw a lightning bolt with unerring accuracy – a lot more experience in fighting for her life.

Jham roared and charged at her, and she flipped easily over his head.

He vanished and reappeared behind her grabbing her in a headlock. She vanished.

She reappeared suddenly, running through his legs and grabbing his ankles on the way tipping him over.

Then she ran up his fallen body and grabbed his head and began banging it on the ground. He reached up and grabbed her by the shoulders and threw her angrily over his head. She careered into the gates with a crash. 'Bastard,' she muttered, picking herself up. She bristled like an angry cat and grew several feet taller.

The gods were watching impassively. It may have been an epic battle between two Djinn, the most powerful creatures in the world, but there had not even been any blood yet. They had all seen worse. And as for Denny, he knew his Tamar. This battle was only the warm up. She definitely had something else in mind. Tamar never got her hair messed up for nothing.

On the surface, they seemed equally matched. One could get the impression that this could continue pretty much indefinitely. But Denny could see the difference. With each blow, Tamar was hurting more and more. She had been right; this Djinn *was* more powerful than her. So what did she think she was doing?

He winced as Jham threw a bridge at Tamar. She fielded it with a tower uprooted from the palace. This was getting out of hand.

And the Djinn were getting bigger and bigger.

Pretty soon they would be using the planets as bowling balls. Denny had had no idea that Tamar was capable of *this*.

What the hell was she doing anyway? It was not as if the Djinn could die.

What he was forgetting, and what Aladdin had never known, was that Tamar knew every line of the Djinn charter by heart. Every rule and every addendum. And there was one very interesting one. Tamar knew what she was doing.

Tamar was down, finally, irremediably. She seemed to have suddenly run out of steam, and the vengeful bulk of Jham was bearing down on her like an unstoppable stream train.

'Why doesn't she *do* something?' shrieked Aphrodite in terror.

Tamar just waited; a slight smile on her face that Denny recognised. He relaxed.

'I just hope this works,' she thought as she braced herself for the last blow.

Then suddenly everything changed. Jham's lamp came spinning through the air and landed by Tamar's feet. With a hideous shriek, Jham was sucked back inside.

Tamar picked up the lamp with a grin. 'Well,' she said. 'That's that sorted out then.'

Rule nine: A Djinn may not, even under the orders of his/her master, mortally wound or kill a human. In such an instance said Djinn will immediately become the property of the injured party in order to make reparation.

'But you *aren't* a human,' said Hecate.

'Yes I am – technically,' said Tamar with a grin. 'It's just that I'm also a Djinn. Or rather I have a Djinn's power.'

'Very clever,' said Denny. 'Machiavellian even.'

'It was risky, though,' said Hephaestus. 'Hey I can hear you,' he turned to where he thought Denny was standing.

'I'm over here,' said Denny.

Hephaestus spun. 'How can I hear you?' he said.

Denny shrugged mischievously, and Tamar laughed.

Hephaestus turned to Aphrodite. 'Can *you* hear him?' he demanded.

Aphrodite looked non-committal. 'You *can*, can't you?' he said.

'Well I can,' said Hecate.

'How?' asked Hephaestus in a bewildered tone.

'It's *her*,' said Aphrodite pointing rudely at Tamar. 'It has to be.'

Tamar shrugged. 'Not as far as I know,' she said.

'What else could it be?' asked Aphrodite.

'Who cares,' said Tamar a little snippily. She was, understandably, put out that her glorious victory over Jham was taking a poor back seat to this new development.

'I care,' said Hephaestus only to receive a warning look from Aphrodite.

'I think I might know the answer,' said Hecate shrewdly. And she pointed to the lamp now currently housing the most powerful Djinn in the vicinity.

'It happened when Tamar trapped the Djinn. It cannot be a coincidence surely. It is the power of the Djinn.'

Suddenly Tamar's face lit up. 'I never had that kind of power,' she said. 'Do you think ...' She turned to Hecate beseechingly. 'Could it ... could he ...?' She was thinking of course, of Denny. She might not have ever had the power to raise the dead, but a Djinn like Jham ... But Hecate was shaking her head sadly.

'He is now the property of Apollo,' she told Tamar. 'That was the deal.' she shrugged. 'I am sorry.'

Tamar shrugged lightly herself. 'Oh well,' she said with rather overdone carelessness. 'I'll get him back eventually, I just thought, he might be handier right now if he were – you know... corporeal.'

'Of course,' said Hecate consolingly. And moved to lay her hand on Tamar's shoulder but Tamar had turned away, a bitter look on her face. To have had hope dangled before her even for a second had only enforced her determination to win this thing and get him back. If she had to slaughter every last deity in the world and throughout the whole of time, she would do it gladly. He was worth more than all of them put together. Not just to her either.

~ Chapter Thirteen ~

'WELL. WHAT NEXT?' said Tamar, recovering her equilibrium with remarkable speed. The question was greeted with blank looks all round.

'Don't *you* know?' asked Hephaestus eventually.

'Well ...' Tamar looked at Nemesis helplessly. 'I thought it would be obvious,' she said.

Nemesis shrugged indifferently. 'The answer is there,' she said carelessly, 'if you care to look.'

Tamar looked at the lamp in frustration. 'What?' she snapped. 'I'm not getting *anything*.'

Nemesis began to laugh softly – a low unpleasant laugh which annoyed Tamar no end.

She snapped. It never took long.

'I'm in charge here,' she said in a dangerously low voice. 'So tell me now, or I will make you wish you had never died.'

'I *already* wish that,' said Nemesis with unconvincing bravado. Tamar had learned from Denny the art of making a threat into a vision of a terrible future that was definitely going to manifest one way or another.

Nemesis was trembling; she was well aware of just what Tamar was capable of doing to her. Sending her to Tartarus was only the half of it. She just had not realised that Tamar knew it too.

'I'm a quick study,' said Tamar reading her thoughts. The truth was that she really had no idea what the power of Hades was capable of doing, but she could bluff with no cards at all when she had to, and she could outstare the Basilisk in a pinch.

Nemesis fell for it anyway. She dropped her eyes and muttered. 'Take a magic carpet ride.'

'Why?' demanded Tamar (instead of saying "how?", as most people would have done).

'I don't know,' said Nemesis, 'that's the next step, that's all I know.'

'And how in the name of thunder was *that* obvious?' said Tamar.

Nemesis looked at her feet.

'A magic carpet ride to where?' said Tamar.

Nemesis shrugged. 'I honestly don't know,' she said.

Tamar glared at her.

'But I do know it has to be a certain magic carpet that will take you to the right place,' she said hurriedly.

'What magic carpet?' said Tamar – it was like pulling teeth she thought.

'Aladdin's of course,' said Nemesis in surprise and a light dawned on Tamar. Of *course*, how else was the mortal, who was expected to be on this ridiculous quest, supposed to get out of here? Those who had set it up originally had not known that the quester would be a former Djinn with powers of her own.

In that context, it *was* pretty obvious.

The magic carpet would then take her to the next challenge, whether she liked it or not.

* * *

'Are you *sure* you don't have any idea where we're supposed to be going?' Tamar asked Nemesis for the fifteenth time. She would far rather have teleported straight there than have all this palaver. Not to mention that balancing precariously on a hovering square of broadloom with a bunch of nervous and, therefore, squabbling gods was not her (or anybody's) idea of a good time.

'Egypt,' this was Denny and he said it because that's where the carpet was gently coming to rest.

Tamar groaned aloud. 'Not the sphinx,' she said. 'Anything but that.'

'I can think of worse things,' muttered Denny.

'Oh really?' snapped Tamar. 'Like what?'

'Like them,' said Denny pointing a ghostly finger at a large band of ... well they certainly were not men, although they stood upright like men and were running along the sand dunes and yelling like men, and as far as Tamar was concerned, they certainly *smelled* like men (urrrgh) the only problem with calling them men was that each and every one of them, was at least fifteen feet high.

Oh and they all had the head of a dog. A minor detail that Tamar was inclined at the moment to consider irrelevant.

Aphrodite, rather predictably, shrieked.

'What are they?' asked Proteus in a tone of careful inquiry.

'I have no idea,' admitted Tamar. Then she squared her shoulders and hopped off the carpet and went forward to greet the ... whatever they were.

'What a woman,' sighed Proteus, as Tamar stood squarely in their path and held up a hand like a traffic cop at the oncoming hordes.

'You have no idea,' said a voice in his ear, making him jump. 'And you had better not be getting any ideas either,' continued the voice of Denny. 'She'll eat you alive believe me. Now that's interesting,' he ended in a different tone of voice.

He had noticed the hordes had stopped short, hit in the face by Tamar's invisible power; this was not entirely unexpected, but every single one of them falling on his knees before her was a little surprising. Tamar's face indicated that she thought the same.

'Interesting,' she muttered.

Well it was.

'What do you make of it?' she asked Denny when, after a few minutes, they still had not moved.

Denny gave a shrug. He could not have cared less really – being dead does that to you.

'Dunno,' he said. 'Cover em with a sandstorm and let's get out of here.'

Tamar frowned. 'You're slipping,' she said.

'Slipping?' he asked.

'Becoming indifferent to the world,' she said. 'Letting go. Don't, I still need you.'

'I can't seem to help it,' he said. 'It all seems so ... small now.'

Denny grinned his old grin at her and her heart ached.

She turned abruptly away. Back to business.

She touched the lead warrior on the shoulder. 'Get up,' she said.

It rose slowly and ponderously to its feet and gazed down at her, a bewildered look in its limpid doggy eyes. And suddenly Tamar understood what she was seeing and was filled with a terrible pity and a raging fury at whoever had done this. Some bored god no doubt. Oh BLAST! BLAST! BLAST!

All magic consists of knowing one extra fact. The legendary army of Anubis was really just this – genetic manipulation at its most cruel and pointless.

There was a faint thudding sound from behind them; they all turned – a man in a long white sheet, as Denny saw it anyway, was running toward them. When he arrived he too threw himself on his knees before Tamar, to her considerable astonishment.

'Please,' he stuttered breathlessly. 'Please ... my master... my master has sent me ... to ask ... please ... call off your army... we will ... we will ...'

'Stop right there,' interrupted Tamar. 'And get up for God's... For the sake of Amun Ra. No one's going to hurt you.'

The man rolled his eyes. 'Amun Ra,' he intoned. 'Amun Ra,'

Tamar pinched the bridge of her nose wearily. 'Oh for fu... for ... Oh *hell*.'

Suddenly she lost her temper. It was all too much. The squabbling gods the stupid quest (oh how she hated a quest) the poor dog men, this blubbering idiot and on top of all this, Denny was dead, *dead*! She kicked the man viciously. 'Take me to your master,' she barked. 'Now!'

* * *

The man could not see the gods, Tamar realised. He took no notice of anyone but her. And it was a few minutes before she understood the reason for this. This man had his own gods. The Greek gods, quite literally, did not exist for him. This was a new spin on mythology that Tamar had not considered before. And it started a train of thought in her head that she decided to put on one side for now to examine later.

It was a palace and Tamar knew that this alone, in this part of the world, was sufficient reason for it to be attacked. Such treasures were the property of whoever had the strength to seize them.

The master of this palace, however, was something of a shock.

Barely 25 years old and ... oh no, it was not fair.... His dark eyes, hair and complexion notwithstanding, the features, the stance, the grin... It was Denny to the life. A negative view as it were. Dark where Denny was fair.

Tamar hated him instantly and unequivocally simply for standing there and breathing in and out as if it were no big deal.

'Evil twin?' said Denny in her ear. He had seen it too. Tamar did not answer. She was clenching and unclenching her hands and grinding her teeth.

She forced herself to calm down. She wanted some answers, didn't she? Besides she was painfully aware that had Denny been standing next to her, in the flesh, as it were, she would have been highly amused at the situation. Particularly as this boy was gaping at her in a manner that was very familiar to her.

It turned out (once she had explained that she was not in command of the horrible army and that she was a stranger in these parts) that it was not his palace that his warlike neighbour was after, he had one of his own even more magnificent. It was his labyrinth, or rather, the treasure held therein.

At this revelation, Tamar's eyebrows went up. A labyrinth sounded like a quest type of thing, particularly one with mysterious treasure inside it.

The boy, whose name was Atsu was more interested in Tamar's apparent ability to control the dreaded army of Anubis, which he had not anticipated would be sent after him. His enemy, the son of a pig, must have made great sacrifice to the god of the dead to have been gifted with such an advantage.

'I guess whatever is in that labyrinth must be worth a lot?' hinted Tamar.

Atsu shook his head. 'It is forbidden,' he said. 'Many of my best soldiers have tried the labyrinth and never returned. It is locked up now forevermore. I have the key hidden in a secret place.' He looked up sharply at Tamar's face as if he regretted saying this and was wondering what had come over him.

Tamar laughed. 'Then why not let your enemy try it if he wants to so much?' she said. 'It would be one way to be rid of him, would it not?'

But again, Astu shook his head. 'We cannot risk that he may find what it is he seeks within.'

'Oh, this is it,' thought Tamar, 'it has to be. I've got to get into that labyrinth.'

'Seduce him,' suggested Denny. 'He's clearly up for it.'

Tamar's eyes widened. 'What?' she hissed. 'Are you kidding?'

Denny shrugged. The dead are beyond jealousy. Denny really did not care anymore.

'Well, *I* still care,' thought Tamar indignantly, as she realised this. However there was *something* in the idea. She would not have to take it too far, just far enough to get into his room where it was almost a certainty that he kept his key. Then she could bash him on the head or something and take it.

This was a plan full of holes as she was well aware. But then again, all their plans were full of holes, and yet they still managed to make most of them work anyway. It was a gift.

She absolutely refused point blank to admit the idea that there was even the faintest possibility that she was remotely attracted by Atsu. That she was lonely, and he was a more than adequate substitute for Denny who was drifting further and further away from her every day now that he was dead.

That he even sounded a little like him, if Denny had been putting on a funny accent for a joke – which he never did actually. Or that if she closed her eyes it would be far too easy to pretend.

He invited her to dinner, which was not entirely unexpected. Then she was shown to a sumptuous room to change.

She sent Denny back to the underworld – this was going to be nerve- racking enough without an audience.

Nerves? Was she nervous? she wondered, and reluctantly had to admit that she was. But why? She could handle this little pipsqueak with both hands cut off and no eyes.

She refused to accept that it was not him she was nervous of, but rather herself.

* * *

Dinner was foul of course; this was a long time ago, but at least, Tamar consoled herself, there were no sheep's eyeballs on the menu. Not that she was eating anything anyway.

She was surprised to find that the wine was not drugged. She had half expected that it would be. The fact that he had integrity enough not to try this was only going to make things harder in the end.

And then of course, she had to allow herself to be persuaded to go to his room. Used to issuing a stark denial and a swift kick in the pants in this type of situation, she was at a bit of a loss here as to how to proceed. Just how much reluctance was too much before it became an insulting refusal, rather than a maidenly evasion?

She needn't have worried. A man like this, a man with power, who has been accepted for a dinner invitation assumes the rest no matter what the woman says. Only the aforementioned swift kick in the pants would have dampened his ardour at this point, and possibly not even that.

She let the pleading go on just long enough, she judged, before he made it an order and pissed her off to the extent that a swift kick in the *head* would not have been out of the realms of possibility. Then she succumbed with a strange mixture of reluctance and desire.

In the end, it was the thought that it was Denny she was doing all this for, after all. He might be indifferent now, but once she had him back in the land of the living he would be hurt and horrified (although he would hide it well) if she let this go any further. And she *would* get him back – mere death was not enough against *her*. She had beaten him before hadn't she?

So, one minute she was lying on satin sheets succumbing to languorous kisses that were, disturbingly, both familiar and alien and the next he was on the floor in a crumpled heap, and she was holding a shining key up to the light triumphantly.

She had spotted the casket immediately so cunningly hidden out in the open. Ha! Like she did not know *that* one. So why had she let it get as far as it had?

She shook her head. 'Never mind that now,' she decided. But in the back of her mind a little voice was saying "Thank God for an iron will – or who knows what might have happened" she ignored it, it was not important now.

She met the assorted gods and ghosts at the gate of the labyrinth as planned and held up the key.

'Okay, she said. 'Let's see what's inside.'

~ Chapter Fourteen ~

'IS THERE something wrong?' asked Stiles nervously.

'N-no,' stammered Hecaté. 'You just look remarkably familiar.' She gave him a sharp look. 'Hades?' she snapped suddenly. 'Is this your idea of a joke?'

Stiles shuttled backwards under the intensity of her gaze. 'What?' he said.

But Hecaté was looking hard at his face and suddenly her features relaxed. 'No,' she said shaking her head. 'You are not him.'

She appeared thoughtful for a moment. 'I have not come to take you to the underworld,' she decided.

'You haven't?' asked Stiles perplexedly.

'No,' she said. 'I have another idea.'

* * *

They all trooped inside to be greeted, immediately, with a sharp drop in the dark.

'Well. That explains the disappearing guards,' said Tamar dusting herself off after a fall that would have killed a lesser woman instantly.

'You know, we never did anything about those dog headed guys,' said Hephaestus coming up behind her. Tamar shrugged – there really was not anything that she *could* do.

'Spooky in here, isn't it?' said Aphrodite and Denny gave a low chuckle which made everybody jump.

'Everybody shut up,' said Tamar. 'Something's coming.'

A bright light appeared at the end of what was now revealed to be a tunnel – well it had to be a tunnel really, if you think about it, but then again, in these magical places you never knew, it could just as easily have been a big pink cloud or a motorway bypass.

The bright light resolved itself into the glowing figure of an elderly man.

He stopped just before he reached them and began to talk in a curious monotone.

'I am the guardian of the labyrinth. All those who seek to enter must pass the first test.'

'What's the first test?' said Tamar, but the man continued talking as if he had not heard her and she noticed that he was not looking directly at her either.

She narrowed her eyes and stepped forward suddenly – the man did not even flinch or appear to notice her action at all.

She grinned and waved her arm right through him.

A hologram. She began to laugh. That would be considered the height of witchcraft in these times she realised, but to her it was merely a very cheap trick.

Then she realised that she was missing the instructions. Damn!

'Er ... reset program,' she tried. The man vanished and once again the bright light appeared at the end of the tunnel. Behind her, she heard Denny laugh softly. 'Cool,' he said.

The spiel began again. And this time Tamar paid attention, despite the twittering of the gods behind her who were distinctly impressed by this display of Tamar's power over spirits and otherworldly beings and her knowledge of the mystical magic words used to control them.

They did not know what "reset program" meant, but each and every one of them resolved to memorise the incantation just in case they should ever need it.

The ghostly man vanished, and Tamar huffed impatiently. 'What a lot of mumbo jumbo she said. 'Nothing ever changes,' she shook her head sadly.

'Face the Chimera, solve the riddle of the Sphinx – I *knew* there'd be a bloody sphinx in this somewhere ...' She turned to Denny's ghost despairingly. 'Can't we just skip all this bollocks?' she said.

Denny shrugged. 'You're asking me?' he said.

'Well you can see the future,' she said. 'Up to a point anyway so ...'

'Look out!' said Denny suddenly. 'Chimera in 5 – 4 – 3 ...'

Tamar spun round with a sigh.

'In the meantime,' said Denny, 'I'll go on ahead and see what the future holds – you only had to ask you know.' And he vanished although only Tamar and Nemesis were aware of it.

The Chimera was an unfortunate beast really, with the head of a lion and also the head of a goat rising from its back, goat's udders and a serpent's tail. It looked, Tamar thought, like a catastrophe in a genetics lab – which was probably not too far from the truth.

As in all these places that exist outside the world, Tamar did not have her powers so she decided to rely on her wits instead.

Fighting this creature without the magical assist was really pretty much out of the question anyway. Besides, when she looked at it, the most prevalent emotion she was aware of was a deep abiding pity. No wonder the poor thing was angry.

She dodged gracefully out of the way as a spurt of flame shot from the creature's mouth lighting up the gloom for a moment and making hideous shadows on the walls of the tunnel.

'Hmmm,' said Tamar thoughtfully, 'why don't you come along with us? We could use a guy like you.'

The Chimera stopped suddenly and looked bewilderedly at her. 'Come with you?' it said. 'You want me to come with you?'

'Why not?' said Tamar. 'It can't be much fun stuck down here in the dark.'

'Huh, you're right there,' said the Chimera in what was, to Tamar, a decidedly familiar tone of whining.

'Stuck here with chumps trying to kill me all the time. I used to try to be friendly you know. Oh I tried, but they always just got out their swords and started hacking away, never gave me a chance. I mean talk about making a snap judgment – it's not my fault that I look like a monster, now is it?'

'I think you look very...' Tamar paused, 'interesting,' she finished lamely.

'Well I will,' said the Chimera decidedly. 'First civil word I've had out of anybody in a hundred years.'

Tamar grinned in the darkness. It always worked – every time. Inside every hideous monster there is a lonely soul who only wants to be understood and to tell their story to anyone who will listen to it. Well she was more than prepared to listen – it beat being roasted alive.

But only just, she was discovering. Boy she had met some moaners before, but the Chimera took the cake. Mind you, he had a lot to moan about, she conceded, but still...

It was a relief when they burst out into bright sunlight, and the Chimera exploded immediately.

'Did you know that would happen?' asked Hephaestus after they had all recovered from the shock.

'Of course not,' said Tamar indignantly. But no one believed her. Maybe it was the slight smile that was playing around her lips as she said it.

'Well either way,' said Hecate. 'I would call it a mercy on the poor creature.' and Tamar threw her a grateful smile.

'Well where are we now?' asked Hephaestus tactfully changing the subject. Having brought it up in the first place.

'Still in the labyrinth,' said Tamar. 'Where's Denny got to?'

'Call him back.' suggested Aphrodite.

Tamar shook her head. 'I think he's got a plan of some kind, 'she said. 'And besides, I'm not the boss of him – or at least ...' she amended, 'I don't think I should be.'

'It looks like a desert,' volunteered Proteus.

'Well?' said Tamar.

'Look' she explained after receiving a quartet of blank stares. 'What it *looks* like and what it actually *is* are two very different things. This is a *labyrinth*. Haven't you ever been on a quest before?'

'Silly question,' she answered herself. 'Well, anyway,' she continued. 'It's not a real desert. I mean we're still underground.'

'Looks like a real desert to me,' said Proteus obstinately.

'That's 'cause you're an idiot,' muttered Tamar under her breath. 'So where is this Sphinx then?' she wondered in a louder voice.

Everyone looked around simultaneously, and everyone saw nothing at all except miles and miles of sand stretching away in every direction.

'Bugger!' said Tamar. The last Sphinx she had met had refused to ask the riddle, because it was bored and wanted some company; it looked as if this one had simply run away, possibly for the same reason.

On the other hand, she had learned a lot since then. The way the universe really worked for one thing.

It had worked before...

'Program reset,' she said, and waited.

'Damn,' said a drawling voice from thin air. 'How *did* you do that?'

The sand blew up around them and coalesced into the elegant figure of the Sphinx and then settled down into a solid shape on the sand. It was wearing an amused grin.

'That's the first time in a thousand years that it hasn't worked m'dear,' he said. 'I congratulate you.'

'*That* was the riddle?' asked Tamar flabbergasted.

'Mmmm,' said the Sphinx. 'Clever isn't it? You might also have tried "run program". Oh do take that look off your face dear, after all you have solved it, you ought to be pleased.'

'B-but it's not fair,' said Tamar angrily. 'You have to know about ... mainframe and programs and all that. Hardly anybody knows that stuff.'

'Quite,' said the Sphinx. 'We can't have just anybody solving the labyrinth now can we?'

Tamar was taken aback. She had not thought of it this way. She realised that he was right.

There was a silence, eventually broken by the plaintive voice of Proteus. 'What's mainframe?'

'Can we *go* now?' wailed Aphrodite like a spoiled child. Tamar half expected her to add, "I need the toilet"

'I don't think we have to,' said Tamar. 'I think this is it.'

'But there's nothing *here*,'

'Wait,' Tamar advised. 'And shut up,' she added warningly.

'Why? What will happen if I don't?'

'I might lose my temper,' suggested Tamar calmly.

'Oh,' said Aphrodite and clamped her mouth shut.

The Sphinx began to chuckle and then without warning he opened his mouth and roared an earth shattering roar that almost knocked Tamar off her feet. She clapped her hands over her ears and felt the world fall away from her. She was – they all were – shooting backwards away from the Sphinx at a tremendous rate, the wind rushing in their ears. Within seconds the Sphinx and was nothing more than a dot on the horizon, then everything went black.

'And we're back underground again,' said Tamar in a resigned tone. 'Figures!'

But it was different this time, this was no magical tunnel in the labyrinth – the air smelled musty and old – it reminded Tamar of the underground lair of the Faeries once the magic had been removed. Nothing more than a very real, very ordinary, very dirty hole in the ground. Above them was the sound of digging.

'Well at least we didn't have to cross the desert this time,' she said to no one in particular.

'But where are we?' asked Hecate, not unreasonably.

'Let's find out,' said Tamar grinning in the dark. 'Everybody ready?'

Above ground, it was the most beautiful garden they had ever seen. Men were running about planting, digging and watering, laying rocks and building walls.

'What is this place?' breathed Aphrodite. 'It rivals Olympia.'

Tamar knew; she had seen pictures. Even unfinished, it was easily recognisable. 'The hanging gardens of Babylon,' she said in a tone that suggested that, for once, even she was impressed. 'Under construction,' she added with a lilt of laughter in her voice.

'Remarkable,' said Hecate. 'Mortals did this?'

'Oh yes,' said Tamar. 'Don't underestimate mortals. In time, they can move the heavens.'

'I am seeing that,' agreed Hecate.

'But what are we here for?' asked Proteus.

Tamar shrugged. 'It'll become clear in time,' she said. 'Just enjoy the view,'

This was such an un-Tamar like remark that Hecate and Hephaestus looked at each other in speechless concern.

'Ask Nemesis,' suggested Hephaestus. 'Threaten her with eternal damnation if she won't tell you. Go on, do your thing.'

'What's that?' said Tamar ignoring this advice completely and pointing at a particularly beautiful flower that was growing all alone in a circular bed in the centre of the gardens.

'That is the scared flower of the Euphrates,' said a passing gardener showing no surprise at her presence at all. 'A treasure beyond worth,' he informed her. 'Without it, the river will die, and all life that springs from it will follow.' And he trundled off in the direction of a grove of trees having given his little speech.

'A treasure beyond worth,' repeated Tamar. 'Oh no,'

She shook her fists angrily at the heavens. 'I won't do it,' she asserted to a passing cloud. 'Not this time.'

'What about your precious lover?' sneered Nemesis. 'Or have you forgotten him? Isn't his life worth a little flower?'

'He's the last person who would want me to do this,' said Tamar, uncertainly.

Hecate came forward and coughed gently. 'There is never just one of any living thing,' she said.

Tamar's eyes widened. 'Of course,' she said snapping her fingers.

I can take the flower and leave it behind too.'

'Hmm, you worked that out awfully fast,' said Nemesis. 'Are you sure that is the answer?'

'Yes,' snapped Tamar. 'Don't bother trying to confuse me. I know what's bothering you. This was the fifth task. Only two more to go and I'll be there, and you can't stand it.'

'It won't be as easy as you think,' said Nemesis.

'It's been pretty easy so far,' said Tamar. 'Stop trying to psyche me out, it won't work.'

'I hate it when she talks to nothing like that,' said Aphrodite.

'Yes,' said Proteus, 'especially when she talks nonsense like that.'

This remark earned him a cold look from both Aphrodite and Hecate.

'*Brittania*?' Tamar was saying. 'What the hell for?'

'You know what, never mind,' she sighed. 'It'll be interesting I suppose, I never saw Britain until the eleventh century the first time around.'

She wandered away muttering something that sounded suspiciously like '– ing magical mystery tour ...'

There was an awkward silence; no one wanted to be the one to tell her she had forgotten the flower.

After a few seconds, she stalked back angrily and plucked the flower from the bed, shook the seeds into her palm, and stalked off again radiating furious embarrassment.

* * *

'Stonehenge,' Tamar said. 'It's bound to be Stonehenge – when it comes to magical nonsense it's always Stonehenge. And I see it's raining – I feel right at home now.'

Hecate nodded. She was really the only one of the gods that Tamar talked to. 'Did not Nemesis tell you the next task then?' she asked, risking instant decapitation.

Tamar only shrugged.

'Where is Denny?' thought Hecate angrily. 'She is faltering without him.'

It was true; ever since Denny's unexpected departure Tamar had been swinging wildly between fury, despair and total indifference.

It was as if she was, only now, grieving for him – now that he was not only dead but also departed.

'You miss him?' she risked, and she did not even step back a pace after she had said it.

Tamar's eyes flashed. 'Miss who?' she snapped.

'Denny,' said Hecate quietly and firmly.

Tamar sagged. 'He just buggered off without a word,' she muttered. 'It's not like him ... What if he doesn't come back?'

Hecate looked troubled. As a goddess of the underworld, she knew this to be a distinct possibility. The dead adapt to their new situation. After a while, the living world no longer means anything to them. Eventually they forget.

'Then you must change his fate,' she said. 'Is that not what this is all about? – this quest that you so abhor?'

Tamar set her teeth at Hecate. 'Right!' she said 'you're right. Just one thing first – you might want to stand back,' she warned. And she threw her head back and howled long and loud and visceral.

The gods looked around startled, birds flew out of the trees and in the distance there was a faint answering howl of wolves.

'That's better,' said Tamar cheerfully as the sound died away. 'I think there may be a bit of Banshee in my heritage,' she joked. 'A good yell always makes me feel better anyway.'

Hecate nodded; she did look happier. As if she had, temporarily anyway, shed a burden. But it would not last.

'Well,' said Tamar apparently to no one, so Hecate knew she was talking to Nemesis. 'What's it to be? Druids? Dragons? Black knight on a bridge?' she laughed. 'A magic sword?'

Nemesis apparently said something and Tamar's face darkened.

'You've got to be joking,' she said eventually. 'I can't do that. It's impossible.'

Now the gods did not know Tamar very well really, but they were, one and all, absolutely certain that this was something she had never said in her life before.

A chill that had nothing to do with the drizzling rain settled over the little group.

'Nothing's impossible,' said a familiar voice. 'I should know, I'm dead.'

It was Denny.

'Or rather I am now data in the wrong format,' he amended. He shook his head. 'I *knew* something was wrong.'

'I can *see* you,' put in Aphrodite suddenly.

Denny nodded briefly at her as if this were a mere detail. He turned back to Tamar. 'See it's like this,' he said 'When a person enters the mainframe, they become mere data. Well, we are all just data actually, but data in its proper format, reads as a living thing. Once I died, this world was not my proper format any more. Therefore, I read as a spirit. Not real – only redundant residual data. And I realised something out there. I saw the truth. The truth of the universe ... The truth about mainframe ...'

Tamar gaped at him. 'Hello to you too,' she said eventually and not without a certain amount of bitter sarcasm. But Denny was not listening.

'I understand it now,' said Denny excitedly. 'I don't know why I didn't see it before, when I was there. The mainframe isn't real. It's a construct put in place to bring order out of chaos. Superimposed on reality to give it a form that could be controlled.

'How you feel, anger, love, sadness, joy, *that's* real, that's chaos – the chaos of the universe. And the chaos is always there, just under the surface, ready to break out. You were right. It's *all* virtual reality. People think that what they can see and feel in the world around them is what's real, and the stuff that goes on in their heads isn't. But actually, it's the other way around. What you feel and think is the *only* thing that *is* real.

And the gods – a product of belief – that's chaos at work. It can't be controlled or held back, not forever. It breaks out all over the place. Gods weren't a product of the mainframe; they sprang from … somewhere else. The mainframe just tried to control them by filing them and boxing them in, but in the end, you can't. The underlying chaos will always break out in the end. You know what. They'll be back, in one form or another, sooner or later.'

'So what?' said Tamar, disappointingly.

'What?' said Denny stopped in his tracks.

'Well I'm sure it's a very fascinating on a philosophical level,' she said caustically. 'But what – practically speaking – has it got to do with our current situation?'

Denny stared at her. 'You mean you don't see?' he said.

'No,' she said stubbornly although she did – she was punishing him.

Denny stared at his feet. I'm sorry,' he said in a muffled voice. 'I didn't … it's so hard to think on this plane ... I didn't mean to … I'm sorry,' he finished lamely.

'Did you find out what the Terastu is?' said Proteus suddenly.'

Everyone turned to stare coldly at him.

'Oh, as if you were not all wondering the same thing,' said Proteus sharply.

Denny shook his head. And Tamar for one did not believe him, but now was not the time to push it, she decided.

'So ...' began Tamar. 'This next part of the quest ...?'

'You *can* do it,' said Denny firmly. 'Since when did you ever believe there was anything you couldn't do anyway?' he asked with a laugh.

'Since I learned that I'm not quite invincible,' she said dryly. 'Even the Djinn ...' she stopped and shook her head. 'What was Apollo thinking?' she said. 'No one ... certainly no mortal could possibly ...'

'But only a mortal would try,' said Denny.

'And die in the attempt,' said Tamar truculently.

'Not necessarily,' said Denny. 'There is a way.'

'I don't think we should put that kind of power into Apollo's hands,' said Tamar.

'Then don't,' said Denny indifferently. 'Keep it.'

'Keep what?' snapped Proteus, now thoroughly fed up with this. 'What kind of power? – What's going on?'

'The stone of creation,' said Tamar. 'It's held by the king of the winter who stole it from the ...'

'I know, I know,' said Proteus testily. 'What a lot of nonsense. Surely no one believes in that sort of thing anymore.'

Tamar burst out laughing. The idea of an ancient Greek god saying such a thing was incongruous at best. How many wise and learned men had said exactly the same thing of him and his brethren, she wondered.

'It's as real as you are,' she said, keeping a creditably straight face in the circumstances. And Denny winked at her so roguishly that she had to look away. Proteus, however, did not appear to notice anything untoward.

'So how are we to retrieve it then?' he said in perfect seriousness.

'We?' said Tamar. 'Oh, of course, I was forgetting what an invaluable contribution you have made so far' she added caustically. 'Go on then, she continued acerbically. 'What do *you* think we should do? Dazzle us with your insights.' There was an awkward silence.

'Thought not,' said Tamar. '*We* indeed.' and she gave an impressive snort.

'Tam,' said Denny warningly. Now was not the time to get the gods offside. Pretty soon, the whole reason they had joined forces with them would be put to the proof – he knew this even if she did not as yet. In fact, it all depended on what she did when she found the Terastu. And even he could not see that although, knowing her as he did, he had a pretty good idea.

In the meantime ...

'The stone is ...' he began, and Tamar interrupted him impatiently. 'It's not really a stone at all,' she said. 'At least ...'

'You have to think of it as a stone,' said Denny. 'It's what a mortal would do and that's your only chance at retrieving it.'

'A mortal wouldn't know any better,' said Tamar.

'Exactly.' said Denny. 'What you believe is all that counts remember.'

Tamar stared at him. 'It's an actual stone,' she repeated like a lesson. 'It's an actual stone,' she took a deep breath. 'And now I know *exactly* how to get it.' She grinned.

Denny grinned back at her. 'I knew you would,' he said.

'Fairy tales, fables and legends,' she said like a mantra. 'It's under the clouds and above the mountains, beneath the earth and above the sky within the air and at the bottom of the ocean.'

'Is it a riddle?' asked Aphrodite *sotto voce*.

Hephaestus shrugged, but Tamar had heard her. 'It's a set of directions,' she said. 'That's how a mortal would read it.'

'It describes the place where the stone resides,' explained Hecate who was beginning to understand. Tamar glanced approvingly at her.

'A description,' she agreed. Then she gave them a wicked glance. 'Ever seen a dragon's lair?' she asked. She pulled a wry face. 'Didn't I say it would be dragons?' she added.

'Ah but which Dragon?' said Nemesis nastily.

Tamar thought for a moment. 'Tiamat,' she said decisively and Denny smiled. He had known she would figure it out.

'Tiamat is not a real dragon,' said Nemesis.

'I know,' said Tamar. 'But try telling the superstitious villagers around here that, and see how far it gets you.'

'What is Tiamat then?' asked Hecate curiously.

'The earth, under your feet, the sky above you, the sea and the mountains,' said Tamar. 'And also, apparently, a bloody great big dragon.'

'Hmmm, gonna need a staff,' she muttered. 'A staff is always impressive. I guess a mortal would use a witch or something, but I reckon I can do it myself ...' She caught Denny's eye he was shaking his head.

'Oh bugger,' she said. 'You can take a thing to far,' she said. 'I'm not *actually* a mortal you know.'

'I feel her,' said Hecate suddenly 'Beneath my feet, above my heart. The Dragon of the Earth. Her heartbeat is the slow rhythm of the seasons, her breath the creeping fog of the winter, the fire of her belly the sunshine of the summer.' Suddenly she slammed a staff into the ground – yet she was not holding a staff – the ground shook and split open. 'AWAKE!' she cried. And a slow creeping fog began drifting up from below the ground. Again the staff crashed into the earth 'AWAKE!' And again. 'AWAKE!'

Slowly the fog coalesced into a recognizable shape that rose high above them into the air. It solidified into a pretty unmistakable dragon. Huge and scaly and seriously pissed off.

'Bloody hell.' said Tamar impressed.

'Cool,' said Denny – well it was all right for him, he was already dead.

Others did not find it at all cool, quite the reverse, in fact, particularly when a thermic lance of white hot flame hit the ground from above turning the pretty woodland into a blasted heath within a matter of microseconds.

Only Tamar stood her ground. She narrowed her eyes. – surely no mortal could survive against this, she thought and was tempted to manifest a twelve foot sword and start swinging. She resisted the temptation. There *was* a way for a mortal to defeat Tiamat – Denny had said so.

No he *hadn't*, she realised. He had only said there was a way to retrieve the stone, which, from the directions, she had surmised was in the dragon's belly.

So how ...? And then she realised it did not matter. A mortal would almost certainly be dead by now anyway. Retrieving the stone was not – had never been – the point of this one. Dying was.

Well she had no intention of dying, but the upshot of dying was a trip to the underworld. 'And *that* I can manage.' she thought.

She vanished – then she reappeared. 'Are you lot coming then?' she said and vanished again.

~ Chapter Fifteen ~

THE BLONDE WAS in trouble thought Tamar, but her antennae were telling her that the blonde was almost certainly a witch. So maybe she was pretty well equipped to get herself *out* of trouble again, as long as Barry did not decide to use Tamar herself against her. What she had yet to figure out was what on Earth she was doing here in Barry's "office"

'I know you took it,' the blonde was saying to Barry. 'Nothing else makes any sense. It had to be you. Personally I think you should give it back.'

'Give it *back*?' blustered Barry. 'I'm the one who sto... acquired it in the first place.'

'He's afraid,' thought Tamar. 'I wonder why?'

'How do you even know about it?' asked Barry eyeing the blonde nervously.

'I just know,' said the blonde. 'I know a lot of things about you Barry Malcolm Evans,'

Barry seemed to hesitate for a moment and then came to a decision.

'Oh all right then,' he said to Tamar's surprise and then she began to laugh softly to herself.

'He thinks she's a goddess,' she realised. 'He thinks he's being called to divine justice for something.' She did look rather like Aphrodite, Tamar considered, but not enough surely to fool anyone.

'I suppose I always knew this day would come,' grumbled Barry. 'I've had a pretty good run of it all things considered. It's in the back. I'll just go and get it.'

'Good,' said the blonde. 'And don't even *think* about slipping out that secret back door of yours with it.'

Barry threw the blonde a terrified look. 'I wasn't thinking any such thing,' he protested.

The blonde merely raised a sceptical eyebrow, and Barry scuttled into the back room without another word.

* * *

Unlike hell, the Grecian version of the underworld was cool and dark and quite a refreshing change after the scorched ground and fiery air of the earth where they had left Tiamat venting spleen – not to mention noxious gasses.

An arm snaked around Tamar's waist, and she was about to turn and strike when she realised it was Denny. Here of course, he had substance; he could touch things. He belonged here. There was pain in this idea of course but oh, to feel his hand on her face again ... his cold, dead, grey hand ... she shrunk back involuntarily. This was wrong.

'I can fight here at least,' he said. He did not seem in the least bit hurt or troubled at her reaction, 'if necessary,' he added. 'If you were also dead,' he explained to her. 'I would seem more alive to you. Isn't that ironic? Now it's *you* who doesn't belong.'

'We just can't catch a break can we?' she said ruefully.

'I believe we already covered that,' he said. 'But at least this is the end of the quest.'

With a start, Tamar realised he was right. It was the seventh and final task.

She turned to Nemesis. 'Okay,' she said. 'What is it this time?'

Nemesis sulked. 'Ironically,' she said, 'it's to steal the Helmet of Invisibility from Hades.'

'Hades is dead,' said Tamar.

'There's a lot of it about,' said Nemesis sourly.

'So that means ... oh for God's ... for the sake of ... the helmet is mine anyway,' she said. '*I* am the ruler of the dead – *pro tem* anyway.'

She summoned the helmet and stood with it in her hand looking disgruntled. 'What's this supposed to prove anyway?' she said eventually.

'I know that Hades used it to walk unseen among the dead spreading fear and wonder etc. But what the hell do I need it for? I can spread fear without props.'

'And wonder,' put in Denny.

Nemesis sighed. 'Put it on,' she said. 'And you'll see. The helmet does more than make you invisible.'

Gingerly Tamar raised the helmet and then, after a moment's hesitation, she rammed it decisively onto her head.

Immediately everything changed. It was as if she had spent her whole life half blind, and now she could see.

She took it off. 'No god made this,' she said. 'This is a product of the mainframe.' And she gave Hephaestus a stern look. 'And you took credit for this?' she said.

'I forged it,' he said. 'But its powers came otherwise. And none, not even Zeus, know from whence.'

'What's the deal?' asked Denny curiously.

'Not sure really,' she said. 'It's a very weird frequency. I can see the unseen though. That's pretty interesting'

'Code breaker,' said Denny. 'The clerks use 'em to decipher broken algorithms in the mainframe. They take you out of phase. Never seen one that looks like *that* though.'

Tamar handed it to him. 'Well it's supposed to be a dead mortal that uses it,' she said, 'according to the rules of the quest. See what you make of it.'

Behind them, they heard Nemesis swear softly. She was just too *good* at this; she should *never* have worked that out – she was not supposed to have got this far at all, in fact.

Denny put the helmet on. After a few seconds he said. 'Nothing's happening. It's not working for me.'

Then he vanished.

'Bugger,' said Tamar.

'What?' said Hecate puzzled. From her point of view, and that of the other gods, Denny had vanished from sight the moment he had put the helmet on. Only Tamar, for some reason (no doubt because she was lord over the dead and the owner of the helmet) had still been able to see him.

Instead of wasting time explaining, Tamar closed her eyes, and after a second or two she also vanished.

'I wish she would stop doing that,' said Aphrodite. 'It's very disconcerting.'

* * *

'Okay,' said Tamar out of the gloom, 'What is this place?'

'You don't recognise it?' said Denny. 'It's the cavern of the Fates – you've been here before.'

'Must have redecorated,' said Tamar.

'This is a different part of it,' said Denny. 'This is where the wheel is kept.'

'The wheel?' said Tamar and then it struck her. 'You mean the *wheel* is what we have been after the whole time? We went through all that for *nothing*? This is where we bloody well *started* from.'

'I know,' said Denny with a wry smile. 'Ironic isn't it?'

'You *knew*? You bugger, you knew all the time didn't you?' yelled Tamar half furious, half laughing.

'Not *all* the time.' he said, laughing too.

'But you *did* know?' she insisted, 'at least for a while.'

'Yes, I knew,' he said. 'Apollo wanted a mortal to have the chance to change the fate of the gods – if anything should go wrong and the prophecy were to be fulfilled. He figured if they were all slated to die anyway then he had nothing to lose.'

'I can see that,' she said. 'He wasn't counting on *me* then, was he?'

'He didn't realise at the time, that the fate of the gods had *already* been changed,' said Denny. 'And that anyone taking the quest would be doing so in order to change it back.'

'That's what I said,' said Tamar happily.

She frowned. 'Why did the prophecy say "it will only exist for a limited time"?' she said. 'I mean it's the Wheel of Fortune, it's not suddenly going to vanish is it?'

'Because *someone* did the translation badly,' said Arachne appearing as if from nowhere like a pantomime demon, as befits a hideous monster in a dingy cavern.

'Figures,' said Tamar with a laugh. Then she frowned again. 'So what *should* it have said?' she asked – she had a bad feeling about this suddenly.

'A one-time offer,' said Arachne. 'You only get one chance to spin the wheel – choose wisely.'

Tamar looked at Denny in anguish.

'Don't,' he warned her. 'Do what you came here for. I will be restored anyway – once the time-line is put back on track.'

'What if it doesn't work though?' she said.

'Tamar – it could all end right now,' he said. 'This is better than any chance we will ever get. If you change the fate of the gods back to what it should have been all along – then this is over – right now. This was what was supposed to happen, and it's the only way. Just *do* it will you?'

Tamar looked at him in an agony of indecision.

He took her by the shoulders. 'Tamar,' he said gently. 'Spin the damn wheel and finish this so we can go home.'

'If I spin the wheel and it doesn't bring you back ...' she began.

'It will,' he insisted, 'because none of this will have ever happened.'

'So many things could go wrong,' she insisted. 'There are too many variables.'

'Bollocks,' said Denny impatiently. 'If the gods die on schedule then we will never have been here in the first place.'

'A paradox,' said Tamar. 'No I can't risk it.

'At least this way I can be certain of getting you back – even if we do end up stuck here for the rest of our lives.'

Denny sighed – he had known it would come to this. Tamar was impatient, impulsive and volatile. She made mistakes all the time, but because of her conscience she rarely made foolish choices out of mere selfishness. This time it was different though. And he knew that there was no point in trying to change her mind.

Arachne came forward a sinister smile on her face that made even the deceased Denny shudder. She was obscenely pleased at the way things had turned out – that was clear. It filled Denny with forebodings.

'Spin,' said Arachne and indicated the wheel.

Without even the merest hesitation, without even a flicker of uncertainty Tamar spun the wheel.

Denny closed his eyes, and for the first and last time in his entire existence – he prayed.

Why are we still in the underworld?' was the first thing he said when he opened his eyes. 'Didn't it work?'

But one look at Tamar's shining eyes was enough to tell him it *had* worked. Besides, he could feel his heart beating.

There was a moment of silence that seemed to stretch out into forever and then they were in each others arms clinging to one another as if they would never let each other go until the world's end.

They finally broke apart at the sound of Arachne's low laughter.

'Well you have got what you wanted,' she said. 'You have changed the fate of one mere man. And may it make you very happy, for you have lost your chance to ever to defeat the gods. A foolish choice as your lover tried to warn you.'

'No,' said Denny surprisingly. 'I was wrong, it was the right choice.'

Even Tamar raised her eyebrows at this – she looked questioningly at him.

'We are stronger together,' he said. 'How can a choice made out of love ever be the wrong choice?' he added. 'I see that now.'

Tamar gazed wonderingly at him for a moment, all the love light of years shining in her eyes and then: 'Well aren't you a soppy git,' she said. And the world returned to normal again.

'Well,' said Denny laughing. 'Don't we have a war to get on with?'

He looked at Arachne. 'Whose side do *you* want to be on?' he asked menacingly.

Reading a terrible threat into Denny's words, Arachne shuddered.

'I wish to remain neutral,' she said.

'See that you do then,' said Denny. 'And stay out of our way.'

~ Chapter Sixteen ~

MOUNT OLYMPUS reared up before them, a shining, glittering spire; its pinnacle hidden among the darkening clouds that glowered dull and heavy and full of menace. The gods were preparing for War.

Lightning flashes erupted from the clouds occasionally, sending the inhabitants of the village below running for cover.

'Where is your savoir now, Arpagius?' demanded the villagers in terrified fury. 'They went to confront the gods and now look ... We shall all be destroyed. All they have done is arouse the wrath of the gods to the destruction of us all. They are most probably dead by now. So much for your heroes Arpagius. You old fool – you have destroyed us all. No one can challenge the might of the gods and live.'

'Oh I wouldn't say that,' said an amused voice from behind the angry mob currently sheltering in (ironically enough) the temple of Demeter. 'I wouldn't say that at all.'

'Sorry we're late and all that,' continued Tamar swinging a gigantic sword with practised ease back and forth past her knees and giving the occasional flourish up around her head while the phalanx of villagers stared at her in wonder.

She was quite a sight to see (a sight for sore eyes under the circumstances for one thing) she looked like a vengeful goddess herself.

The belt of Orion glittered and flashed like the lightning of Zeus over the costume of the Amazons, taken from the traditional hunter's garb of Artemis.

A large golden bow was draped over her shoulder and on her midnight hair rested a laurel crown that glinted and caught the light like a shower of stars. Her eyes glittered like sapphires, and there was the promise of cold death in her glance.

Those villagers who dared to catch her eye looked away immediately in fear and confusion.

'Impressive entrance,' admitted Aphrodite.

'Incredible,' muttered Proteus. He nudged Denny. 'How does she do it?' he asked.

Denny grinned. 'She's just being herself,' he told him.

'Well it won't impress Zeus I can tell you that for nothing,' said Hephaestus. I wish it would.' There was a tinge of regret in his voice. He was wishing he had never started this now – it was far too late to change his mind. His defection, and that of the other gods, was by now certainly well known on Olympus. He was a marked man – god.

'He is right about that,' said Aphrodite reluctantly. 'Impressing a bunch of ignorant villagers is a very different proposition to overawing the King of the gods.'

Denny grinned again. 'Don't bite your nails,' he said. 'It's unladylike.'

Aphrodite whipped her fingers away from her mouth and glared at him.

'You are not at all concerned?' asked Hecate in some surprise.

Denny turned to her. 'After all you have seen her do,' he said. 'How can you not have faith?'

'Gods do not have faith,' said Hecate, after a moment's thought. 'We *are* faith. That is people have faith in *us*.'

'For all the good it does them.' It was, surprisingly enough, not Denny who snorted this disparaging remark, but Prometheus.

'Everyone needs to believe in something,' muttered Denny and he looked at Tamar who was currently the centre of attention.

'They believe in her – don't you see?'

The gods looked at Tamar, realisation finally dawning.

'You mean ...?' began Hecate who was generally the quickest at working out what Denny or Tamar was driving at.

'An army.' said Denny. 'She's good at building armies. It's a natural gift.'

'But they are *mortals*' snorted Hephaestus in deep contempt.

'Believers,' corrected Denny. And the gods shuddered. They knew what *that* meant.

'Too few though,' said Prometheus grimly, 'far too few.'

'About four hundred, give or take,' said Denny.

'Too few,' repeated Prometheus.

'Not necessarily,' said Denny. 'Depends on what she has in mind.' And he grinned again.

'Do you *know* what she has in mind then?' demanded Hephaestus.'

But Denny just grinned irritatingly.

Tamar came back over to them a satisfied smile on her face.

'That went well,' she said.

'What did?' asked Hephaestus

'What do we do now?' asked Hecate a little more circumspectly.

'We wait,' said Tamar. 'This shouldn't take long.'

'*What* ...' began Hephaestus, but Aphrodite nudged him into silence.

'Right,' said Denny in the awkward silence that followed. 'Who wants to eat?'

'We'll have to tell them sooner or later,' said Denny as they sat by the fire in Arpagius's cottage.

'They aren't going to like it,' said Tamar sagely. 'So for now I think the less said the better.'

'It doesn't matter whether or not they like it,' said Denny. 'There isn't a damn thing they can do about it now anyway.'

Tamar bowed her head and muttered. 'There is *one* thing.' And Denny nodded.

'I want to go *home*,' wailed Tamar. 'I miss our *proper* friends – I don't trust this lot. I miss Iffie, and I miss our life.'

'Me too,' said Denny. 'It won't be long now – make or break eh?'

'Make or break,' repeated Tamar, and in the reflected firelight in her eyes there was the familiar light of battle.

* * *

It began around midnight. There was a flash and suddenly, without warning, a glittering god stood in the firelight of the large bonfire that had been built, on Tamar's orders, in the centre of the village.

'Friend or foe?' hissed Tamar menacingly.

The god gave her a supercilious glance. 'Friend of course,' he drawled. 'What else?'

Tamar nodded.

'Which one is that one?' hissed Denny in her ear.

'Narcissus,' said Tamar with a grimace. 'I know I know,' she forestalled him. 'But at least it's a start.'

Denny nodded uncertainly. If this was going to be the general calibre of the gods they could expect they might as well give up and go home now.

'Has it started?' said Hecate appearing beside Denny. 'Oh my goodness,' she exclaimed, 'who on earth ordered *Narcissus*?'

Other gods were starting to appear. Minor deities. Leto, Eros, Amphitrite, Asclepius, Themis, Helios, Ilithyia, Pan, They were less powerful than the Olympian gods, but, on the other hand, there were a lot more of them.

A number of even more obscure deities included Aseco, Acheron, Acte (the goddess of two in the afternoon – no really) Aeolus, Angelia, Akratos (the god of incontinence – a fact that caused much hilarity when it was revealed)

Kairos, Karmanor, Chremetes, Khrysos – The god of gold. Chloris – The goddess of flowers. Daeria, Doris (and it has to be said Denny had a hard time keeping a straight face over this one) Dysnomia – The female personification of lawlessness. Ersa – The goddess of the dew (they really did have gods for just about everything). All twelve of the Horai including the rather weird, and Denny's personal favourite of these – Gymnastika, The fourth of the twelve Horai (Hours) – the goddess of the morning hour of gymnastics.[*]

And far too many more to mention. Right to the end of the alphabet in fact, to Zelos - The personification of rivalry. Which Tamar took as a good sign.

'Told you she was good at building armies,' said Denny to Hecate.

'Indeed,' said Hecate gazing in disbelief at the hordes of minor divinities thronging the open field behind the village.

There was a sudden explosive noise from the fire-lit area, louder than any previous entrance and everyone turned.

There was a shocked silence while everyone stared in utter disbelief.

Then Tamar stalked forward purposefully. 'F-Friend or – or …' she began.

'I'm on your side of course,' boomed Poseidon heartily. 'Didn't believe me eh?' he snorted pointing a massive horny finger in the general direction of Olympus. 'Thought I was seeing things. Going mad! Ha!'

This seemed a good enough explanation to Tamar who had seen gods do things for far pettier reasons.

'Ah Hephaestus,' said Poseidon noticing him suddenly and hailing him with enthusiasm. 'Good to have you on our side

---

[*] I'm not making this shit up honest – look it up.

eh? That should tip the balance eh? What are our weapons then? What have you got for us? Something new and improved I'll wager.'

Hephaestus looked blank.

'Ah yes,' said Tamar into the awkward silence. 'I was going to get to that. You see I had this idea ...'

* * *

'Can you do it?' she asked anxiously. 'Is it possible?'

Hephaestus stroked his chin thoughtfully reminding Tamar irresistibly of a plumber looking at a leaky faucet and trying to determine how much he could get away with charging.

'Well,' he said. 'The labour would be ...' He stopped at the look on her face. 'Yes,' he conceded 'I can do it although I never in my life heard of such a thing ... ahem well it would be extremely difficult to ... about a month in the forge to get the ...'

'Tomorrow,' said Tamar flatly.

Hephaestus opened his mouth to procrastinate further, but something in her face made him stop. She had won. From the moment he had admitted he could do it, her uncertainty had vanished.

He gave a put upon sigh. 'Very well,' he said, and vanished.

Tamar gave a triumphant smile. 'We can't lose,' she said to no one in particular.

'It's cheating,' pointed out Denny.

'Of course it is,' she said. 'That's why it's going to work.'

The temple of Demeter had been rather hurriedly converted into a temple to small gods on Tamar's instructions. All the minor deities, in fact, that did not have temples of their own. And then Tamar had explained to the villagers the concept of control through belief.

The gods had been drawn there like moths to a flame. All gods, major or minor, were ambitious, and this was their chance to elevate themselves. To take over from the main pantheon and rule in their stead. They did not realise that they were under the control of the villagers – only by their belief and prayers did they have any hope of success. What the gods also did not know was that the villagers, primed by Tamar, were well aware of this fact.

All the villagers had to do throughout the battle was stay in the temple and pray as hard as they possibly could for victory. And of course believe.

Four hundred villagers all praying and believing at the same time would, Tamar estimated, be more than enough.

As long as Hephaestus came up with the weapons in time. Once the people had seen those, they would *all* believe.

It was going to be a long night.

~ Chapter Seventeen ~

'WHAT'S THAT?' asked Denny, as the blonde called Cindy triumphantly placed a grubby looking bottle on the counter before him.

'Isn't that it?' she faltered.

'No.' said Denny. 'That's an old bottle.' He grinned at her. 'It doesn't matter,' he said. 'I appreciate what you did anyway … I guess the Falcon is long gone

'I-I'm so sorry,' stuttered Cindy. 'I was sure that must be it, the man was so reluctant to give it up.'

'Was he really?' said Denny looking at the old bottle in wonder. 'That's odd, isn't it?'

'Well I must be going,' said Cindy with rather overdone carelessness.

'Well wait a minute,' said Denny. 'Don't you want to know what's in it? I mean it must be something or else why would Barry have kept it all these years?'

'It's probably just a Djinn,' said Cindy carelessly. 'They're of no use to ... but you are a mortal of course, aren't you? I was forgetting.'

Denny felt his brow crease in consternation. 'What do you mean, *I'm* a mortal?' he said.

Tamar had not felt the change of ownership until the witch had handed the bottle over to a mortal. Then she looked up nervously at the top of the bottle and tensed herself for her new master.

This was always a stressful time. Barry might have been a swine and a stupid swine too, but there was always the chance that the new one would be even worse.

She was never to know.

* * *

As dawn faded in above the peak of mount Olympus, turning the clouds from silver and black to rosy red and gold, there rose up from the mists below what at first appeared to a swarm of tiny insects, but as they rose higher and higher the shapes resolved into hundreds of warrior clad figures some on winged horses and some merely flying without apparent support of any kind and led by a fierce figure in a chariot – her long hair flying behind her from under her golden helmet. All were brandishing weapons of a strange and disquieting design.

A terrifying battle cry split the air, and the Gods on the mountain top trembled.

Never had the gods known such terror. None of them had imagined in their wildest dreams such a day would ever come, and they reacted with all the terrified fury of those who have nothing left to lose.

The sky darkened and lightning cracked the heavens open. Tamar laughed triumphantly and swerved her chariot out of the way smoothly.

Then, all at once, the whole of Tamar's battalion opened fire.

The darkened sky lit up – flashes of fire filled the air and the sound of a thousand thunder claps assaulted the ears of the gods.

'What are these things called again?' shrieked Hecate over the sound of the firing.

'AK-47's' said Hephaestus proudly. 'Wonderful aren't they?'

'Amazing,' agreed Hecate firing wildly and ecstatically.

'Fire in the hold!' yelled Tamar and fired a rocket launcher at the summit.

Everyone backed off rapidly as the top of Mount Olympus exploded in a vast mushroom of flame sending varying gods and extras tumbling through the air in crazy somersaults.

'Yee –har!' yelled Denny getting a little over excited for a moment.

This earned him a "look" from Tamar. They looked, in fact, at each other for a moment and then burst out laughing together.

Then Denny surged forward on his mount spraying gunfire as he went, the joy of battle was in him; he was back in his element.

A battalion came forward out of the clouds of dust and smoke, led by Ares. Tamar urged her chariot forward to meet him and smiled evilly as she shot him in the head, sending him tumbling to the earth where it could just be seen that he exploded as he hit the ground in a shower of red lights and vanished.

'HA!' she yelled. 'Take that!'

'This thing is heavy,' moaned Proteus, clutching at his gun and hauling it up over his shoulder with a pained expression.

'Suck it up,' yelled Aphrodite in joyous delirium. 'I've never had so much fun in my life. This is fantastic. I was *born* for this.' And she charged away yelling and swearing like a trooper, spraying gunfire with glorious abandon.

'You think you know someone,' muttered Hephaestus shaking his head.

Athena came forward to take the place of Ares, but arrows, no matter how accurately they are shot, are no match for automatic gunfire.

'Take that you stuck up cow!' screamed Aphrodite firing with savage glee at Athena. 'Who's stupid now?' she crowed delightedly as Athena fell forward and then spiralled like a run-down firework down to the earth below to join her brother.

It was, Denny realised, not the time to question, since the whole thing was running on pure faith. That the gods could be killed and their home reduced to rubble by mere bullets was patently ludicrous really. But now was really not the time to allow access to those kinds of thoughts. And it all, he realised, depended on your point of view.

These weapons were pure magic of a powerful and mysterious kind to the people of this age – they had been told in no uncertain terms that they would work – and so far, the belief was holding.

It was a massacre. The gods of both camps were falling like flies.

So far though, there had been no sign of Zeus. This was nagging at Tamar like a bad itch. She badly wanted to get her hands on the King of the Gods. Preferably to wring his neck with her bare hands.

Ares, Athena, Hera, Demeter, Hestia, Dionysus, Persephone, Apollo. The death toll grew longer.

One by one they fell. Poseidon fell to an arrow of Hera, Prometheus to a seven sided attack from the Harpies that had risen from the underworld to avenge Hades. He fell in defence of Denny, who took revenge for his death by slaughtering the Harpies with a furious vengeance.

When only Aphrodite and Hephaestus were left from the original pantheon, Tamar called a ceasefire.

Silence fell over Olympus and as the smoke cleared the extent of the devastation was slowly revealed.

'Zeus!' called Tamar. 'Come on you old coward. I'm calling you out.'

There was a silence while everyone held their breath.

And then, with slow dignity Zeus appeared through the smouldering air. He inclined his head haughtily at Tamar.

'It would appear that I surrender,' he said, and he held up his hands.

'Duck!' yelled Tamar as a lightning bolt streaked across the sky. At the same moment, however, perhaps even a split second earlier, Tamar opened fire.

And Zeus staggered back clutching his chest and fell over – dead.

Tamar closed her eyes and smiled in relief as a massive cheer went up around her. The age of the Greek Gods was over.

~ Chapter Eighteen ~

'ONE, TWO, three – heave.'

The villagers were pulling down the newly converted temple to the small gods.

'No more gods,' Tamar told them, and they were only too happy to comply.

The minor deities themselves would, no doubt, be extremely pissed off to discover they had been tricked and betrayed, but Tamar shrugged it off. She had said "whatever it takes" and she had meant it.

There was only one last thing to sort out now, and they could go home.

'We promised not to kill you,' Denny told Aphrodite and Hephaestus. 'But we never said that we were going to leave you as gods. And he held up a hand in which the Athame gleamed in the sunlight.

Aphrodite took it surprisingly well. 'Our time is over,' she said. 'As it was foretold. A few more years on this Earth is a just reward for our part in this. We might have died like the others had we not joined with you, and accepted our fate.'

'You speak for yourself,' blustered Hephaestus. 'I don't want to be a mortal.'

'You prefer death?' asked Aphrodite.

'It all comes to the same thing, doesn't it?' he snorted. 'I notice that Hecate isn't here facing this choice. Playing favourites?' he sneered.

'It's not her fate,' Denny shrugged. 'But it is yours.'

'We shall simply have to achieve immortality the human way,' said Aphrodite.'

'Steal the Ambrosia?' said Hephaestus hopefully.

'Through our children,' Aphrodite corrected him gently, 'and our children's children.'

'Oh,' Hephaestus huffed disdainfully. 'Descendants.'

She smiled conspiratorially at Denny. And he moved forward, the Athame in his upheld hand.

'You look different through mortal eyes,' Aphrodite told Denny after it was over and Denny grinned to himself.

'I bet,' he said. 'Less ... attractive?' he calculated.

'No,' she said, to his surprise. 'Just different.'

There was a silence. Aphrodite licked her lips a little nervously and then took a deep breath. 'Oh what the Hades,' she said, and grabbed his face and kissed him hard on the mouth.

He was too stunned to think of pulling back, but he really did not need to, as an outraged Hephaestus grabbed her by the hair and towed her away muttering oaths under his breath.

'I wish those two luck,' said Tamar from behind him – she sounded amused. 'They're going to need it.'

Denny spun round in agitation. 'I didn't mean ...' he began babbling. 'She just ...'

And Tamar grabbed his face and ... Well it's obvious really.

'Let's go home,' she said on finally pulling away from him.

'Yeah let's,' he said. And they closed their eyes and clicked their heels together – just for the fun of it.

There's no place like home …

~ Chapter Nineteen ~

HECATE PLACED HER hands on the corpse of Jack Stiles (a sight which his spirit found extremely disturbing to watch) and as she gave back to him the gift that had been taken, suddenly ...

Denny pulled at the cork and with a flash and a bang Tamar appeared in the room. They took in each other for a moment before suddenly ...

The world blew away.

~ Epilogue ~

'AND *YOU* WERE there and *you* were there and ... Well no, ok *you* weren't there,' Denny finished, looking at Iffie who, along with the others, had been listening open-mouthed to their tale.

'What do you mean, *I* was there?' said Stiles in perplexity. 'I mean I can see how Hecaté was there but ...'

'I don't quite see how I could have been there either,' said Cindy. 'But with you two, I'd believe just about anything.'

'Ain't that the truth,' said Stiles with a laugh.

'He was joking,' said Tamar giving Denny a look that promised trouble later on. 'He's just been dying to say that – that's all.'

Denny ran his thin fingers through his long untidy hair until it stuck up like a bottle brush. 'Yeah, that's right,' he agreed. 'I couldn't help myself.'

'So,' said Tamar jumping up and rubbing her hands together. 'What are we going to do about mainframe?'

* * *

'He *knows*,' said Clive nervously to his colleague. 'And whatever *he* knows, *she* knows too. You can count on that.'

'Knows what?' asked the colleague indifferently.

'About us,' snapped Clive. 'About the origin of mainframe. Its true purpose.' He sighed. 'I suppose it was always inevitable. If only he hadn't *died*. That was *not* supposed to happen. Chaos at work again. It's always trying to break through.'

Now his colleague looked alarmed. 'B-but it can't break through,' he stammered. 'We've always managed to hold it back.'

'Until now,' said Clive gloomily. 'If she gets involved who knows what will happen. I really ...'

'Pfft,' said the colleague. 'What can she do?

'It's that kind of overconfident bravado that keeps getting us into trouble,' said Clive sternly. 'It's time we learned our lesson. I really wouldn't underestimate her.'

'I wouldn't turn my back on her for too long either,' he added *sotto voce.*

'But why would she ...? I mean if she ... Well everyone suffers that's all. Surely she can't be so ...'

'We can't take the chance,' interrupted Clive. 'You don't know her like I do. She's a human – well, she is now – they can't help themselves. They just *have* to interfere, even if it makes things worse. That's free will for you.'

'So what shall we do?'

'We'll just have to distract her that's all.' said Clive. 'And remember, this is just between you and me. If we get the others involved, they'll have committees and endless meetings and by the time they have come up with some stupid idea that probably won't do anything more than annoy her in the long run, it'll be too late to do anything anyway.'

'All right,' said the colleague. 'Distract her how?'

'Ah well,' said Clive with a sly grin. 'I did have a rather good idea about that actually. Just fetch me that bottle over there will you?'

He held the bottle up to the light and turned it over in his hands a few times. 'There's nothing quite like an old enemy returned to keep your mind occupied for a while you know.'

The colleague looked at the bottle in awe. 'You mean that's ...? But if you put *him* back in the world ...' He trailed off as his mouth went dry at the horror of it.

'Exactly,' said Clive. 'I wouldn't normally do it of course. But we have to look after ourselves now.'

'And,' he added as if he had just thought of it, 'if he kills her then so much the better. But I suppose that would be too much to hope for,' he ended regretfully.

'Now, where shall we put him? Nowhere too obvious of course. I mean she's bound to work it out in the end, but it would be helpful if she blamed that sidekick and his messing around in our files, at least at first.'

How about a nice desert island somewhere?' said the colleague.

'Perfect.' said Clive. 'I can see you are getting the hang of this already.

And he hurled the bottle back into the world and watched with a satisfaction that was awful to behold as the lonely castaway discovered it.

'Let the games begin,' he said.

INTRODUCING ...

Iphigenia Black – Dragon's Teeth

Time heals all wounds...

"Not if a thousand years were to pass, would I ever forgive you"

It's been twenty-five years since Tamar and Denny left for the end of time. Now living alone, Iffie is visited by a sinister figure from her past – the enigmatic Isabelle Wilde – who recalls to her the terrible events of those far off days that led up to her self imposed isolation of the present.

But perhaps by finally facing the past Iffie can put it behind her and learn not only to forgive those who trespassed against her, but also to forgive herself for letting it happen.

Also by Nicola Rhodes

SCI 'ON The Shadow Worlds

The first book in the SCI 'ON Trilogy

Whenever a decision is taken that is of significance to the world, the world divides and two alternate futures are created. In the beginning, there was only one world. That world we name SCI 'ON. All other worlds that sprang from it, we name the shadow worlds. Some believe SCI 'ON is the only real world and that all others are mere reflections, hence the name. Others believe that all the alternate worlds are equally real and important – however they may have come into being.

Whatever the case, one thing is certain. If SCI 'ON itself – the cradle of creation– were to be destroyed, all other worlds would cease to exist. For SCI'ON is the mainspring and without it, the shadow worlds would have no point of origin.

Johnny Hammond is not your ordinary computer nerd. He has the makings of a hero. When a mysterious man shows him the way To SCI 'ON, Johnny becomes obsessed. And only he can find a way to get there through the myriad shadow worlds that stand in his way. But someone doesn't want him to get there.

From earliest childhood, Ryan and Kai have been best friends. The fact that they come from separate universes is not allowed to stand in their way.

As they grow up, they realise that this ability to travel between the worlds is no mere coincidence, as their ultimate destiny unfolds.

SCI'ON II - Legacies

Even his own mother, from the moment he was born, was afraid of Talvas, for she knew whence he had come and wondered what his power would be.

Talvas Firebrand, later known as Talvas de Bellême and "The Destroyer of Worlds" was the son of Toros the fire god. His story and that of the other Undying begins on SCI 'ON back at the beginning.

Watching him from his citadel beyond time is Johnny Hammond, the only man in all creation capable of defeating Talvas and stopping the slaughter of millions.

What will happen when these adversaries finally meet again in a new cycle of time?

About the Author

Nicola Rhodes often can't remember where she lives so she lives inside her own head most of the time, where even if you do get lost, it's still okay.

She has met many interesting people inside her own head and eventually decided to introduce the rest of the world to them, in the hopes that they would stop bothering her and let her sleep.

She has been doing this for ten years now but they still won't leave her alone.

She wrote this book for fun and does not care if you take away a moral lesson from it or not.

You have her full permission to read whatever you wish into this work of fiction. As she says herself:

"Just because I wrote this book, doesn't mean I know anything about it."